PLAYERS
BUMPS &
COCKTAIL SAUSAGES

Natasha Preston

Acknowledgements

I want to again thank Hilda from Dalliance Designs and Mollie Wilson from MJ Wilson Design for the gorgeously hot cover. To Eileen Proksch for editing, and the fabulous Emma Mack for proofreading Jasper.

For Roy.
Grumpiest, silliest old sod I've ever
met but with a heart of gold.
I love you, Grandad.

CHAPTER
One

Jasper

"**E**verleigh!" I shouted. Jesus, my niece was like a fucking ninja! She just appeared and disappeared whenever she wanted to, and when I least expected it.

"It's not funny anymore, come out." I walked into the kitchen again to see if she was hiding in a cupboard, although she didn't like to hide in the same place too often. "Everleigh, I'll give you chocolate ice cream."

My phone vibrated in my pocket, and I prayed it wasn't my sister calling to talk to her daughter. I was running out of excuses as to why a three-year-old couldn't come to the phone. If I told Oakley it was because I had – yet again – misplaced her only child in my house, she would flip the fuck out.

I sighed in relief when my wife's name flashed up on the screen: Abby.

"Hey, babe," I said.

"Hi. I've been invited to dinner with a few colleagues, is that okay? We don't have anything on, do we?"

Great, I'll fend for my-fucking-self then!

I frowned and replied, "Yeah, it's fine. I'll probably hang around Oakley's until she feeds me when I drop Everleigh off."

Or eat alone. Again.

Abby laughed. "Lucky Oakley! How is Everleigh?"

If I could find her, I could ask...

"She's fine," I replied, and opened the downstairs bedroom wardrobe to search for her. I couldn't quite remember how long ago it was that she hid in her bedroom, so I wasn't sure if looking here was productive or not.

Bloody kids!

"Is she being good? Didn't Cole and Oakley say she was having a 'no' phase?"

She was. There was no getting her to do what she didn't want to. I think it was Oakley's fault; she had always told her she never had to do anything she didn't want to. We all knew it was because of what she'd been through, but it did mean Everleigh got away with murder sometimes. Plus, all she had to do was look up at me with her big blue eyes and I was done.

Everleigh's high-pitched scream made my heart stop and the hairs on the back of my neck stand up. Shit! I turned on my heel and sprinted towards the noise.

"Everleigh?" I shouted as I ran to the living room, shoving the door open.

She jumped off the sofa, landing in front of me and shouted, "Roar!"

"What the...!" She burst into a fit of giggles and jumped up and down. "What was that? Why did you scream? You scared the sh-sugar out of me!" I scowled.

She shoved her hands on her hips – a mini diva. Oakley was never like that when we were kids, even before... "You were taking too long to find me."

I blinked, shocked. "So you screamed bloody murder to get my attention?"

"What does bwoody mean?"

Damn it. "Err, that doesn't mean anything. I said… blonde."

"No, you didn't."

"I did," I countered.

"No, you didn't."

"I did."

"No, you didn't."

Sighing, I ran my hand through my hair. "If you pretend I didn't and don't tell your parents I'll give you sweets."

She smiled and skipped out of the room, replying, "Deal, Uncle Jasper."

I just got owned by a three-year-old. Abby shouting my name made me realise she was still on the phone which I was clutching in my hand, so now I was in trouble with my wife. I grimaced.

"Hi, beautiful."

"Jasper Dane, what on earth was that? Is she okay?"

Is she okay? I almost had a heart attack!

"She's fine. I'll see you later tonight then."

"Okay."

"I love you."

"Love you, too," she replied and hung up.

"Uncle Jasper, where are the sweeties?"

"Change of plan, we're going out," I called back.

Everleigh appeared in front of me, making me jump.

"Where?" She asked.

"You do realise you're the child and I'm the adult, don't you? You have to do what I say."

She shook her head. "Nana said you're as mature as a two-year-old."

"Did she now?"

"Yep, and she said I looks after you more than you looks after me."

I grabbed her coat off the bannister. "Well, I'll be having a word with Nana later. Shoes on. Let's go."

Everleigh was quiet in the car. She always looked out of the window, silently taking everything in. Sometimes I would take her for a drive just for a little bit of peace and quiet. As exhausting as looking after her was, I wouldn't have it any other way. I loved hanging out with her.

I pulled up at Cole's office and noticed that Oakley's car was there, too.

"Are we seeing Daddy?" Everleigh asked.

"Yeah, but only for a minute, he has to work. Mummy's here, too."

Everleigh cheered and pulled at her seat belt.

"Don't take your belt off yet!" I said. "Remember what I told you could happen?"

"I fly out of the window, and my brains will fall out."

I nodded once. "Exactly. You want to keep your brains in, right?"

"Yes."

"Good girl."

I parked beside Oakley's car and unbuckled Everleigh's seat. Okay, so telling a kid her brains would fall out if she didn't wear a seat belt wasn't exactly appropriate, but sometimes you had to use scare tactics to get the little buggers to play ball.

Cole had his own office which Everleigh skipped to, waving and saying hello to her dad's colleagues. She walked through the building as if she owned it.

"Come on, Uncle Jasper!"

"Sorry," I muttered, rolling my eyes.

Everleigh pushed Cole's office door open and skipped up to Oakley, shoving her arms out to her.

"Hey, baby," Oakley said, picking her up.

"Mummy, what does bwoody mean?"

Oakley looked up and scowled.

"You're not getting those sweets now," I told Everleigh.

"Jasper," Oakley said, sounding just like our mum when she told me off. "Stop using inappropriate language around my daughter. And stop bribing her not to tell on you!"

Everleigh stuck her tongue out, and I glared. We were usually a team. I was cool Uncle Jasper, and she usually sided with me. Traitor.

"Slip of the tongue. Anyway, I wanna take the little angel swimming. That okay with you?"

She bit her lip and looked torn.

"You promise you won't leave her for a second?"

"You know I won't."

"She'll love it," Cole said, looking at my little sister in a sappy, loving way that made me want to throw the hot drink he held in his face.

To say I was overprotective of my grown-up, twenty-four-year-old sister was an understatement. After what happened to her as a child I never wanted to let her out of my sight. I looked hard into everything, making sure there were no signs I was missing again. Cole was all right though. We'd been friends since we were kids, and then there was him being pathetic and pining after her when we moved to Australia for four years thing. Anyone else and their tea would be scolding their face right now.

Oakley nodded. "Yeah, she will. Do not let her–"

"Out of my sight," I said, holding my hands up and finishing her sentence. "She's safe with me. You know that."

"I know. I trust you."

Trust was a huge thing for Oakley. For me, too. My sister didn't trust her daughter with many people, and Everleigh had never been to nursery or playgroup. I worried how Oakley would cope when she went to school. Not well, probably. But then I think I'd worry myself sick over it too.

"Good." I sat on the desk. "You wanna go swimming, Everleigh?"

"Yeah! And Auntie Abby?"

My jaw tightened.

"No, Auntie Abby's at work."

Then she was going out, again. I was all for her spending time with colleagues and talking about whatever boring teaching things they talked about, but I was getting tired of spending quality time with the T-fucking-V.

Oakley gave me her there's-more-to-this-you're-not-saying look, and I knew I was telling her all about it, whether I wanted to or not.

"Cole, why don't you take Everleigh to get a biscuit from the staff room?" She said.

Subtle, Oakley...

"Uncle Jasper, is Mummy making me leave so she can talk to you?" Everleigh asked me.

I smiled. I had taught her well.

"Yep, exactly. Mummy wants to talk to me, so she's getting you and Daddy out by secretly bribing you with a biscuit."

"Is it about you saying bwoody?"

"Okay, off you go," I said gently pushing her shoulders. She skipped out with Cole.

"Kids, huh?" I shrugged, grimacing.

"I'll let that one go. What's going on with Abby? That's five Fridays in a row she's cancelled plans with you or just gone out."

I shrugged. "Nothin' really. She's just going out with work people."

"Right, but you're not happy with that."

"I'm not one of those bunny boilers, Oakley. If Abby wants to go out, I'm not gonna tell her she can't."

"I know that. You know we're going to get to it soon, so let's skip the 'I'm a good husband' bit – because I already know you are – and get to the part where you're honest."

My breath left my lungs in a rush, and the words came out.

"What if she's…"

"Cheating?"

I nodded. I forgave her the first time; we were teenagers, and she was stupid. After five years apart we'd grown up, and I thought she was ready to be serious. She was the only girl I had ever been serious about, and now she was my wife. Getting over a cheating teenage girlfriend was one thing, getting over a cheating wife was another. And no way in hell was I going to forgive that again.

"Do you honestly believe she is? After the last time? I'm sure she wouldn't be that stupid to risk losing you again."

"I don't know what I think. All I know is that she's going out more and is distant at home. We haven't had sex in–"

She held her hands up. "Okay, that part you can speak to Cole about!"

"Prude," I muttered under my breath.

Oakley shook her head.

"Jasper, if you're worried you need to talk to her."

"I can hardly come out with *are you fucking around again*, can I?"

"Maybe be a little more grown up about it… If that's possible." Oh, ha fucking ha! "You should be able to talk to her about anything."

"Well, sorry my marriage isn't as perfect as yours."

"Mine's not perfect. I want to kill Cole fifty per cent of the time, but I'd sure as hell ask him if I thought he was cheating."

It was easy for her; she knew Cole would never cheat. The guy had been in love with her since they were kids. He waited four years for her. They were each other's firsts. They were pathetically perfect for each other. Me and Abby had hot sex and then we fell in love. And then she cheated and turned me into a whore; which was fun through my twenties but now I was twenty-seven if I had to be single again, sleeping around would just make me feel like a sad old man. A fun sad old man, but still a sad old man.

"Maybe I should do some snooping."

"No, Jasper, just talk to her."

"Yeah, I'm pretty sure I'm gonna snoop first."

She sighed. "If she finds out you've been checking up on her rather than just–"

"La la la. I've made up my mind."

"Oh my God, my daughter's more mature than you."

"Mummy, I got two chocolate biscuits, and Daddy said I don't have to share with Uncle Jasper," Everleigh announced as she strut into the room. She was three going on fifteen.

"Well, Daddy's a–"

"Do not finish that sentence," Oakley snapped. I grinned.

Everleigh and I swam for an hour – well, I raced around after her and constantly had to wipe the water she splashed at me out of my eyes – and then I dropped her home.

Oakley had told me to be grown up about things and speak to Abby, but let's be honest, where did that ever get you? Pussy-whipped and fucked over, that's where. Not a place I wanted to be, so I was snooping. Abby was in the shower, possibly getting ready to screw another man, so I reached into her jacket pockets and found just a lipstick.

Her bag was on the kitchen table. I got told off for leaving stuff on there, my surf board mostly, but her bag, new shoes, make-up, and umbrella was fine – inequality at its bloody finest. The bag was open. If she left it open she was inviting people to look, and if I didn't touch anything, technically, I wasn't going through her things.

I peered in and saw the usual crap women kept in bags and a watch box. Armani watch at that, not a shabby one. My stepdad, Miles' birthday present, no doubt. I hoped.

Standing back, I took a swig of my beer. There was nothing incriminating. Maybe it really was all in my messed up head.

"Babe, I'm going now," she said, grabbing her bag off the table and kissing my cheek. "You're sure you don't mind? Perhaps we can do something the day after tomorrow? Or we can stop off in a bar after Miles' party tomorrow? I feel like we never spend time together anymore."

Oh, whose fault is that!

"Sure. Day after tomorrow sounds good. I volunteered us to look after Everleigh tomorrow night."

Abby smiled. "Yeah? That sounds great. We can rent a Disney film and make popcorn. Let her have a late night." Abby loved having Everleigh over. She wanted a kid as much as I did; we couldn't wait to be parents but recently she'd spoken less about it.

"She'll love that."

"Good. I gotta run. Love you."

"Love you, too." I watched my wife walk out to spend her Friday night with people who were not me again and sighed. I didn't care that she was going out. I cared that her going out made things different between us. I was now the one that she fit into a tiny slot in her schedule, rather than her friends. She might as well be married to her job and colleagues.

What the hell was I doing waiting in every night while my wife is out having fun? Shaking my head at how whipped I really was I pulled my mobile from my pocket and dialled Brad's number.

"Jasper, 'sup?"

"Wanna go out and get shit-faced?"

He chuckled. "I'm in. I'll drop Ben and Cole a text and meet you at the pub in thirty."

I snorted. Like Cole would go.

"Right."

I hung up and went to have my own shower and spend the night getting wasted with the guys. I love my wife, but I sure as hell wasn't sitting around for her. If she didn't give a crap about our marriage, which was clearly in trouble, then why the hell should I?

CHAPTER
Two

Jasper

I walked into the bar and Cole, Ben and Brad sat on a table in the corner. Well, fuck me, the pussy came out! "Let you out then, did she?" I said to Cole as I sat down and took the unnatural green-coloured shot that was waiting for me.

He rolled his eyes. "So what's Abby done that's caused me to leave my horny wife at–"

"Cole, I swear to God if you finish that sentence…"

He lifted his eyes to the ceiling and shook his head.

"My sister's clothes stay on."

"Yes, Jasper. Everleigh was an immaculate conception."

I nodded my head. "That's what I thought." I was even more protective with my little sister than my mum, but then I had never caught Oakley and Cole, so it was easier to pretend it didn't go on. I shuddered at the future therapy memory.

"Seriously, what's going on?" Brad asked, checking his phone again.

"Who're you sexting?" Ben asked.

My eyebrow arched. "Did you just say sexting? Are you fifteen?"

Ben held his hands up. "That's what it's called."

"Stop trying to keep up with the kids, man, it's over."

"Alright!" Brad said. "I'm not *sexting* anyone. My sister's home from Uni for summer and doing my head in. She's bored and apparently has no friends here anymore. Well, not any that are in the country until next week."

"Invite her to join us," Ben said.

"I don't think I'll be doing that."

"Either invite her or keep replying to her all night," he replied.

I was going to point out how this was a boys' night, but we technically hadn't said anything about it only being us guys.

"Is she even old enough to get in?" I asked.

"She's twenty, Jasper."

"You're shitting me! Holly's twenty now?"

"I shit you not."

I sank back in my chair, feeling like a grandad. The last time I saw her was shortly after I met Brad when we moved back to England, about five years ago. She was a teenager that wore too much eyeliner, spent her life glued to her mobile and was so painfully shy she barely spoke to anyone outside her friends and family. Now she was twenty and at Uni.

"She's coming," Brad said as his phone beeped again.

I turned my nose up.

"Great, we're babysitting tonight."

"She's twenty, Jasper," Cole said.

"Right, five years older than my sister was."

"What the fuck does that have to do with Holly?" He asked, shaking his head.

"It has everything to do with everything whenever I want to bring it up." He laughed and took a swig of beer. "Now can we please get me shit-faced?"

"What's going on with Abby? Kerry said you're pissed off she's always out," Ben asked, eager to change the subject.

"Your wife talks too much," I replied. Did everyone know about Abby barely staying at home in the evenings anymore?

Ben nodded. "Spill."

"No. Women talk. Men drink, so, Cole, it's your round."

"I'd ask why it's my turn first, but I have a feeling it's to do with the fact that I'm sleeping with your sister." He's smirking as he got up and walked to the bar. "You need to get over that, by the way," he called over his shoulder.

Not likely.

Ten minutes later, Brad pulled out a chair. "Hey, Hol," he said.

I looked up and apart from being a bit older Holly hadn't changed much at all. She still wore dark eye make-up that would scare the shit out of you if you woke up beside it – the panda eyes would be immense. She did have a rockin' body though – mostly hidden under a long top – and no longer dressed like she was on the set of a Marilyn Manson video as much.

"Holly," I said. *Good job growing up, minus the make-up thing.*

She smiled and blushed. Still just as shy.

"Hi, Jasper. Hey, Ben."

"Alright," Ben replied and stood. "What're you drinking? Cole's just gone up."

"Um, vodka and lemonade, please?"

He nodded and took off to the bar.

"Thanks for inviting me; I was going crazy at home with mum and dad."

"Just don't embarrass me," Brad replied.

"Whoa, let's not be so hasty," I said. "Share with the group, Holly. Has he ever done anything like getting his old chap stuck in a hoover?"

Holly's cheeks flamed, and Brad frowned.

"Jesus. What's wrong with you, Jasper?"

I laughed.

"That's a yes. So, what's Uni like? I really hope it's all American Pie. Do you get a lot of action?"

Her eyes widened.

"Oh, are you a virgin?"

"Jasper, for fuck sake!" Brad punched my arm. "You are, though, aren't you?"

I couldn't help the big grin on my face as Holly looked down at the table. I couldn't work out if she was embarrassed – which she shouldn't be anyway – or she wasn't and didn't want to talk about it in front of her brother.

Cole – inadvertently becoming Holly's saviour – returned to the table with a tray with far too many drinks for five people. Holly blushed again.

"Thank you," she said as she took her drink from Cole.

"You're welcome," he replied, not even noticing her pink cheeks.

"Shots. Three for Jasper and two for the rest of us. Holly, I got you some too, but if you don't want to take them Jasper will."

"Oh, will he?" I replied sarcastically.

Cole held his hands up. "You asked us to get you shit-faced."

"I did. Hand them over." I was getting drunk because my wife was off with God knows who again. I hadn't met all of her colleagues. Well, I had, but I never paid any attention to them because they all seemed boring. Apparently I wasn't giving them a chance because I had only met them at the school where she worked, and they were fun outside it. I hadn't failed to notice how I never got invited out with them to witness said fun.

"I'm not really a shots kind of girl," Holly said and smiled at me. "You can have mine."

I narrowed my eyes. Were you even allowed into Uni if you didn't do shots?

"Thanks." I lined my five up and took them one after another. "The hell is this, Cole?"

He shrugged. "I asked for eleven of their strongest shots."

Jesus, did they give him paint stripper?

Holly sipped her drink. She definitely wasn't doing the Uni thing properly.

"So, what is tonight in aid of?"

"Jasper's having wife issues," Cole replied.

"Oh," she said, wincing. "Sorry, Jasper."

I shrugged.

"You're married now, too, right?" She asked Cole.

He nodded. "Two and a half months."

"Congratulations."

Cole smiled in response and got that blissful look on his face.

"I bet you know the hours, too," I sneered.

He stuck his middle finger up, and I laughed. Yeah, he definitely did.

"Anyway, I thought I said no more talk of women and marriages? Holly, tonight you're a man."

"Thanks," she said sarcastically.

"Sorry, I just mean I don't want any girlie talk."

"Not really a girlie girl," she replied. *Yeah, I can tell.* She was a good girl that was still half living in a badly done rebellious phase. Growing up she would dress like she wanted to rebel but never actually did anything wrong. It was like she didn't know who she was yet. Although, who was I to judge? I wasn't really sure I knew who I was any more, either.

Things were easier when I was happily married, but now I didn't know what Abby wanted, I didn't know what I wanted. Well, that wasn't true. I did know: I wanted to have kids and grow old with my wife. But I couldn't if she wanted something or someone else.

"Cole, more shots," Ben said.

Brad stood. "I'll get these."

"When do you go back then?" I asked Holly.

She scooted over and sat on Brad's chair, next to me as the DJ turned up the music.

"Not until October, so I have a long, boring summer here."

Almost four months off! She didn't know how damn lucky she was; I wish I got that much time off work. How the hell could universities charge so much money when you were hardly there?

"Where are your friends?"

"I didn't have many friends in high school, and the ones I did have either settled down or moved away. I'm catching up with Amy when she's back from Tenerife soon though."

Do I know who Amy is? "Right," I replied, not knowing what to say.

"Well, your brother's coming to my stepdad's barbecue on Friday. Come too, if you want."

"Yeah? He wouldn't mind?"

"Nope." Miles was too laid back to care if I brought an elephant along with me. My mum, however…

Mum would love Holly. In a way, Holly reminded me a little of Oakley – the shyness and how she looked almost as if she would shatter if you shouted boo at her.

"Thank you."

I shrugged. "No worries."

"So… do you want to talk about your wife issues?"

I arched my eyebrow. "You're going to give me advice? Have you ever been in a relationship?"

Her cheeks reddened.

"Thought not."

"I have a while ago, but it wasn't really serious, we were together for eight months before school finished, and Uni is really full on."

"Of course it is. Holly, you don't have to be embarrassed, you're still really young."

"I'm not embarrassed." Then why did you go beetroot? "Anyway, if Brad tells me correctly, you've not exactly had any meaningful relationships apart from Abby."

"What the hell has he told you?" I asked, smiling tightly.

"That you slept around and broke hearts."

I held my finger up.

"Uh-uh. I may not have been a *good boy*, but I never promised anyone anything. They knew the score as well as I did. It was just sex."

"Such class," Ben said, shaking his head. I glared but let it go.

Now I wasn't exactly proud of sleeping with as many women as I had – sixty-eight – but I wasn't exactly ashamed either. Sure, I would have preferred Abby to not have cheated on me when we were teens, ripped my heart out and left me an empty mess, but she did, and then I slept around. But that was in the past, and I had no desire to go back to that.

"I think it's sweet that you changed so much for your wife," Holly said, sipping her drink as if she was afraid it was the last one she would ever get.

Technically, I had changed because of Abby twice. And I really wanted this to be it.

"Yeah, or pathetic." Ben grinned. "Although not as pathetic as Cole."

"Good," I said, "Because Oakley deserves the best." And the most pathetically in love idiot, I added in my head. She deserved someone that was willing to wait for a thousand years for her.

"Aw. The nicest thing Brad has ever said about me is that I'm not that ugly," Holly said.

Ben laughed, and I felt like I should have said something to explain, but I didn't want to bring up the past. Tonight was supposed to be fun and what had happened to my sister made me violently angry.

Me and Oakley were close, and I would die for her in a heartbeat. We'd been through something that meant we could never have a distant brother/sister relationship, not that I wanted that anyway. My mum, sister, and niece were three people I would kill for, no questions asked.

"Brad's a dick. You're definitely not ugly," Ben said. She definitely wasn't, but no one found their sibling attractive – well, some probably did, but those were the people that would have eleven-fingered children.

Holly blushed at Ben's back-handed compliment and muttered a shy, "Thank you."

"God, you and Brad are so different. You sure you're related?" I said.

"Hold up," Ben said, "you and Oakley couldn't be more different either. She's smart, beautiful, funny, and you're...."

"Thank you," I said sarcastically. "Anyway, can we please cut the small talk and get me so drunk I can't even remember my own name?"

They did.

I woke up and groaned. My head was pounding, and my tongue felt like sandpaper. How fucking much had I drunk last night?

"How're you feeling?" Abby asked, leaning over me. She sounded pissed off. Why was she pissed off? I was the one who was allowed to be pissed off here.

"My head... It hurts."

"Not surprised. Brad and Cole had to carry you home. Some girl gave me your phone." She raised her eyebrow, waiting for an explanation. *Yes, Abby, I brought the girl I cheated on you home with me. Jesus!*

"Holly," I said. "Brad's sister."

"She's pretty."

Dangerous fucking territory.

I shrugged. "She's alright." Holly was pretty under the eye make-up. Her naivety and that good girl thing she had going on made me doubt she would ever cheat. If anything she would be cheated on, like I was.

"How old is she?"

"Twenty."

Abby sat down, and I knew I'd said something wrong.

"You know a lot about her then?"

"Are you for real? Ben said we should invite her because she knows no one here and I asked if she was old enough to be drinking in a pub and Brad told me her age." Was she seriously quizzing me? I would never do anything to hurt her, and she knew that. Or she should know that.

"Okay, I'm sorry. I just don't like women thinking they have a chance with my hubby, that's all."

Since when did carrying a phone become payment for animal sex in a pub bathroom?

"You trust me?"

"Of course I do, baby, I just get jealous. I wouldn't be normal if I didn't."

But jealous of someone holding my phone?

"Alright. What time is it?"

"Almost eleven. We need to leave in an hour so take these," she replied, handing me two white painkillers and nodding to a glass of water on the bedside table. "I'm gonna have a shower. Do you need any clothes ironing for today? Know what you're wearing?"

"Jeans and a t-shirt." *Miles' birthday, not dinner with the queen.*

"Okay." She kissed my cheek and left the room. I hated that we were stressed at each other more than we were happy now. We needed something to get back to how it was just a few months ago; things had become mundane and pretty shit. A dirty weekend away. That would do it. I wanted a whole weekend with no clothes and my wife in as many positions as possible.

I heard the shower turn on and got hard. Abby in the shower seemed like a damn appealing idea right now. After downing the pills and taking a huge gulp of water, I went to the bathroom. She was washing her hair in the shower; the suds streamed down her back making my mouth water.

"Room for me?" I asked.

She spun around as if she thought I was a murderer. "Jasper, you scared me. I'm almost done, babe, we don't have long."

Another rain check then.

I stripped as she quickly finished washing her hair and got out.

"So, what did we get him?" I asked Abby as I drove over to Cole and Oakley's place. It was Miles' birthday but since my sister's garden was massive the party was at their house.

Abby put herself in charge of presents after the condom incident on Cole's birthday after Everleigh was born.

I rattled the neatly wrapped present. It wasn't a watch-shaped present. Why wasn't it watch-shaped? Watches weren't flat and floppy, but this was.

"A shirt your mum picked out when we were shopping last weekend."

Okay, a shirt definitely wasn't a watch. I looked at Abby and mentally cursed her blank expression. Why wasn't she giving anything away, and why couldn't I just man up and ask her? *Have you turned back into a cheater, Abby?*

"Did you pick up Everleigh's headband?"

"Damn it," I muttered.

Abby sighed. "Jasper, we've had that almost a week now."

"Sorry. She can get it tonight."

"I'll make sure she gets it."

How had Abby changed so quickly? She'd been acting weird for a little while now. At first I thought it was just because her parents were separating, but I don't think so now. Her parents fought for most of her life, and she said she was relieved they were finally breaking up. So what the fuck was up with her? Another man was the only conclusion I could come to. I hated it because I'd finally reached a place where I could trust her one hundred per cent again, and she was seriously screwing with that.

Feeling deflated, I looked out of the window as we approached Oakley's house. I should have just kept whoring around rather than forgiving her and settling down. That was much easier.

"Ready?" Abby asked, smiling at me as she opened her door.

I nodded and got out, plastering a smile on my face. As soon as the front door opened and Everleigh ran outside my smile turned real.

"Uncle Jasper," she screamed. And I knew that no matter what happened with Abby, I would always have my favourite girl.

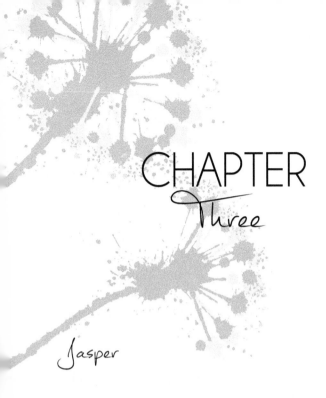

CHAPTER
Three

Jasper

I plucked Everleigh out of the air as she jumped at me. The kid could properly clear the floor. It was terrifying.

"Hey, kiddo."

"Don't eat the chicken. Daddy said Grandad don't cook it right," she said, getting straight to the point. "Chicken that don't cook right makes you hurt, doesn't it?"

It was hurl, and it was me, not Cole, that had told her when I was sick once that bad chicken made you hurl, but I was glad she'd got it mixed up. Saved me from Oakley's yelling.

"That's right. Bad chicken makes your belly hurt."

"Hey, girly," Abby said, taking her from me. Everleigh started telling Abby about the chicken too, so I took the opportunity to say hi to my mum who was waiting by the front door – on granddaughter duty.

"Hi, sweetheart," Mum said, hugging me.

"Hey. How's it going?"

"Good. I'm so happy everyone can be together again. It's been too long. Abby," she said, pushing past me. "How are you? It's been a while."

I tried not to think about why she wasn't at my mum and Miles' for dinner last week. It seemed that while I just wanted to knock her up and have a family, she just wanted to be young and go out again. I thought we were on the same page. When we got married, I thought – because she'd *said* – that we were going to start thinking about trying to have a baby. Usually, I was quite good at finding the real message between what a woman said and what she actually fucking meant, but clearly I had mistaken 'I can't wait to have a family with you' for 'Sod off, I want my freedom.'

I followed them into the back garden, saying happy birthday to Miles before I grabbed my first beer of many.

"Hey, man," I said as Brad walked out to join me. Holly was just behind him, almost hiding. I nodded my head. "Holly."

"Where's the beer?" Brad asked, heading over to the cooler by the barbecue that I pointed out.

"Hi. Thank you again for inviting me," Holly said, biting the inside of her mouth.

I shrugged. "No worries. Let me introduce you to my sister. Oakley!" Holly flinched, not realising I was about to shout, even though Oakley was at the other end of the garden.

Instead of my sister, my niece ran over and stood in front of Holly, checking her out with a little scowl.

"Do you like purple?" Everleigh asked her.

"Um," Holly muttered at the random question and then smiled, bending down a little. "I love purple, it's my absolute favourite."

"Mine, too." Everleigh beamed and skipped off, and with that brief exchange, Holly had been accepted.

"She's cute. Your niece, Everleigh, right?"

"Yeah, and yeah, she is. She likes you."

She smiled. "You can tell from that?"

"You like purple, and if she didn't like you she would have held onto my hand and glared at you."

Holly laughed. "Alright."

"Hi," Oakley said, finally getting to us. "You're Holly, right?"

"Yeah, hi. Thanks for letting me come."

Oakley waved her hand. "Of course. You want something to drink? My mum's making cocktails, can't guarantee they'll be nice, though."

"Holly's not a big drinker," I said.

"Okay," Oakley replied slowly. "Well, we have non-alcoholic stuff too. Come with me and we'll find you something." They walked off, leaving me alone, chatting as they made their way into the conservatory that now looked like a brewery. How fucking much alcohol did they buy?

"How come Holly's here?" Abby asked, doing Everleigh's ninja thing and just appearing in front of me.

I frowned.

"Because her brother's here. I said she could come rather than hanging out at her parents' house alone. Plus, I thought she would get on well with Oakley, and I was right."

Jesus it wasn't like I'd asked her on a date.

"Right," she replied. "Are you going to introduce me too?"

Shrugging, I nodded my head and walked into the conservatory after them. Abby's mood swings were beginning to piss me off. In the car over she was okay, minus the headband thing; when we arrived she was a loving wife, but now she was acting pissy.

"Holly," I said, "this is my wife, Abby. Abby, this is Brad's sister."

Abby stepped forward. "Nice to meet you, Holly."

"You too." They shook hands, and Holly took the cocktail from Oakley's hand, thanking her.

"Drinking today?" I asked.

She shook her head. "It's a non-alcoholic cocktail."

"You don't drink?" Abby asked as she poured herself a glass of red wine.

"Not much."

"How do you survive Uni without alcohol?"

Holly laughed. "I have no idea. Did you go, too?"

"Yeah, to study teaching and English Literature and Language. Now I work at the high school. What about you? What do you want to be after Uni?"

"A pharmacist in a hospital," she replied.

"Wow, that's great," Abby replied. I was glad they had something in common because if they hadn't Abby probably wouldn't have tried that hard to get along with her. She could be kind of selfish like that. She wouldn't necessarily ignore Holly, but she wouldn't have bothered to make her feel at ease.

Holly smiled shyly, and I realised the men were outside, cooking the meat on the barbecue with a cooler of beer beside them and I was inside chatting to the women who were drinking girlie drinks. I shook my head and backed away. "I'll be outside."

I walked to the man area and grabbed a beer.

"Tell me there's Jack Daniels in that?" I said to Cole.

"Just coke," he replied, and I raised my eyebrow.

"Well, since my wife is now on her third cocktail I'm guessing I've been nominated the designated responsible parent for today."

"She's getting drunk?" I frowned. She never got drunk, drunk. "Is everything okay?"

"Everything's fine, Jasper."

I didn't like it. Oakley didn't drink until she got drunk, just tipsy. The last time she was drunk was when that bastard sperm donor we were supposed to call Dad sent her a letter from prison. It was almost two years ago. She got in such a state that Mum and Miles took Everleigh for the night so she could calm herself down. I hated seeing her like that. I'd wanted to kill him more than ever.

"Seriously, Jasper, she's fine. It's Miles' birthday, and she wants a few drinks. She's twenty-four, old enough to have a few cocktails."

My shoulders relaxed. If Cole wasn't worried, I wasn't going to be. He knew her better than I did now, and he was a real worrier when it came to my sister. If he was cool and not concerned, then everything was fine.

He smiled sadly, understanding exactly why I freaked out. Oakley had dealt with a lot, but as strong as she was it would always be there. Therapy couldn't take away the memories of what those bastards did to her when she was just a few years older than Everleigh.

"So everything okay between you and Abby now?" He asked, flipping over the burgers.

I shrugged. "I guess. Women drive you crazy, right?"

He laughed and shook his head. I could tell that was just for my benefit. Oakley didn't drive him as insane as Abby drove me, but he didn't want to disagree and leave me feeling bad. I wanted to pull my damn hair out. What the hell was going on with my wife? I knew I was going to have to do the mature thing that Oakley suggested and talk to her, but in my experience, ninety per cent of the time talking to a woman left you no less confused than before. I think they enjoyed it. They loved messing with our heads; it was like a damn hobby.

"You up for going out tomorrow?" Cole asked.

Was he trying to keep my busy?

"Can't. Doing something with Abby. Soon though?"

He nodded. "Sure."

"Jasper, refill the cooler, please?" Miles said, handing me a bucket of water and balancing Everleigh in his other arm. Miles was her hero; she worshipped him. He had more right to be her grandad than that bastard rotting in prison did. She didn't even know about him, and we wanted to keep it that way for as long as we could – forever, if that was possible.

I took the cooler from him and curtseyed, earning me an eye roll.

"So, when am I getting my second grandchild?" Mum asked me, smiling like a psycho as I walked into the house to get some more beers.

I shrugged. A baby seemed so fucking far away now. I wanted to be a father and have a tiny person call me Daddy. Whenever Everleigh called Cole Daddy it put a smile on my face, she worshipped her dad – I wanted that, too.

"Dunno, ask your daughter," I replied.

Oakley frowned. "We're not trying for another one until Everleigh's settled in school full-time."

"What?" Cole whined, walking through the door and pouting at my sister. "Not now?"

She laughed and threw her wadded up napkin at him. "Sorry, but you've gotta wait at least another year and a half for baby number two. Unless, of course, you want to give birth?"

He smiled and then his mucky paws were all over her.

Mum pouted at me and Abby, more effectively than Cole.

"Come on, you two, I'm not getting any younger."

I wrapped my arm around my wife. "We're happy with the way things are for now," I said, not wanting to put Abby in an awkward position if I said I wanted tons of them but she was more focused on her career.

She smiled up at me, and I felt like she'd jammed a knife into my heart. She believed what I said, even though we'd had a few conversations where I said I was ready, and so did she. What the fuck was wrong with women? How could you go from being ready one month to suddenly wanting to focus on other things the next? The last time she said she was excited to have a baby of our own was less than six weeks ago. What had changed so drastically in six weeks?

"We'll give you another grandchild one day, Sarah, but we're just enjoying being together right now."

Just enjoying being together? When the hell were we 'just together'? If we hadn't committed to Miles' birthday she would probably be out with her colleagues, and I would be at home. We hadn't enjoyed 'just being together' in months.

I wanted to tell her she was being unfair, but I didn't want to get in the way of what she wanted. If she wanted to wait another five years for kids while she concentrated on teaching, that was fine, but she shouldn't have told me otherwise.

My smile – which probably looked like a pissed off grimace – fooled everyone except my nosey sister.

"Uncle Jasper," Everleigh screamed, and I wanted to thank her for interrupting right when I could sense Oakley asking for my help with something in the kitchen. "Come and help me and Leona make daisy chains! You said you would!"

I held my hands up. "Alright, diva, I'm coming." How the

fuck do you make daisy chains? I filled the cooler with beer and we headed back outside. "You have far too much attitude for a three-year-old."

"I'm almost four," she replied as if that made all the difference. Everleigh growing up sucked. I had no idea what I would do on my days off when she was at school. Me and Oakley rotated our shifts at The Centre, the place Oakley opened after the trial was done so we could look after Everleigh. I loved spending time with her, so it was going to suck when I couldn't do that as much.

After handing Miles the refilled cooler, I let Everleigh lead me to the corner of Cole and Oakley's perfectly cut lawn where Cole's niece, Leona, and Holly were sitting cross-legged on the grass. I frowned.

"They've not left you to be the babysitter?"

She smiled up at me. "No, it's okay. I like hanging with them."

"You can join the adults when you want."

"Really, it's fine. I love spending time with kids."

I sat down and prepared to bullshit my way through making a necklace out of flowers.

"You know how to do this?" I asked.

"Daisy chains? Everyone knows how to make daisy chains," she replied, brushing her light blonde hair out of her face.

"Uncle Jasper don't," Everleigh said and sighed.

"Wow, really?"

"I'm a man."

Everleigh giggled. "Remember when you wore Mummy's dress? You looked like a girl."

"Yes, thank you, Everleigh." I winced as I watched Holly try not to laugh.

"Hey, I'm comfortable with my masculinity, that's how I'm

able to put on a dress and not have it shrink the boys," I replied, giving myself a mental high five at changing *my balls* to *the boys* before I'd started saying it.

"Of course," Holly said wryly. "Perhaps the stories I've heard about you were less about a broken heart and more about hiding in a closet."

My mouth dropped open. Sweet, shy, innocent little Holly made a joke like that – and a good one. If it wasn't aimed at me, I would have laughed.

"There's nothing PG I can think of to reply so just imagine my response."

She laughed and shook her head as Leona tried to figure out what we were talking about. She was at that age where she was starting to understand what we didn't say.

"Will do. Ready to make a daisy chain, girls?"

Leona and Everleigh nodded. I was sure Leona knew already, but she looked up at Holly like she wanted to be her.

"Okay, take your daisy and with your nail make a small slit in the stem. Everleigh, do you want me to help you?"

I looked on at them, picking grass because I would rather boil my own head than make a daisy chain. Holly was great with kids; she would be an awesome mum one day.

"How come you're so good with children?" I asked. "You don't have younger brothers or sisters, right?"

"No, but I have a lot of younger cousins."

"You want kids when you're older?"

She beamed and looked prettier, even with the overly dark eye make-up.

"Definitely."

Why couldn't Abby be that sure? She had already taken back saying she wanted them now, and had postponed our family. What the hell was I going to do if she decided in a couple years that she wanted to wait another couple of years?

"You do, too," she said overly confidently. Did it show that much? I didn't really care, having children was so important to me now. A few years ago I would have laughed if someone told me I would end up desperate to be a dad.

"Yeah, I do."

"When do you think you will?"

I shrugged.

"I would tomorrow, but apparently that's not an option now."

It was a woman's prerogative to change her mind. Pissing never satisfied, mind changing, evil, heart breaking women!

CHAPTER
Four

Jasper

Abby was already out of bed when I woke the next morning. I groaned. It was only seven in the morning and on a Sunday. What the hell was she doing up?

"Abby?" I called to see if she was just in the bathroom before I forced myself to get out of bed.

She poked her head around the corner of the door.

"Oh, you're awake then?"

No, I'm sleep talking!

"Yeah." I rubbed my eyes, trying to wake up. "What're you doing up so early?"

"I'm meeting Carol and Brett at Wendy's Cafe to discuss the Thorpe Park trip. Two parents have pulled out, and we're having trouble with the coaches now too. We're grabbing breakfast and sorting through the issues. I won't be long, and then we can do something. Want me to bring you bacon rolls back?"

Sunday. It was the official day of rest, and she wanted a working breakfast. Leaving your bed before ten on a Sunday should be illegal and here was my wife, dressed and ready to leave the house at seven.

"Right. Bacon rolls would be awesome."

She blew a kiss and grabbed her handbag off the dressing table. "Only be a couple hours. Love you." And then she was gone.

I wanted to call someone to complain, and normally I'd call Oakley but she was getting bored of me complaining and not doing anything about it. I was scared of doing anything about it. Actually, I was fucking terrified. If Abby was cheating we would have to get divorced, sell the house and divide everything up. I would be a divorced man. I would have an ex wife. Abby would be fine with her new man, but I would be screwed. No one wanted to be the one left behind. I didn't want to be in love with someone that left me for someone else.

The only thing that I knew would take my mind off what was possibly going on – yes, I was a fan of burying my head in the sand – was Everleigh. I dialled my sister's house knowing they would already be up.

"Hello," Oakley said down the phone.

"Can I have Everleigh for a couple hours? Pancakes at the diner."

"Good morning to you, too, Jasper."

"Please?" I said.

She paused. "Sure. Any reason?"

"She's my favourite person, and I want to take her to breakfast."

"That's the only reason? Is Abby going, too?"

"I'll pick her up in twenty," I said and hung up. *Damn mind-reading sister.* There was going to be a lecture. There was always a lecture. I should speak to Abby about it; that's what she'd say. Of course, she was right, but I wasn't gonna do it.

I dressed and grabbed my keys. Abby had left one of her many handbags on the kitchen table – the one the watch was in. We had nothing coming up – not my birthday or an anniversary – so if the watch was gone that meant she took it with her today. To this Brett twat? I backed away, needing to trust her.

*

*

*

Oakley opened her front door as I pulled up. Great, she was ready to preach. She raised her eyebrow as I walked towards her.

"Don't start," I said.

"I'm not starting. I just don't get many early morning phone calls from you on a Sunday. Actually, I've never received an early morning phone call off you on a Sunday."

"Abby's working for a couple hours, so I thought I'd use the time to treat my niece."

"Abby's working?"

"Something about sorting out school trip shit." I shrugged my shoulders. "I dunno. Everleigh ready?"

"Cole's just putting her shoes on. Do you want to talk about it?"

I glared. "There's nothing to talk about."

Oakley smiled one of her smiles that made me want to throw tomatoes at her.

"Seriously, it's fine. If she wants to waste Sunday morning talking about work, that's her stupid choice."

I could see in my sister's eyes she was thinking *but what*

about spending time with you, blah, blah, blah. Would I prefer to spend time with my wife in the morning, yes, of course, but she had stuff to do. I'd survive.

"Everleigh," I shouted past Oakley, ignoring her questioning look. If she kept raising her eyebrows at me, I was going to shave them off.

"Uncle Jasper!" Everleigh screamed, jumping up and down as she made her way to the front door. "Pancakes! Can I have chocolate?"

I grinned. "You can have whatever you want."

"Yeah," she cheered, jumping outside in one big leap that made Oakley tense up. "Let's go, Uncle Jasper."

I unlocked my car and she ran to her door, letting herself in. Cole appeared behind Oakley, wrapping his arms around her.

"No kiss goodbye?" He said to Everleigh. She turned, shook her head, waved and got in the car.

"Too eager for food. She takes after you," Oakley said, kissing Cole's cheek over her shoulder. That was my cue to leave. I didn't need to be seeing any of that soppy crap right now.

"So what's wrong, Uncle Jasper?" Everleigh asked, leaning her elbows on the diner table she barely reached so it looked more like she was just laying her arms out, but I knew the effect she was going for – 'tell all'.

"Nothing's wrong, Noodle. I promise."

She sighed and shook her head. "Uncle Jasper, you just told a lie."

My three-year-old niece was disappointed in me. Wow.

"Just grown-up stuff. Nothing for you to worry about."

"But I love you."

There was nothing that could keep me down when she said

that. I smiled like a fat guy locked in a McDonalds overnight. I was suddenly so glad Oakley didn't have anything planned and let me take Everleigh for a bit. This kid was my antidepressant.

"I love you, too, but you don't have to worry about me."

"Are you sad?"

"If you ask your dad..."

She frowned, my joke going over her head.

"Never mind. I'm not sad."

"Is it Aunty Abby? Are you in the dog house?"

I laughed, my eyebrows shooting up.

"What?" Where the hell did that come from?

"Mummy said Daddy was in the dog house when he broke her favourite mug. Did Aunty Abby break your favourite mug?"

I loved her weird little innocent mind.

"Yeah, she broke my favourite mug."

She nodded. "Don't worry, Uncle Jasper, I'll buy you a new one. Ooh, can I have a chocolate milkshake? I promise won't tell Mummy and Daddy."

"Sure. You can have whatever you want."

She grinned a face-splitting smile and pushed her empty plate away.

Oakley informed me that she and Cole had popped to The Centre to sort out an air conditioning issue in the ballet room, so I was to take Everleigh there. Going into work on your day off felt wrong.

"Where's Mummy and Daddy?" Everleigh asked as soon as we got out of the car as if I had some radar.

"Office, probably. Let's go find them."

I walked into reception with Everleigh hanging off my arm – literally. Blinking in shock, I shook my head. Holly sat behind the desk with Oakley.

"Hey. What's going on?"

Oakley looked up, her eyes lighting up as she spotted her daughter. "Hey, baby, you enjoy your pancakes."

Everleigh nodded theatrically.

"Yep. Where's Daddy?"

"In the office, go find him." The only reason she let Everleigh go off alone was because the office was behind the reception desk and she had to pass her to get to it.

I walked up to the desk and leant my arms on the surface. "You're working here now?" I asked Holly.

She nodded, blushing. Jesus, I only asked if she was working here, not what colour her underwear was.

"Yes, part-time until I go back to Uni. Your other receptionist started maternity leave early, apparently."

Wow, no one tells me anything!

"Yeah," Oakley said, her attention now back on us. "Olivia's not been feeling well and decided to start maternity two months earlier than planned. She'll take nine months off rather than six now."

"Oh. She okay?"

"She just needs rest. Thankfully, Holly's available, so I don't have to advertise for the maternity cover position until September. I'm just going to check on Cole and Everleigh, make sure she's not rearranging the paperwork again. Can you show Holly the booking system?"

I shrugged. *Not like I have anything better to do.*

"Sure."

Oakley smiled and left.

Holly bit her lip and whispered, "Thanks."

"It's fine. Okay, budge over."

Holly moved her chair, and I pulled the other one up. It was clear that she wasn't used to being so close to men by the way she let her hair fall in her face, half hiding her face. So shy.

"This your first day?"

"Yeah. I'm scared I'll do something wrong and get fired."

I rolled my eyes. "You'll probably do something wrong, who doesn't? You won't get fired."

She smiled and her shoulders relaxed. Wow, she was really worried about messing up. Christ, if I had a pound for every time I screwed something up I'd be rich.

"Thanks, Jasper," she said. Her eyes had less black kohl around them today. It made her look softer and not like she was about to gut me and eat my insides.

I grinned, winking, which made her blush again.

"Alright, if you click booking..."

When I'd finished being Holly's teacher, I left The Centre and went home to see if my wife was back yet. Her car was in the drive, along with another one I didn't recognise. My heart beat at a thousand miles an hour. Who the hell was that? I didn't want to think the worst. I'd forgiven her and we'd agreed to move on, but I couldn't help it. Recently I'd been wondering if she was bored of me and looking elsewhere.

Opening the door, I slowly walked inside.

"Jasper, in the kitchen," Abby said. It couldn't be bad if she yelled to me.

A guy was sat at my kitchen table. Brett? What the hell was he doing here if they'd sorted everything out at the café?

"Hey. Babe, this is Brett and, Brett, this is my husband, Jasper."

I held my hand out, and we shook, both squeezing slightly to test who had the biggest balls.

I won.

"Brett."

"Good to finally meet you, Jasper. Abby's talked about you a lot." Saying what?

"Really." I wanted to say she's not mentioned you much at all, but that would make me a child. "You two get the trip stuff sorted?"

Abby nodded, flicking the kettle. I looked in Brett's mug – my mug – and saw it was empty. Was he staying for another one?

"Want one, babe?"

"Please," I replied, even though I didn't.

"Brett?"

"Are you sure? I don't want to get in the way." *Good. Fuck off then.*

Abby frowned and waved her hand. "Oh, you're not in the way."

Speak for yourself.

"Did you go to Oakley and Cole's?" Abby asked, grabbing the mug off Brett to refill it.

"Yeah, took Everleigh for pancakes."

She smiled. "I bet she loved that. Your bacon rolls are in the fridge."

"Thanks, I'll eat them later."

Brett stayed silent. *See, arsehole, our lives may not be rock n roll, but we work. Back off.* I wanted to laugh at myself. Technically, he hadn't done anything wrong, but I didn't like his pissing-contest handshake. She was my wife, and he needed to back the hell away.

Brett stayed for one more cup of tea, and the whole time was in a deep conversation with Abby about work before he left.

They'd occasionally tried to include me, but I didn't work in a school – thank God, or I think I'd end up killing some of them – so I didn't have much to say. I did try to talk sports with him and make an effort but apparently he didn't follow any of it.

Abby turned and handed me a box. "Here," she said.

I frowned, taking it from her. Shit, had I really missed something? I opened it, and *that* watch stared back at me.

"What's this?"

"It's a watch, Jasper," she replied sarcastically. "I know things have been a little strained recently, there's a lot going on at school. I just want to show you how much I appreciate your support and understanding. I love you, baby."

I am the worst man on earth.

"Abby," I muttered. Damn, all this time I had been thinking the worst of her. I'm such a dick!

"Do you like it?"

"I love it. Thank you." Grinning, I pulled her into a kiss.

Work got her for the morning, but for the rest of the day she was mine.

CHAPTER
Five

Jasper

I woke up on Monday morning, and after a long night of what I could only be described as crazy animal sex, I was pretty fucking happy. Abby was already up and in the shower; I could just about hear her strangled-cat singing.

It wouldn't be long before Oakley would call and yell about me being late, so I dragged my satisfied arse out of bed and went to the bathroom. My naked wife was facing the tiled wall; her body was lathered up, completely covered in bubbles. I watched her with wide eyes and an open mouth as she ran her hands over her stomach and across her breasts. In record time, I was hard. *So what if I'm a little late…*

She stepped under the water spray, and the bubbles slid off her body. My mouth went dry. She looked over her shoulder and winked, turning the shower off. No, she was done!

"You should've got up earlier if you wanted to join me."

"What?" I frowned. That was not fair; I was asleep and didn't know shower sex was up for grabs. "Get back in."

She laughed and shook her head, wrapping a towel around herself and, unfortunately, ending my perving.

"Can't, I've got to get to school. If you're up on time tomorrow though–"

"I'm there," I said, making a mental note to set my alarm earlier.

"I'll leave you to it then," she said, sauntering out of the room, trying, and succeeding, to look sexy.

Considering I'd missed some wet naked time I was in a really good mood. And it wasn't just the sex last night either. Things were finally back to normal between us. There'd been something missing for a while, she was distant, and I'd stupidly doubted her but she'd just been stressed and overworked. We had one last thing to discuss now that things were back on track – children.

I made no secret of the fact that I wanted them immediately, but she'd said she now wanted to wait. I had to know if that was just the stress talking or if she really meant it. Either way was fine, but we needed to talk about this stuff.

By the time I was ready for work, Abby had left, leaving a note that she'd be home before me tonight and would cook my favourite dinner and then take me to bed. I didn't mind that she hadn't said goodbye. I couldn't bloody wait for tonight.

"Morning," I said, yawning as I walked into the building.

Holly looked up and smiled wide, lighting up her whole face.

"Good morning, Jasper." She was very perky for half past eight in the morning. "Did you have a good weekend?"

"I had a good Sunday. You?"

She shrugged, blushing.

"I know that look," I said, pointing my finger at her. "Who is he?"

"No one."

"Bull. Details. Now." I pulled up a chair next to her, grateful that no customers had come in yet but the early seven a.m. classes had finished by now, and the next ones weren't until nine. I had about twenty minutes being me before I had to act professional.

"*Nothing happened*, but I met this guy and we're going to lunch."

"Oh yeah, where'd you meet him?"

"At the library."

"What were you doing there?" I shook my head. "Forget him, he's boring."

She tilted her head, and her golden hair fell in her face. She sat back up. "Just because he reads doesn't mean he's boring."

I raised my eyebrow. "Would you prefer him to read about an orgasm or give you one?" Her face turned the colour of the Santa's hat that still sat behind the monitor. Me and Kerry couldn't work out who took the hat out of the Christmas decoration box – I said her and she said me – so now it's a battle, and there was no way I was putting the damn thing in the loft.

"You're so crude," she hissed, pretending to look at the booking screen on the monitor so I wouldn't see how embarrassed she was.

Was that crude? "Sorry," I muttered, trying to keep a straight face. "What's his name?"

"Harry."

"And where is Harry taking you?"

"Carlton's."

"Ooh, the stuffy, posh place. Wanna take my number so you can text me to save you when you're so bored you want to stab yourself with their shiny, fancy silverware?" Carlton's was bloody boring. I took Abby there once, and I regretted it the second I stepped into the place.

"I think I'll be fine, thank you."

"You'll be bored. Get him to take you to the diner, eat crap and have an ice cream fight."

"I'm not eleven," she replied dryly.

"Nope, you were definitely born thirty." She frowned, and I knew I'd gone too far. "I didn't mean that in a bad way. You're not boring; you're just too shy and too scared to let your hair down. When was the last time you did anything impulsive?"

She opened her mouth and closed it again. "So what. So I don't have ice cream fights or jump out of planes, that doesn't mean I'm–"

"You want to jump out of a plane?" I asked, shocked.

"Yes."

"With a parachute attached, right? You're not that upset by what I said?"

She rolled her eyes, and a small smile tugged at the sides of her mouth. "Of course with a parachute." I would never have guessed she would want to do anything even remotely dangerous.

"If things go well with Harry, get him to jump with you." She needed someone that was going to challenge and push her. Brad was outgoing, an idiot and would do pretty much anything for a twenty or a shag. I had no idea why Holly was so reserved.

"I don't know."

"Why not. You want to do it, and you're an adult, so…"

"Uncle Jasper!" Everleigh screamed, coming to Holly's rescue. I shoved my chair out in time for her to leap up and land on my lap.

"Hey," I said, rustling her hair and grinning like a moron. I really missed her. Oakley walked in behind, carrying Eveleigh's Snow White bag. "Wait, have you just got here? And after all the crap you give me about being late."

She let the bags drop down on the table and raised her eyebrow. "I was here at seven. Cole went into work late today, so I let Everleigh stay at home for a bit longer. I've just been home to get her before Cole leaves."

Damn it. "Holly has a date," I said to get the spotlight off me.

Holly gave me an evil glare. Without all the eyeliner, she didn't look that scary though. Her looks matched her personality when she wore only a little make-up. Perhaps that was why she wore so much black around the eyes, to appear more confident.

"Really? Quick work," Oakley said, winking. "You've not been back long. Who is it?"

"Some boring dude she met at the library. By the way, what were you doing in a library?"

"Buying paint," she replied sarcastically.

"Ha ha. I meant because you're on break from Uni. Surely being around books is the last thing you want to do now?"

"Shut up," Oakley said, hitting the back of my head, making Everleigh gasp.

"You're not allowed to hit, Mummy," she said, shaking her head as if she was the parent and deeply disappointed.

"Go in the back office and watch TV for a minute," Oakley said, lifting her off my lap. "I'll come and get you when your class starts."

Everleigh skipped off, pulling her bag, which fell to the floor and scraped along the ground, behind her.

"It's great that you have a date, Holly. Jasper, why don't you make sure the gym is ready for the class?" She grinned. "Everleigh'll only tell you off if it's not."

She bloody would, too. If anyone came between her and her gymnastics time, she'd freak. It was like looking at Oakley when she was Everleigh's age. I knew that although Oakley hoped Everleigh would carry it on, she didn't think she would; the kid just liked climbing and jumping off stuff. It wouldn't surprise anyone if in a year or so, she stopped wanting to go.

"Am I in trouble?" I asked, grinning, "Or do you just want her out of the way, so you don't get in any more trouble?"

"Shut up, Jasper."

"You two sound just like me and Brad," Holly said and laughed. Flashing them a smile, I went to see if Marcus wanted any help.

After chatting with Holly and taking a million instructions for the new equipment that was being delivered for the new football pitch, Oakley left to take Everleigh swimming then to some messy play group. I'd take my kid to all that crap, too. I was sort of looking forward to it.

Holly kept to herself most of the day, working hard and doing everything exactly as she'd been taught. She worked like a newbie, before long she'd be on Facebook between booking customers in and filing. If she even had a Facebook account. Surely she would have.

The day dragged by so, so slowly. It didn't usually, but I was on a pretty sweet promise tonight, so I wanted to get home as soon as possible. Finally though, Oakley was back for a few hours while Cole gave Everleigh a bath, so I was free to leave. My sister also had a sweet deal tonight; she made the mess with Everleigh and her husband had to scrub the paint off her skin and hair!

Abby's car was in the drive. I practically abandoned my car on the street I was so excited to get this evening under way. My heart was racing and jeans were tightening with the excitement. I threw the front door open and legged it into the kitchen. The smell of steak and peppercorn sauce hit me as I walked through the door.

"Hey, babe," I said, grinning from ear to ear. My wife looked stunning in a summer dress with her hair pulled back, revealing her kissable neck.

She turned and handed me a bottle of beer. "Hey. Dinner will only be two minutes so why don't you sit down and I'll bring it over."

"Thanks." What the hell did I do to get this lucky? I sat at the table and watched her and her sexy arse as she finished up and brought our dinner to the table. My mouth watered as I flitted between looking at the big, fat juicy steak and my gorgeous, juicy wife. I couldn't wait to get her into bed and potentially make our baby. My heart suddenly dropped a little. We had to talk about what was going to happen on the baby making front.

I took a huge swig of beer, gathering as much courage as I could. *Man, I'm such a pussy. Grow some balls and ask your damn wife when she wants kids!*

"Abby, did you really mean it when you said you don't want children yet?"

She froze; her wine glass suspended in the air and then she put it down. That wasn't a good sign.

"How come you're bringing this up now? I thought we were having a relaxing evening together."

"We are." What did that mean? We can't talk about things like that because we were supposed to be having lots of sex later?

She sighed, pushing her food around on the plate. "Jasper, right now just isn't a good time. There's so much going on, and if we have a baby now it'll be ten times harder to go back to work after."

"Of course it will, but it'll be harder whenever we have one. You know we'll work out childcare with Oakley."

We split having Everleigh between us so we could both work at The Centre, so I knew she'd do the same with her niece or nephew. Abby wouldn't even have to give up work. I wasn't a chauvinistic bastard, and I didn't expect her to give up on her career goals. I wanted to do as much as I possibly could. Hell, I'd do it all if I had to.

"Right. So you want to wait a year or…?"

"Maybe we can talk about it again in a year." Just talk about it again in a year. What if she decided she wanted to talk about it again in another year? I nodded, pretending that I wasn't so disappointed it was crushing me.

"Okay, we'll talk next year," I whispered, forcing a smile. Our night was ruined; I could feel it by the way she dropped her eyes to her dinner and refused to look at me. Did she not want children at all now or was it really just not in the next couple years? I'd wait a few years if that was what she needed, but not having them at all would be too much. I couldn't do that.

I gulped and forced in another mouthful. If she didn't want kids at all, it was over.

CHAPTER
Six

Jasper

To say I was in a bad mood was an understatement. I was pissed. My wife was being fucking impossible, and I had no idea if she was bullshitting me and didn't want a baby at all or genuinely just wanted to wait.

I tried bringing the subject up again, but all I got was her cutting me off and telling me we'd agreed to talk about it in a year's time. And we hadn't had sex since the night before our should've been romantic evening. We were back to another dry spell.

"Jasper, I think the chip and pin machine is broken," Holly said, frowning and shaking it as if that was going to magically make it work.

"Some twat is coming to change it tomorrow," I replied.

Her eyes darted up to mine at my choice of words.

"What's wrong?" She asked.

Sighing, I took a seat next to her. Holly had been working

with us for a week, and she was doing a great job: she was also a better agony aunt than the ones in Abby's magazines.

"Nothing, just the usual."

I'd told Holly all about Abby's change of baby plan. I hadn't even told Oakley. There was something about Holly that made you open up, probably because she was the first girl that I wasn't related to that I didn't try to pick up – before I was married of course. I didn't have a girl friend. There was Kerry, but we were only friends through Ben. I wouldn't admit it to her and let her get a big head, but I really valued Holly's friendship.

"I'm sure she just needs time, especially if her career is going well."

I knew I couldn't be pissed at Abby for that; she deserved to do what she wanted, and I was happy for her, but she had no consideration for the plan we had already made and what I wanted. I hated that she could just change everything on her own without even talking it through with me first. She was all for making decisions together when it suited her.

I nodded. "Yeah. Not much I can do anyway. It's not even the fact that she needs more time – I get that – it's that she didn't tell me for ages."

"I'm sorry," she said and offered me one of the chocolate biscuits she had in a packet on the desk. I took one and smiled. "You know, it's really nice to meet a guy that wants to start a family so much, it's usually the other way around."

"Well, I've done the being young and sleeping around thing. Before Everleigh, I wasn't sure I wanted kids, but she won me over."

Holly smiled. "She is adorable."

"She is," I agreed. "I keep worrying that Abby's one year will turn to two, then three, and I'll end up childless with a wife that's always working. Most of my teachers were old; I know they don't give it up until they're Zimmer-frame bound."

"I don't think she wants to wait until she's retired, Jasper. Perhaps promotion opportunities are coming up, and she wants to go for those before she takes a year out to have a baby?"

She did say she wanted to concentrate on her career, so that's what I took that to mean. *When she's moved up a bit more, she'll want to have a kid.* At least that was what I was telling myself. "Yeah, I know. I just hate that we were always on the same page. We made all these plans, and now I feel like she's going down a completely different road."

"No," Holly said, "she's just taken a detour."

"You're a wise one," I said, patting her head and making her let out a shy laugh. Physical contact with men always made her blush; she even did it when the deliveryman touched her hand as he passed her a pen. It was the reason me and Ben made sure to nudge her or innocently touch her arm whenever we could – it was just funny.

"You're out tonight, right?" I asked.

Holly nodded. "Oakley's making me."

"Cool."

It'd been ages since we'd all been out together. Mum was having Everleigh overnight, so Oakley and Cole could both go, and I was planning on getting my sister drunk. I'd only seen her pissed a few times, but it was hilarious.

"Anyway, I better go see what Oakley's left me to do today," I said as I walked into the office behind reception.

I flicked open the daybook and groaned as I saw what Oakley had written:

Jasper, Helen has an appointment so won't be in until 12,

*please clean the equipment after the Over 50's Fit Club – I
know how much you love doing that!*

*Vending machine mechanic's coming at some point to service
it – mention the dodgy C2 button – I won't be happy if I don't
get my Munchies!*

She was hilarious! The thought of cleaning off sweaty dumb-
bells made my stomach turn. Why did the cleaner, Helen, have to
make her appointment for today? I bet it was done on purpose.
Some women in the Over 50's Club were like dogs on heat, and
they had no issue with the fact that they were old enough to be my
mum!

I walked back out. Holly was printing some summer class
flyers for the teenage boy that thinks he's the dog's bollocks to
hand out tomorrow.

"You done something different with your hair? It suits you,"
I said, giving my award-winning smile.

She turned, blushing shyly, and then her eyes narrowed. "No,
I'm not cleaning the Over's room for you."

"Damn it! Did you read the daybook?"

"No, I just learn. As if I'm going to fall for that again."

"Think I could pay that kid to clean too? His number written
anywhere?" He was handing out hundreds of flyers for cash, so I
had no doubt that I could sling him twenty quid and he'd clean. He
was desperate to get tinted windows on that tin can he called a car.

Holly grinned, suddenly very amused. She picked up a pack-
age from the desk.

"These came today. I was going to put them in the cleaner's
cupboard when you came in. Good thing I waited."

She handed me a pair of yellow rubber gloves.

"You're so funny," I muttered. "If I'm not back in twenty

minutes come and find me, you know how they are."

She laughed, taking too much pleasure at the thought of my impending pain.

"Hello, Jean," I said, taking a subtle step back. She was the worst. Jean was about a stone overweight, wore clothes about a size too small and had straw-like mousy hair, cut into a bob. She also had a heart of gold. But she really needed to watch where she put her hands.

"Jasper, dear, when are you taking me to dinner? I've been waiting two years now."

I laughed. "Jean, that's George's job."

She waved her hand. "Oh, that silly old fool'll never take me. Don't like the way other people cook, apparently. Doesn't help that he smoked like a chimney for near thirty years. His taste buds are shot to bits."

What could I say to that?

I laughed nervously as she took a step closer, now invading my personal space.

"If I were ten years younger, I'd eat you alive."

I winced. Only ten years younger? That would still put her in the could-be-my-mother category.

"I believe that," I replied, trying to keep my voice light. I really didn't want to think about her 'eating me alive'.

"Are you all done in here now?"

"We are in *here*. Right, ladies?" Jean said, giving me a wink.

I didn't ask where she wanted to go, which was obviously what she was hinting at.

"Great, have a lovely day," I said and sidestepped them all, walking over to the floor mats. They all looked like sweet, al-most-old ladies, but they were vultures. One of them, Noreen, even grabbed the electrician's arse when he was working in the hallway. We were lucky no one had tried suing us because of the old cougar club, yet.

"Jasper, dear, how long is that lovely young lady here for?" Jean asked.

They still hadn't left.

I hauled the pile of mats up and straightened my back, trying not to show anyone how heavy they were.

"She's here for the summer, then back to Uni at the end of September."

"Oh, such a shame. I was hoping we could hold onto her. She looks fun to corrupt."

"Now, now, Jean, leave the poor girl alone."

She pointed at me. "You think I don't know your reputation, mister? A few years ago you'd have had her crying over you."

All right, I wasn't that much of a bastard. I'd never lead any-one on.

"I'm a respectable, married man now."

She laughed from her diaphragm, cocking her head back.

"You're married, Jasper, I'll give you that one."

"Hey, I'm respectable!"

"You're up here flirting with us fogeys every week."

My mouth dropped. Did she honestly believe it was me that flirted with them? That was, nor never, would be the case.

I smiled, now conscious that a bit of friendly banter and cheeky smile was considered flirting. Was it?

She waved her hand dismissively. "Don't you worry, I won't be telling George or that wife of yours."

She laughed again and walked out, followed by the last of the stragglers. Abby was always 'that wife of yours'. But then Abby didn't really make time for idle chitchat with strangers, so they never warmed to her.

"Your usual?" I asked Abby as we walked into the bar.

She bit her lip as if I'd asked her what the square root of pie was. Actually, she probably knew; she'd listened in school and had gone to Uni. Whereas I'd pissed about and had a laugh.

"Um. Yes, please," she finally replied.

See, that wasn't so hard, was it.

I spotted Oakley, Cole, Holly, and Brad on a table so nodded my head towards it.

"Why don't you take a seat, and I'll bring it over."

I watched her eyes drift over and settle on Holly who was looking much better with less of that heavy eyeliner. Less is more.

"I'd prefer to stay with you."

I shrugged. "Alright."

"Double JD and coke, red wine and six shots of whatever's closest, please," I said to the bartender.

Abby's eyes snapped to me.

"Six shots? Does Holly even drink?"

"Brad's ordered a taxi for them all, so I assume she's drinking tonight. If not, I'm sure someone will do hers."

If Abby was going to be a dick around Holly all night, I was going to need extra shots. I wanted to have fun, not referee her bitchy comments. Abby was usually so sweet about everyone, but if she was jealous she could turn in a second. I didn't like it, and I had no time for it. At least guys would give each other a black eye and move on.

I paid, and we walked over.

"You're all doing one," I said, putting the shots on the table. "Ben and Kerry coming?"

"No, they're on a date," Oakley replied and grabbed two

shots, handing one to Cole. "We're child free tonight and tomorrow morning, so let's drink up."

Who took over my reserved sister's body?

"Let's do it," I said, and clinked my glass against Oakley's. I loved to see her relax, have fun and act her age. "If you don't want it I'll do your shot, Holly."

She smiled. "Thanks. I'll have one. You can do the rest for the evening."

An hour later and I'd done it. Mixing shots with beer had got me well and truly wasted. Abby, who wasn't that drunk at all, pretty much refused to acknowledge Holly's existence now, which annoyed me. Since my lengthy conversation with Holly, Abby had turned arctic as if we'd been having sex the whole time and not just talking. Holly was cool, and as our friend's sister she should at least be civil.

Holly sat awkwardly, talking and laughing with Oakley. She'd noticed the tension, and she didn't seem like the type of person to come out and ask Abby what the deal was.

I was so when Abby went to the bar I followed. "What's your problem?" I hissed in her ear.

"My problem?" She asked, turning her nose up like I was something she'd stepped in. "What's with the 'I'll have your shot, Holly' crap?"

"What? She doesn't drink much." Jesus, I was just trying to be nice to the girl who barely knew any of us! She was a friend, just like Brett was hers! "Everyone can sense the tension so cut the shit. Holly's alright, just give her a chance."

"You would think that."

"What? Abby, have you lost it?"

"She's your type."

It was then that I realised my wife didn't know me at all.

The women that were my type were confident women that dressed sexy and wore light make-up, nothing heavy. Holly was not my type and even if she was; I was married, there was no way I'd be chasing her.

"Whatever," she said.

"Yeah, whatever." I walked off to the bathroom, grinding my teeth.

Something niggled at the back of my mind: *Abby's cheating.*

Wasn't it the people who were always accusing others the ones that were doing it? She thought I had a thing for Holly because she had a thing with someone else and was trying to shift the spotlight off herself. I didn't want to believe that was true but I bloody couldn't stop myself coming back to the same conclusion.

Laying my head back against the wall, I took a deep breath, pushing those thoughts further down inside. It was just in my head. We were just going through a rough patch, that was it.

CHAPTER
Seven

Jasper

"You giving up alcohol when Abby's pregnant?" Oakley asked as we sat in her living room going through the new gymnastics equipment we needed and what it'd cost.

The Centre was doing really well, and the gym coach, Marcus, was keen to update some of the stuff. Since Oakley got away, he was determined that another potential Olympian wouldn't. He thought he had one in eight-year-old Aleah.

Cole had stopped drinking when she was pregnant with Everleigh. Well, when they were out together anyway. On lads' nights out he was as trashed as the rest of us.

I shrugged. "I won't have to worry about that for a while."

She put down her pad of scribbled notes and figures. "Oh? I thought you were trying soon."

Yeah me too.

"No," I replied. "Postponing for a year."

Or longer.

"Ah. Okay. I thought you were all set but at least you get more time together without being woken up in the night or at the crack of dawn."

I smiled tightly. "Yeah."

She could see right through me. Her eyes narrowed the tiniest bit.

"This wasn't your decision, was it? I thought it was odd; you've been so excited."

"Abby wants a career."

"That's understandable. Believe me, everything is harder with a baby."

"I'm ready for harder. I want harder. This fu–"

I stopped myself as Oakley's eyes widened. We both looked over at Everleigh who was too absorbed in Beauty and the Beast to have heard my near slip up.

"This sucks," I said quieter. "I hate that she just decided on her own. We were ready. She said she was ready. Christ, we'd even picked out the soft lime paint for the damn nursery." I scratched my forehead.

Why couldn't I let it go? I was stuck on having a baby. It was on my mind most of the time, driving me crazy.

"Jasper, why are you so desperate for a family? It's not like either of you are pushing fifty. There's plenty of time to have children. Trust me, enjoy the peace while you still can!"

My grip on the mug tightened. "I'm not desperate."

My once sweet little sister raised her eyebrow. "Sure you're not."

"I'm not."

She looked up, pained. What was going through her head?

"Our family was ripped apart in the worst possible way."

"Oh, fuck that." I stood up, raising my hands. "I'm not trying to recreate a family because I feel like I've lost out on something."

"If that's not it then why are you reacting so badly?"

"Because I don't want to talk about that arsehole," I hissed and spun around, ready to make a quick exit. But I couldn't leave. No one else was here, and I didn't want to leave her alone if she was thinking about what our sorry excuse of a father did to her.

I turned around and sat down. She smiled half-heartedly, eyes watching Everleigh who was still too into her film to notice us.

"Do you want to talk about him?" I asked, praying she'd say no.

"Not him. I want to talk about you."

"I'm fine."

"You're not, but you're too stubborn to admit it. Come to therapy with me."

I laughed and shook my head. "I'll pass, but thanks."

"Please? I think it'd be good for you. For both of us. Since the trial that subject's been pretty closed–"

"And it still is."

She sighed and her eyebrows knitted together.

"Whatever you say and however much you try to be the strong one that's not affected by anything, I know how badly it's hurt you. Jasper, you don't go through something like that and get to walk away without scars. He was your dad–"

"Shut up, Oakley!" I clenched my fists and took a deep breath. My world turned red, and I wanted nothing more than to smash something up and go get wasted.

"Please, come with me. I hate seeing you like this. Just go for a couple times and if it does nothing for you I'll never mention it again."

She gave me her pleading look, and I groaned.

"Fine, I'll give you two sessions and then I'm outta there."

"Thank you. You're not going to regret it."

Carol wasn't what I expected. I thought she'd be in a black suit, notebook and pen in hand and instruct me to sit back on a reclining chair. Her office was relaxed, warm and welcoming with cushions, pictures on the walls and crystal figurines on a bookshelf.

Carol herself was a welcoming person too. She had her long wispy hair pulled back in a bun. She looked as if she was about to bake for us, not tell me where I was going wrong and how to fix my life.

Oakley sat beside me, leaning back on the sofa with her legs crossed at the knee. She looked the picture of ease while all I could think about was getting the hell out of there.

"So, Oakley tells me she practically had to drag you here," Carol said, smiling.

I glared at my sister out of the corner of my eye. She wasn't supposed to tell her that! "I don't need therapy."

"What do you need?"

"A drink."

Carol laughed. "I've heard that one before. In our sessions, Oakley has expressed concern for how you're coping with what happened."

"I cope fine."

"He doesn't," Oakley said. "He's too stubborn and selfless to think about what he's feeling or what he needs. Drives me crazy."

"Sorry, should I be a selfish prick?"

She frowned and elbowed me in the ribs. "You should be more selfish, yes. I don't want you to hold it all in because you're scared of what it'll do to me and mum. You can talk about him."

"Why would I want to?" What possible reason could I ever have to think about that man ever again? After everything, I didn't get why Oakley would want to keep on going over it.

"Because he hurt you, too! It wasn't just me, Jasper. He hurt all of us."

"Okay," Carol said, "let's cool down for a minute."

I didn't want to 'cool down' I wanted to leave. I scratched my jaw and took a deep breath.

"Jasper, how do you feel about your father?"

"How the fuck do you think?"

Oakley scowled at me, telling me to stop, but I carried on regardless.

"I hate him. He could drop down dead right now, and I'd throw a party."

Carol said nothing. Oakley lowered her head. She couldn't tell me she didn't feel the same.

"Have you grieved for the loss of your father? You're allowed to miss that part of him; it's only natural."

I stared at her. Had she lost it? "He stopped being my father the day he let his sick pervert friend touch my little sister." I heard Oakley's gulp, and I took her hand. "I'm sorry."

"Don't be. I want you to talk about how you feel, remember. I just want you to be okay, Jas."

I'd not heard her call me Jas in a fucking long time, not since we were really little kids and she used to say it to annoy me. "Well, I'm fine, so stop worrying." I looked back to Carol. "She thinks I want kids to recreate a family I lost. Crazy."

"That doesn't sound crazy at all. In fact, it's natural to want a family, Jasper, especially if it's something you feel you've missed out on," Carol said.

"I have a family." Beside me, I felt my sister tense, growing frustrated with my lack of cooperation. I had to keep reminding myself that she worried about me and was only trying to help. "Look, I want a family because I want one. Not because I'm trying to fill some hole."

I should have told her that as excited as I was to have children I was also terrified. I would never hurt my kids the way my father hurt Oakley but what if I hurt them indirectly? If I didn't protect them from something else? The way I didn't protect Oakley.

I was haunted by a vision of Oakley as a child, scared, alone and crying every single day. Then when Everleigh was born she was standing right beside her, scared, alone and crying. And when me and Abby were all set to start trying before she changed her mind, a girl that looked half like me and half like Abby joined them.

I didn't want to admit that out loud and have Carol analyse it, and I didn't want my sister to know it at all.

Carol nodded. "Good. Oakley mentioned you and your wife have put those plans on hold."

"Did she now," I muttered.

Oakley winced. "Sorry. I know I shouldn't have said anything, but Carol asked if you were trying now, so…"

Apparently I featured in Oakley's sessions a lot. I had no idea how much she worried.

I shook my head. "It's fine. That's the point of therapy, right, to talk?"

"Was that a mutual decision, Jasper?" Carol asked.

I looked at my sister and knew she'd not discussed why me and Abby had stopped trying.

"No. Abby was being shady about it until I asked her outright. She wants a career first, and that's fine."

"Is it fine?"

Oakley sank back in the sofa, into the background as Carol fired her questions.

"Yes. What's not fine is her making the decision before discussing it with me. We were all set for Operation Knock Up, then she avoids the conversation and then she tells me it's on hold."

"Your anger is understandable but have you considered that it may have been difficult for her to tell you how she was feeling?"

"Maybe. I hadn't thought of that. We've always been able to talk about anything though."

"What is it?" Carol said, prompting me to explain what my deep frown was about.

"Recently I've not been feeling like I can talk to her either."

"Why do you think that is?"

"I'm not sure. She's been working a lot more. Sometimes I feel like she's moving on and changing and I'm still the same guy I was when we got back together."

"Back together?"

"Yeah, we went out when we were teenagers."

"How did it end?"

Oakley looked up at me, and I could tell what she was thinking. Maybe Abby was distant because she was cheating again.

"She slept with my friend."

"But you're past that now."

"I am."

"Am or was? Is that why you don't feel like you can talk to her any longer? The distance you feel as a result of her focusing on something else is creating doubt in your mind."

I hated her for being able to talk me round and make me look at something in a new light. Or for just getting the truth out of me from what I didn't say.

"I guess," I replied, half sulking. "But it's not because she's concentrating on something else and not giving me enough attention. I'm not that self-absorbed."

"That's not what I was suggesting."

"Then I suppose you're right. A part of me does think she could be seeing someone else and I hate myself for it. When I forgave her, I made a promise to myself that I'd let it go and never throw it back in her face, and until now I haven't."

"Have you spoken to her about your fears?"

"No. She has no idea what I'm thinking, and I don't want to tell her."

"Why not?"

"Because if I'm wrong she's going to be crushed."

Carol nodded once. "And if you're right you're going to be crushed."

"You have a knack for hitting the nail on the head."

"I hope so," she replied, "or I'm not doing my job right."

"So is this the part where you tell me what to do?"

"I can't do that. What you do with your life is entirely up to you, Jasper. I'm here to listen, help you identify the root cause of your issues and suggest ways you can address them. But I can't do any of it for you."

"Alright, what do you suggest?"

"Having an open conversation with your wife is a start."

Oakley played with her fingers, and I knew she wanted to know Carol's thoughts on what I should do about the man rotting in prison. He was locked away, so he wasn't a concern. All I wanted was for things with Abby to go back to normal so we could be happy again.

My father was nothing. My wife was everything.

CHAPTER
Eight

Jasper

"I'm home, sweetie," Abby shouted from the front door.

"In the kitchen."

"Okay. I'm just going for a quick shower then I'll be down. I've had a nightmare of a day, had to fill in for a double period of year ten PE. I'm sweaty and exhausted. Won't be long."

Her footsteps thudded up the stairs. I ran my finger around the rim of my mug.

What the fuck is going on?

She never ran straight to the shower from work. What the hell was wrong with me? She'd just explained why. Everyone wanted to shower after exercise. I would, although I would've said hello properly and given her a kiss before going.

Here I was all ready to take Carol's advice and talk to Abby and hopefully get us back on track, and she was running off upstairs to shower.

Since I admitted out loud that I was worried she was cheating, it was constantly in my head.

All I could think was that she had to be cheating. And along with Oakley, Everleigh and my child's terrified faces all I could see was my wife in the arms of someone else.

"What would you like for dinner?" She asked, kissing the top of my head as she walked by ten minutes later. I was so grateful for her coming back at that moment and stopping the mental images that plagued my mind.

"Since you've had a long day why don't we order Chinese?" I replied.

"Sounds good to me. Shall I order?" She asked, ruffling up her damp, dark blonde hair.

I nodded.

She was being weird, acting as if we were practical strangers. I'd seen her be warmer towards traffic wardens. "Are you okay?" I asked.

"Yeah, fine. Sorry, I just need to relax and forget about work. Why don't you pour me a glass of wine, and I'll call the take-away."

I stood up, eyeing her suspiciously as she unlocked her mobile. She used the house phone to call landlines. Why was she keeping that so close to her? I forced myself to look away and get on with making her a drink. Second-guessing, everything she did made me feel like shit.

I trusted her. Nothing was going on. Nothing could be going on because it'd crush me and end us. I wanted our marriage to work. She left the kitchen, but I heard her placing our usual order. My stomach turned. What if she was cheating?

There was no way I could forgive her again. We'd be over. The thought of her with another man was painful. Did he get her fun playfulness and leave me with the withdrawn distant woman?

"Abby," I called as I heard her say bye.

She stepped out from the living room. "Yes?"

"What's going on? You're distant, and it's more than work."

She froze for a second and then frowned. "It's not more. Nothing is wrong. I'm tired, Jasper, that's all."

Tired all the time? I didn't believe that. It was a cop-out.

"No, you either treat me as if I'm in the way, or you're indifferent. Have I done something?"

She sighed. "You've not done anything. I have."

The colour drained from my face. "What?" I whispered.

"All of our plans have changed, and it's my fault. Do you think it's easy to see the disappointment in your eyes knowing that I'm the cause? I'm angry because I hurt you and I'm angry at you for not understanding."

"That's shit. How many times have I told you I understand? I do, Abby, and I've never tried to make you feel bad about it. I am disappointed; I can't help it, but I've never tried to make you feel worse about it. If you're feeling guilty, that's on you."

Now I was pissed off. How dare she blame me when all I'd done was support her? I'd encouraged her to go for the Deputy Head of English and then the Head of English jobs. I was the one waiting in the car after her interview and taking her out to dinner after. How fucking dare she suggest that I want a child over her career aspirations?

"Well, thank you very much! Now I feel a whole lot better!" she shouted.

"Why're you being like this? I'm not fighting with you so lower your voice and talk to me the way you used to. What is going on?"

Her face reddened. She was angry. Well, so was I.

"You're making me out to be the bad one."

I threw my arms up in exasperation. "I'm not making you out to be anything!"

"Don't think I don't know that look your mum gave you when you said we're waiting to have a baby."

"What look?" *Jesus, I swear she sees what she wants to.*

"She knew it was because of me."

"So!"

Abby glared. "So?"

"Yeah. So? It doesn't matter whose idea it was. We're married, Abby, so I'll fucking stick by whatever you want to do. I don't care if my mum or your parents want a grandchild now if one of us isn't ready, for whatever reason, we're waiting."

Tears filled her eyes, and she leant back against the wall. What the fuck now?

"I hate the way things are between us," she whispered.

"So do I. Why is it like this? I don't resent you for wanting to wait."

"I feel like you do."

"Well, I'm telling you I don't. What more can I do, Abby? Why can't you believe me?"

She shrugged. "I don't know. Maybe because I know how much having a family means to you."

"It means a lot, but I don't need it right this second. I thought it meant a lot to you too?"

"It did." She closed her eyes, and when she opened them again they were distant. "It does, but I can't even think about it right now. There's too much going on. I'd rather get my career to where I want it now. It'll be harder to do it with a baby."

"Fine," I said. "That's fine. I've never said it isn't. You're making this a much bigger deal than it has to be, and I don't understand why. If you're worried about what my mum thinks, I'll have a word with her, but you know she loves you, too. As long as we're happy she's happy."

"Oh, come on. She's much closer to Cole."

"What? Is this jealousy because you think my mum prefers her son-in-law to you?" *Fuck, is she eight?*

"Don't look at me like that!" she growled. "You have no idea!"

"You're right, I don't, but that's because you're not making any damn sense!"

"I'm just sick of being the one that's making you unhappy."

"I'm unhappy because you've been cold and distant recently. We're waiting to have a baby, fine. Let's leave it at that and not mention it for a year or so. Can we please just get back to normal now?"

"So that's it? Topic closed and everything's fine?"

Wasn't that what she wanted?

"Yeah," I replied. "I'll warm some plates, I hate chow mien cold."

Turning around, I walked deeper in the kitchen and away from her. Hopefully, she'd calm down now. That had to be one of the most ridiculous and pathetic arguments we'd ever had. I still didn't get the crap about my mum preferring Cole; she'd never treated them any differently. She saw them both more because of Everleigh. And because Abby worked a lot!

I shoved two plates in the microwave, ready to turn on when the Chinese arrived.

After our awful evening yesterday I'd arranged to drop Everleigh off at mum's and for Oakley to pick her up from there. Me and Abby needed a weekend away, somewhere we could relax without the monotonous everyday life stuff. We hadn't talked properly or had sex in three weeks, and I was starting to feel like the distance between us was unfixable.

I had to do something so I'd booked a Bed and Breakfast near the coast for Friday and Saturday night, and I was on my way to the school to surprise her.

She shared car rides with another teacher so I'd spoken to Louise about not waiting around for Abby after school was out.

Everything was planned, apart from her weekend bag. There was no way I was going to pack for her because my choices would just end up being wrong and/or inappropriate for public. We had time though. It was only three-thirty.

I'd learnt not to come until fifteen minutes after school was out as it was hectic before. I also didn't like the young girls looking at me, and Abby didn't like getting comments about her 'hot' husband. Ten years ago I would've been eating it up.

I walked through the front entrance and nodded to the girl still at reception. I knew her, so she waved me through, but I couldn't remember her name, so I didn't stop to make an idiot out of myself. Abby's classroom was at the back of the school – about as far away as possible. Surely English was an important subject; it should be closer.

Strolling through the halls brought back so many memories of me and Abby in school. We were inseparable from the minute we got together; that seemed like such a long time ago now. I'd give anything to get that back again. I wanted her to look at me like I was the only guy on earth again, and I hoped this weekend would help with that.

"Hello, Jasper," Louise said as she stepped out of her classroom and closed the door.

"Hey, Louise."

"On your way to pick her up?"

No, just here for the view! "Yeah."

"I've been so excited for you all day. It's been torture not telling her. She's going to love a romantic weekend by the sea."

"Yeah, I hope so. You didn't tell her, right?"

"Course not. Anyway, I'd better go, I've got my own romantic weekend planned with a stack of marking!" She nodded her head towards her bulging, oversized leather bag.

"Sounds fun."

"Doesn't it," she replied sarcastically and smiled. "Have a good weekend."

"Thanks, try to relax too."

"I will. Bye."

I watched her disappear around the corner then made my way to the English block. Abby's door was shut, and I tried to picture her face as I told her where we were going.

I pushed the door opened and immediately wished I hadn't.

CHAPTER
Nine

Jasper

My stomach lurched. I stood there staring at my wife with her tongue down another man's throat. I'd been suspicious of her for a while but even so, I couldn't quite believe she'd do it. They hadn't seen me yet. I wanted to scream at her and knock that bastard the fuck out, but I couldn't move. I was stuck watching her cut my heart out and piss all over the life we'd planned.

She pulled away first and smiled at him the way she used to at me. Brett. Then, finally, she looked over and her face fell.

"Oh no," she whispered, pushing the prick away. "Jasper…"

I held my hand up; there was no explanation for what she'd done.

"Look, man," Brett said, and before he got any further, I launched myself forwards. Abby screamed for me to stop, but I couldn't. I was panting.

Adrenaline mixed with fury and betrayal coursed through

my veins. My heavily clenched fist collided with his jaw, and he stumbled backwards, falling over the desk he'd just had my wife leant against.

"Fuck you!" I spat at him and then looked at Abby. "You made me forgive you and trust you again. You promised you'd never hurt me like that, but your word means shit. Our marriage means shit. I'm filing for divorce. You stay the hell away from me and my family."

Usually, when she cried it made me feel like crap, but I didn't care now – in that sense – she hadn't changed at all. He was welcome to her.

I turned on my heel, ignoring her pleas for me to come back and talk about it, and stormed out of the school.

I got to my car, and it was only when I turned the key in the ignition that it hit me. She'd cheated again, and my marriage was over. Swallowing hard, I pulled out of the parking space and drove off, just in time for her to come running through the double doors.

My eyes were heavy, and I leant against the bar, propped up by my arm, downing yet another double JD – straight. My phone had been ringing non-stop until I blocked her number. Then it started ringing non-stop from my sister's number. I didn't want to speak to anyone. I wanted to drink myself into oblivion.

Minutes, or hours, later – I could no longer tell which – Cole sat down beside me. My sister had sent her husband out searching for me.

"She a fucking bitch," I slurred, holding my hand up to get the bartender's attention.

"What happened? Oakley's been going crazy trying to get hold of you. Abby called and told us to find you; she's worried, too."

I laughed humourlessly. "My wife is worried, is she?"

"What happened?"

"Went to meet her from work. Saw her kissing that Brett twat."

"Shit," Cole hissed. "I'm sorry, man." He shook his head, and I knew he was trying to think of something else to say. I would've been the same. What the hell do you say in situations like that?

"I think I should get you home."

"Home. I don't have a home now."

"Come on, you do. I don't think Abby is there, she said she was at her mum's and that we should find you."

"I don't care where she is."

She could be with Brett. I clenched my jaw and shoved away the image of them together.

"I can't go back there now. How do I know she's not had him back there? I don't want to be around anything that reminds me of her."

"Come to ours then."

I snorted. "And let Everleigh see me like this?"

"It's almost one in the morning, Jasper," he replied.

"You got anything back at yours?"

"Bourbon and Southern Comfort. And some girlie shit Oakley drinks, tastes like fruit."

I laughed. "Bourbon's mine. No mention of Abby to Oakley." He frowned.

"I mean it. She'll want to talk. I just want to drink."

"You're not going to be able to do that for long."

"I know. I'll deal with it tomorrow."

He held his hands up. "Alright. Let's go, and you'd better be able to walk because I'm not carrying your arse out of here."

"Cheers, man. Your support is just what I need right now."

He smiled and chucked some money down on the bar, downing my shot that had just been placed in front of me.

"Jasper, where the hell have you been?" Oakley asked sounding more like Mum than I had ever heard her before.

I shrugged with one shoulder, hoping that I didn't look too drunk.

"Bar."

"Why?"

"To get a drink."

She glared.

"Jasper, why don't you go through to the kitchen? You know where the booze is kept," Cole said.

"What?" Oakley hissed. "Someone needs to tell me what's going on."

I held my hands above my head and walked past them to the kitchen. I did not need to have that discussion tonight. I did need a drink though.

Opening the cupboard slowly so it wouldn't creek, I honed in on their conversation. Now I'd see if Cole was going to tell his wife or keep his word. There wasn't fucking much keeping of words lately.

"What on earth is going on? Why is he in that state?" She asked.

"Calm down. He's fine. He doesn't want to talk about it tonight, so we need to go in there and have a drink with him."

"Like he needs more drink! You know what's wrong, don't you?"

I practically heard him gulp. "I do, but he's asked me not to say anything, so please don't ask me to tell you, baby."

She sighed. "Fine. He's okay though, right?"

"He will be."

Would I? I had no idea what I was going to do next, apart from necking the Bourbon.

Cole and Oakley joined me just as I sat down and poured myself a drink. Oakley got herself a glass of water, and I was about to protest when I realised that Cole was going to drink with me, so one of them would have to have a clear head for Everleigh in the morning. Shit, I was going to have to stay in the spare room until I'd sobered up tomorrow.

"Okay?" Oakley said and sat beside me. She tried to keep her voice light, but I could see the worry in her eyes. Something I think would've been easier if we weren't so close. Worrying about the people you love was exhausting.

"Fine," I replied with a smile. I downed the glass in two large gulps.

No one knew what to say. I could tell my little sister was desperate to start the Spanish inquisition, but I knew she wouldn't because I didn't want her to.

"I hope you weren't saving this for anything," I said to Cole, raising the bottle before pouring myself some more.

"What's mine is yours, mate, you know that." I had a feeling if I hadn't just been cheated on he would be wrestling some of it off me for himself.

I downed another glass.

Shortly after sitting down, Oakley went up to bed. She had to be up at the arse crack of dawn with Everleigh, and she wasn't getting anything out of me. And I expected she thought I would open up with Cole and have a man chat, or whatever it was women thought men to do.

I drank until the sun came up.

My head pounded and my mouth was as dry as a desert. I'd never felt so rough after a night on the drink before. Groaning, I rubbed my temples to try to stop the throbbing pain.

Downstairs I could hear Everleigh gibbering away and as much as I love that girl, I couldn't face playing hide and seek just yet. I closed my eyes and willed my hangover to go.

"Jasper?" Oakley called quietly outside the door.

"Yeah, I'm awake."

She walked in, carrying a plate and mug. The smell of coffee hit me, and I sat up.

"Here," she said, "eat this and take these." She put the plate of toast and coffee on the bedside table and handed me a packet of pills from her pocket.

"Thanks," I replied, popping the tablets out of the pack as soon as they'd landed on my lap.

"Everleigh doesn't know you're here so Cole is taking her to his sister's for a bit. Apparently, Mia bought glitter play dough for the girls so Everleigh's excited."

I looked up, knowing what that meant. "So you want to talk."

"I do, but only when you're ready. You look like shit right now."

"Thanks," I replied. Just what I wanted to hear on top of everything else. Siblings really didn't sugar coat it. "Abby is cheating."

Her mouth fell open, and she sat down, making the bed bounce at how she dropped down onto it. "She what?"

"Yep, I was right. Isn't that fucking fantastic."

"I don't…" She shook her head. "With who? How did you find out?"

"Walked in on her kissing that fucker Brett at school."

"Oh my God. I can't believe it."

"Yeah, well, me too."

"I'm so sorry, Jasper." Her eyes filled with tears. I looked away from the pitying expression. "I can't believe she did that to you." She suddenly looked murderously angry. "Like you needed that after everything. You can stay here as long as you like. You know that, right?"

Like anyone needed that ever.

I looked back and saw her trying to control her emotions. "Yeah. Thanks."

"What're you going to do now?"

"You know a good divorce lawyer?" I asked, laughing with no humour.

She bit her lip. "Have you spoken to her since?"

"No, and I don't want to. She'll hear from me through our lawyers. She can have the house; I don't want it. She'll either have to buy me out, or we'll sell and split what's left."

"Are you sure? That's your home."

"Not anymore. It's all hers. I want nothing to do with her. Has she called you today?"

Oakley shook her head, and I took a gulp of the boiling hot coffee.

"Good."

"This is all happening so fast. Are you sure you don't want to talk to her?"

I stopped mid-swallow. "You think I should forgive her again?"

"God, no! I think you should talk it through though. You bottle everything up and move on without ever dealing with anything. Don't you have questions for her?"

Oakley was now a deal-with-things-and-find-the-answer-by-talking-the-shit-out-of-it, and I was a deal-with-it-and-find-the-answer-on-the-bottom-of-a-bottle kind of guy.

"You're supposed to be on my side, you know?"

"I am, Jasper. You have no idea what I want to do to her right now, but I just want you to be all right. I worry about how you deal with things."

"Well, I will be fine, after the divorce." I shrugged. "Having a wife was just holding me back anyway. I mean, come on, it wasn't really me, was it?"

She looked away and tears pooled in her eyes. "Don't. You know you don't really think that. You love her, and you're hurt but going back to your old sleep-with-anything-that-moves ways isn't going to help. You're better than that. Please don't shut us out. Speak to Carol again. She can help you. I know she can."

"I don't need to talk about it, I need to forget it and move on."

She sighed sharply. "But forgetting it isn't really moving on. I tried that for eleven years and look where that got me. Other people were hurt because I bottled it up—"

"That wasn't your fault."

"Fact is, if I would've spoken sooner things would have been... dealt with sooner."

They would have been behind bars sooner. But that wasn't strictly true. The only evidence proving what they'd done to her started when she was eight. If she'd have spoken up straight away they might've got off, a child's word against an adults may have meant they walked free.

And it wasn't her fault.

"You were just a child, Oakley."

"We're getting off topic. You know what I'm getting at. It was only when I spoke up that I was able to move on. Mum too. That just leaves you."

"I'm fine. Men are hard and all that."

She rolled her eyes. "Don't give me that stereotypical man crap. Neither of us believes you don't feel just as much because you have a penis."

I laughed and wanted to hug her for being one of the only people that could make me laugh right now. "The word penis sounds wrong coming from you."

"Well, I'm glad I amused you. Now eat your breakfast and have a shower – you smell like a brewery – we're going out."

"What? Out where?"

She stood up and left, ignoring me. That was just great. I didn't want to go anywhere today. If she thought that I was going to speak to my soon-to-be ex-wife, she was very, very wrong.

After finishing a slice of toast – as much as I could eat without wanting to hurl – I hopped in the shower. The night Abby and I showered together immediately sprang to my mind, kicking me in the gut. It hit me then that I was going to be solo in the shower – and everywhere else it really mattered – for, probably, the rest of my fucked up life.

Leaning against the cold tiled wall, I sunk to my knees and did something very stereotypically un-manly, I cried.

CHAPTER
Ten

Jasper

"Where are we going?" I asked Oakley as she drove us…
somewhere. I had a throbbing head, what felt like knives
stabbing my heart and a sick feeling in the pit of my stomach and
she was taking me on a bloody field trip!

"I'm going to deal with the one thing that still haunts me.
We're going to be strong together," she replied. "Then you're going to deal with your wife."

"What still haunts you?"

"The place where we camped," she whispered. Her hands
tightened around the steering wheel.

The sick feeling multiplied. "What? Why do you want to go
back there?"

"I've not told anyone this, but I dream of that place sometimes. It's the one thing that I still hold on to because it's too painful to face."

I gulped. Did I want to go there? "So today is all about exorcising our demons?"

"Yes."

"You make it sound easy."

She gave a short, humourless laugh. "I'd love it if it was. Going back over things is the hardest thing I've done – closely followed by leaving Cole – but it's also the only way I've been able to move forward. Jasper, you can't expect to sweep everything that happens under the carpet and not have a breakdown at some point. There's only so much a person can take. So I'm facing this and then you're speaking to Abby."

"I want nothing to do with her."

"I know, and I support you one-hundred per cent. I wouldn't want to get back together with someone that had cheated on me either, but you have to speak to her. A marriage isn't something you can ignore."

I hated it when she was right. There were so many questions I wanted Abby to answer.

"Can't I just call her?"

She shrugged. "If you want. Either way, you have to have that conversation."

"You don't have to do this, you know? I get your point, and I'll talk to my whore of a wife, but you don't have to go first."

"Actually, I do." She bit her lip. "I'm tired of being scared of a scrap of land."

It wasn't just a scrap of land though. It was the place our bastard father took her to and photographed his friend abusing her. It was where she lost her innocence and most of her childhood. That scrap of land started her eleven-year silence.

"How come you've not told Cole about this?" I asked. He knew more than anyone – besides Mum probably – but she hadn't told him. They had a tell-all rule that I was sure was Oakley's idea after living with too many secrets and lies.

"I've not told anyone, not even Carol. I wasn't ready to deal with it, so I pretended it wasn't an issue. You're the only one who knows about the nightmares, so, please don't say anything."

"How does Cole not know about your nightmares?"

"He'd sleep through an earthquake! They're less frequent now, maybe one every few months. I don't wake up screaming, so there's no reason he'd know, but I can't go back to sleep afterwards. Maybe if it's not haunting me in the back of my mind any more, I won't see it in my dreams."

"You think that will work?"

She shrugged one shoulder stiffly. "I'm hoping. It's worked with the rest of it well enough."

"Well enough?"

She sighed. "There's no miracle cure, Jasper. It'll always be there, but it's no longer in my head all the time."

"Good," I whispered, not daring to admit it was still in my head all the time.

We fell silent. Oakley seemed somewhere else, and I desperately wanted to know what was going through her head. She kept her eyes focused on the road, still gripping the steering wheel too tight. She said she wanted to do this, but it sure as hell didn't look like she did.

She pulled into the forest and turned down the track to the camping site. Her hands gripped the wheel so tight I could see the tendons in her inner wrist.

"Hey," I said softly. "It's okay."

Nodding, she gulped and parked in a space at the edge of the car park.

"I'm coming with you," I said. I wasn't sure if she planned on going there alone, or if I was here to be with her the whole time. Either way, I was staying by her side.

Her grip loosened a touch. "Thank you."

I stared at a piece of grass nearby a stream. Beside me, Oakley stood deadly still, clutching my hand as if it was her lifeline. She was thinking about what happened to her, but I couldn't. I wouldn't let myself think about it. I couldn't think about the man that was supposed to be there for us but had let us both down.

She took a deep breath. "It's less overgrown now. The grass was longer. A few bushes have been cut down too." I wanted to ask if we were in the right place, but her fear vibrated off her. This was the place.

"How do you feel?"

"Sick. Scared." She frowned. "Actually, less scared. Seeing it as an adult makes it seem smaller. When I was little everything was huge, and I don't just mean size, I know I was smaller then, too. I'm not explaining it well, am I?"

"You're explaining it fine. I think I get it."

"This is just a bit of land with grass and mud and trees." She nodded once, and her eyes glazed over. As strong as she was trying to be it was still hard for her.

"What did the bastard do when he saw how scared you were of this place?" My hand tightened around hers. Whenever I thought about him, I wanted to rip his head from his shoulders. Hate was a strong word but not nearly strong enough for what I felt for him.

"Nothing." She gulped. "By the time it got...really bad I wasn't talking, and he didn't care."

Okay, we were done with that conversation. I was having trouble breathing evenly. I wanted to kill him so badly it hurt.

"Did, er, did Frank stay all weekend?"

"Yes. He was in a separate tent though. A bigger one."

"You shared a tent with Max?" I asked. He wasn't Dad to me, and he hadn't been for a long time.

"Yes."

"And he definitely never did...anything."

She shook her head. I knew he hadn't; she'd said many times before that the man that created us never touched her like that – he'd just let his sick friend do it and Max took pictures. What we didn't know was that the place it happened still haunted her. Secrets had plagued our family for years. I didn't want any more.

"He was a different person when we were away. The change was instant. As soon as we were in the car he was cold and detached. Like he was severing our relationship in his mind so I was no longer his daughter."

"Hope they fucking rot," I growled.

"Calm down," she said, squeezing my hand. "Don't let them get to you like this. We're here, and they're not. I never think of it as winning, but I suppose that's the easiest thing to compare it to. If you let them rule you then they win."

He'd already won. He may well spend the rest of his life in prison, but he'd screwed us up forever. Like Oakley said, it would always be there. I was a man; I was supposed to protect the women in my family. I failed my baby sister and all the time our dad was hurting her I was hero-worshipping him. I hated myself.

"What can't you get past? The guilt?" She asked. Her voice was so low I barely caught it.

"That's the main one."

She squeezed my hand again; opting to not tell me I shouldn't feel guilty for the seven millionth time. I loved that she didn't blame me for not knowing; it would kill me if she did, but that didn't mean that I didn't blame myself. Who didn't notice something like that?

"I think I'm ready to go now."

"Yeah?" I asked through clenched teeth, trying to calm myself down.

"Yes. I expected to feel… more. I don't know if that's good or bad."

"Good. I think good."

She looked up at me and smiled tightly.

"I think maybe it is too."

I turned, and it took her a second to move but then we were walking back to the car. We'd been there less than five minutes. It wasn't over; I wasn't stupid enough to think that demon had been exorcised already. It was more like opening the door for her to talk about it.

"Now, how do you want to deal with Abby?" She asked.

"Time machine so I can go back and not marry her. What the hell is wrong with me? I never should have given her a second chance."

Oakley stopped, grabbing my arm and pulling me around to face her.

"Don't you ever blame yourself for what that bitch did. Even if you were growing apart, that doesn't give her the right to cheat. It's *not* your fault, Jasper."

"I don't know what to do now. I want to hate her."

"I'm so sorry," she whispered, wrapping her arms around me. I hugged her back, swallowing the rising lump in my throat.

Her betrayal hurt like hell. The thought of her with another man, kissing him, underneath him, telling him what she wanted, made me want to hurl.

"What am I going to do? I can't get the image of them out of my head. I can't stop thinking about her."

"You're going to be fine. You're going to talk to her and sort out what you need to. Then you're going to pick yourself up and start again. We're all here to help, and you know you can stay at mine for as long as you like."

Back at Oakley's house, I excused myself from drinking tea with her and went up to 'my' room. She'd just dealt with something bigger than a cheating spouse, so I had to grow a pair and call my wife.

As ready for this call as I thought I should be my heart still raced.

"Jasper!" Abby said, sobbing down the phone. "Thank God. I've been trying to reach you. Baby, I'm so sorry."

"Stop." I gripped the phone. Hearing her cry was shredding me. "Stop crying, you have no right to cry." *And I can't stand it when you're upset...even now.* "I just want to know why."

"I don't know why. Please come home so we can talk."

"I called you so we can talk. Tell me why."

"Jasper," she whispered.

I clenched my fist. "Abby," I snapped. "If you're not going to give me what I want and tell me why, then I'm just going to hang up. I didn't call to hear you cry. I called to ask you why you cheated on me and destroyed our marriage."

"Don't say that." She started sobbing, and I wanted to throw my phone at the wall. "Please don't tell me we can't fix this. We've been through so much. I believe in us. I messed up, big time, but don't–"

I hung up. She was about to blame me for ending it and tell me that *I'd* given up, and I couldn't hear that. I loved her, and I didn't want to hate her completely but if she blamed me for all of this I was going to. But at the same time a part of me wanted to hear that because maybe hating her would stop it hurting.

For the next two hours, I laid on the bed, staring up at the ceiling. Oakley came in once not long after I'd spoken to Abby to tell me that she was popping to Cole's sisters to drop Everleigh's bag off because her and Leona had decided they wanted a sleepover.

I was glad of the time alone, but as I moved into an hour and a half as a hermit, I wished Oakley was back to distract me.

Finally, when I was just about to go out of my mind or go looking for Brett, someone knocked on the door.

"Jasper," Cole said. "Can I come in?"

I sat up. "Sure."

He walked in and leant back against the wall. "You okay?"

"Nope."

"Sorry, stupid question. You need anything?"

"Everleigh's with Mia and Leona for the night?"

Cole nodded.

"Then I need something strong."

"Coming downstairs? Bit too pathetic drinking alone, isn't it?"

"Thanks, man, you always know what to say," I replied bitterly and stood up. He was right though; I couldn't drink alone in the spare bedroom at my sister's house. That was a level of pathetic I wasn't quite ready to sink to.

I followed Cole downstairs.

"No lovey stuff tonight," I said. The last thing I wanted to see was him stroking Oakley's hair, playing with her fingers or kissing her.

He looked over his shoulder, grinning. "You're telling me to keep my hands off my wife?"

Oakley laughed, hearing the last bit of our conversation.

"No, I'm ordering you away from her. For tonight, you're not all in love." I turned my nose up and reached in their cupboard. "Tonight the only love to be shown is to this great man. Mr. Jack Daniels."

Cole held his hands up. "Fine."

"Good to see you out of that room," Oakley said, putting two glasses down on the table.

"You're not drinking with us?"

"Not that. I'll have a glass of wine, but I need to be able to drive to pick Everleigh up in the morning."

"You're supposed to be working tomorrow." It was me that should be looking after her while Oakley worked. I loved the days I had her, but right now it was a struggle to do anything, I had no idea how I'd pretend to be happy for her sake.

"It's fine. Marcus is going to stay until the afternoon when Mum can take Eveleigh for a few hours."

She'd sorted everything out then.

"Marcus doesn't mind?"

She shook her head. "Of course not. He's just concerned for you. And besides, he's teaching classes until twelve anyway, it's only an extra hour."

"Sorry," I said. I hated letting anyone down but when I let my sister or mum down I felt like crap.

"Pour your drink, and I'll pretend I didn't hear you apologise," she replied.

"Jasper," Oakley called from the front door.

From the tone in her voice, I could tell that it was Abby. Cole and I had moved our drinking session into the living room. I wasn't sure if he was being a baby about drinking or letting me have it all, but he'd only had two, small measure JD and cokes. It was almost like he didn't want to get rat arsed at four in the afternoon.

"Tell her to fuck off."

"Jasper, please," Abby shouted. "Come on, please just let me explain. You owe me that much."

What the fuck? Again with the I owed her and blame in my direction. I jumped off the sofa and flew out of the door. Abby stood outside and Oakley just inside. "Are you fucking kidding me? I don't owe you shit!"

I stopped behind my sister who took her exit and closed herself in the living room.

"I'm so sorry. I never planned to hurt you. It was a mistake, I swear. Brett means nothing to me. You have to believe me."

She looked like shit. Her eyes were bloodshot and puffy. Her hair was all over the place, and she was wearing the clothes she put on at home to relax in. I hated that she still looked beautiful, and I still wanted her.

"I love you so much, Jasper."

I closed my eyes and gripped the door frame. "Don't say that. If you loved me, you wouldn't have screwed someone else."

"It was just one time." She held her hand up. "It only happened once, and when he kissed me I should have pushed him away. I was weak. I'm sorry. Tell me what I can do to make it up to you. You're my husband, and I want us to work. I'll do whatever you want."

"Did you fuck him in my house?"

"No! Of course not."

I believed that about as much as I believed it only happened once.

"Do you love him?"

"No."

"So it was just sex? Or was it the thrill of something new? Am I not enough?"

"Don't do that. You're enough, of course you are."

"Then why, Abby? I thought this was past us. I thought you wanted us."

"I do! I made a huge, huge mistake, and I'm sorry. I wish I could take it back, but I can't. Please, just come home with me and we'll talk it through. I swear I will never hurt you again."

"I don't trust you. It took years to build that back up, and you've pissed all over it. I don't even want to try. I love you, but I won't let you cheat. You knew I would never forgive that again, and yet you slept with him anyway."

Tears rolled down her face, smearing her mascara. I wanted to hold her, and I hated myself for that. Why couldn't I just hate her?

"Why him?"

"I don't know. He was nice. We got talking, and we have a lot in common."

"I have a lot in common with Cole, but I'm not going to screw him!"

She wiped her tears and sniffed. "I suppose it was exciting. We've been distant recently; you know we have–"

"And that gives you the right to sleep with someone else? Fucking hell, Abby, if you feel something is missing in our marriage, tell me! I would've done anything to make it feel exciting for you again. I would've done *anything* for you."

Her face crumpled, and she sobbed. "I know, and I know I hurt you, but we love each other. Jasper, we can make this work. We'll try for a baby now."

"Don't. You have no right throwing that at me. You honestly think I'd want a child with you when all I see when I look at your face is you and him? How sick would that be? Kids aren't stupid; they pick up on shit like that. Jesus, we'd fuck that kid up more than you've fucked us up."

I couldn't believe she'd said that. She was getting desperate, offering me the thing I wanted the most. There was no way I could have a baby in a situation like that. I didn't want a child with her at all, not anymore.

"We'll go to therapy and talk it through. We can fix this."

"You're not getting it. I don't want to."

She recoiled as if I'd hit her. "You don't mean that."

I took a deep breath as my heart ripped to shreds. "I'll have my lawyer contact you, and I'll pick up my stuff while you're at work. There's no need for us to talk to each other anymore. Good-bye, Abby."

I slammed the door and fell to the side, hitting the wall.

The living room door opened, and Oakley rushed to my side as I slumped to the floor and cried. Before she could get anything out of me, I told her I wanted to be alone and picked myself up.

I went up to the spare room and climbed into bed, hoping I'd sleep until the morning.

CHAPTER
Eleven

Jasper

I sat in Oakley's living room drinking my second tea – even though I wanted something stronger – and stared at a picture of me and Abby in a huge family collage photo frame on the wall. It was mine and Abby's wedding. The picture of us made me feel sick; we looked so happy. How did we get from there to here?

I should've been at work, but Oakley had Marcus cover us both so she could babysit me.

"Can you call Mum and ask her for the number of the divorce lawyer she used?" I asked.

Oakley looked up. "You're sure? You don't need to do any of that right now. If you need time to think everything through..."

"I don't need time."

"Sure?" She asked.

"If Cole cheated?"

"I'd cut it off and then divorce him." She reached over to her phone on the coffee table. "I'll call Mum."

I watched as Oakley called our mum, and I mouthed a refusal to speak to her on the phone. She'd probably cry, and I hated when Mum cried, I didn't need to deal with that, too, right now. Oakley jotted down a number, promising Mum that she would look after me.

She blew out a sharp breath as she hung up. "You owe me one. She was almost in her car before I convinced her to give you some space."

"Thanks. She can be intense."

"She worries, that's all."

I nodded. "I know, but sometimes you need to not be okay, and I can't do that in front of her."

"Can you do that in front of me?" She asked.

"A bit."

She bit her lip and turned her body to face me.

"I want you to be able to be honest with me, Jasper. You don't have to pretend around me. I thought we were past that."

We'd never be past that. I would always want to protect her. She was upset when I was, so how could I let it all out in front of her?

"I'm good, Oakley."

"You just found out your wife is cheating on you. You're not good! Don't lie to me."

"Fine, I'm not good. I feel sick, and I just want to..." I trailed off, gripping my hair as Abby's betrayal pierced through my heart again, taking my breath away.

Oakley threw her arms around me. "Shh, you're going to be okay."

I wished I shared her optimism because right now everything I'd worked for was gone and I was going to have to start right back at the beginning.

"Uncle Jasper!" Everleigh screamed, running at me full pelt. I threw my arms out and caught her as she leapt up.

"Hey, did you have a good time at Auntie Mia's?"

"Yep, we made Peppa Pig cupcakes and Leona let me ride her scooter."

"Yeah, and you got most of the cake mix on you, so upstairs for a bath," Cole said, pointing to the stairs.

"Okay, Daddy," she replied, jumping like a rabbit towards the door.

"Alright?" Cole asked.

I shrugged. "I guess."

"Why don't I give Everleigh her bath and you two can talk," Oakley said.

I stood up and shook my head. "Why don't I do the bath and you two can talk."

Those were the magic words to get Cole to agree so I wouldn't have to deal with talking about Abby or my sodding feelings again.

"Talk about what? Everything okay?" Cole asked.

She smiled. "Everything's fine. Jasper's right though."

I left the room as Cole walked over to her with a deep, concerned frown. It was time for them to talk about Oakley's nightmares.

Everleigh had just finished hopping to the top of the stairs when I started going up. "Don't turn the water on yourself," I called up.

"I know, Uncle Jasper, I don't want to burned my skin off."

I winced; hoping Cole and Oakley didn't hear that. They tell her 'don't do that because it'll hurt' and I go in for the kill and tell her exactly what'll happen. But she's never had an accident when

I've had her.

I ran Everleigh a bath, adding lots of bubble bath so she could build her castle out of it and sat on the toilet while she played.

"Where's Auntie Abby?" She asked after a few minutes.

How should I handle that? I wanted to tell her Auntie Abby was a whore who couldn't keep her knickers on, but Everleigh loved her, so I knew I couldn't, plus, she was three.

I swallowed the hurt and anger and replied, "She's busy working."

"Is she marking papers?"

I smiled. "Yeah, she's marking papers."

She was probably with Brett. Were they together now? In my house? I ran my hands through my hair and rubbed my eyes. The image of her in his embrace burned into my memory, haunting me every time I closed my eyes.

"Uncle Jasper?"

"Yeah?"

"Can you make me have bubble hair?"

I got down on my knees in front of the bath and scooped a handful of bubbles to put on her head. "Sure I can."

Everleigh was the best. I hung out with her, watching old Disney movies and eating popcorn. I loved how I wasn't required to talk about anything deep or painful. Her favourite topic was *what's Timon and Pumbaa going to do next.*

Cole and Oakley flitted around the house, occasionally joining us but after Oakley's nightmare confession they'd had a lot to talk about. I preferred it being just me, and Everleigh anyway – she didn't give me pitying looks.

"Are you sure you want to go to Sarah's tonight?" Cole asked. No.

"Yeah."

"They'll understand, you know."

"I know, but it's Miles' night. If Mum starts fussing, I'm out of there."

Miles had just landed a promotion that he'd been working towards for the last year. The old office manager finally retired, and he was sure he wouldn't be picked, but he was, so we were celebrating.

"Plus, someone has to eat some of the cocktail sausages and stop Everleigh from devouring them all," I added.

The kid must have eaten about a thousand pigs all herself in her three years.

"I'll race you to eat them all up, Uncle Jasper!"

"No, you won't," Oakley said quickly. "You'll be sick."

Everleigh pouted and stomped towards the door where Cole was now holding her shoes up.

"We can leave at any point if you want to."

"Thanks, but I'll be fine."

She watched me for a minute, trying to decide if I was fine or not. I wasn't, but I returned her stare, trying to look like I didn't just want to drown my sorrows away in the closest bottle I could find.

Mum opened the door, and after being attacked in a big hug with Everleigh, she moved on to me.

"Oh, sweetheart," she murmured against my shoulder. "I'm so sorry this happened to you. Are you okay?"

I pulled back and with every ounce of energy I could muster, I smiled.

"Sure. Let's not talk about it today though. This is about Miles. Where is he?"

"Just finishing up his new recipe canapés."

Everleigh ran through to the kitchen shouting, "Grandad, did you make my cocktail sausages?"

"Cool. I'm hungry." I sidestepped Mum and headed to the kitchen to talk to Miles. He wouldn't mention Abby, so I knew I was safe in his company.

"Jasper," Miles said, balancing Everleigh in his arm and putting what looked like sick on top of tiny little toast. "How's it going?"

I nodded. "Not bad." He knew the truth, but unless you came to him he wouldn't pry. I liked that about him. "You?"

"Good. Want to be guinea pig and try these?" He nodded to his canapés.

"Err, what's on it?"

"Spicy meatballs."

"Alright, not what I expected."

"Your mum loved it on pizza, so I thought I'd try something different to salmon."

At least if I got food poisoning it'd take my mind off my wife.

"Sure, I'll give it a go."

Just as I was about to eat one, I heard the door opening and Oakley saying something I couldn't make out.

"He doesn't want to see you," Mum said, and I knew it was Abby.

"Please, Sarah."

Miles, Everleigh and I walked into the living room.

"Let her in, Mum," I said. "This should be interesting."

In the background, I heard Miles say he was taking Everleigh outside to play on the swing. I didn't plan on causing a big scene, but she definitely didn't need to be around this.

"I'm sorry to interrupt your evening," she said, stepping past Mum, who was shooting daggers at her with her eyes, "but you won't answer my calls or texts."

"Because I don't want to talk to you."

I felt like shit, and I looked like shit. Whenever I saw her or thought about her, I felt ten times worse. Why the hell would I want to take her calls? I wanted her to leave me alone so I could try and forget about how much I missed her and how much she ripped my heart open.

"Mum. Kitchen!" Oakley said, ushering everyone out of the way. At least one of them respected my privacy...

"Jasper, we have to talk about this. I can't apologise enough, and I'm not going to give up on us. You're angry, and I understand that. I'm angry with myself, too. I can't believe I was so stupid. We can work this out. Our marriage deserves a second chance."

What? I gritted my teeth, and willed myself not to cry like a baby. "You cheated before. This was the second chance."

"We were merely kids before."

"Such a fucking cop-out! Don't pretend it was okay before because we were young. I managed to keep it in my pants. If you wanted to see other people you could've ended it with me."

"Oh my God, I'm sorry, Jasper! Are you really going to give up before we've even tried?"

I held my hands up and clenched my fists. Turning around, I grabbed the closest thing to me – the plate of cocktail sausages – and launched them across the room.

Abby gasped, and my eyes widened. They flew across the room, pelting to the floor, in the fireplace, up the wall and behind the radiator like a sausage rainfall.

Grease stained the feature wallpaper on the chimney breast.

"Jasper!" Abby said, her voice a squeaked whisper.

"Get out. I can't do this, Abby. I love you so much, and I want nothing more than to go back to how it was, but I've lost all respect for you. If you care about me at all, you'll leave me alone."

She gulped audibly. "Don't do this."

"I didn't. We're over, Abby," I replied and walked into the kitchen.

She didn't follow, and I heard the front door close seconds later.

My family were lined up along the counter, waiting.

"How did it go, honey?" Mum asked, stepping forward to give me a hug.

"Like you weren't listening."

She squeezed me tight. "Are you okay?"

"Sure. I don't want to talk about it though. Can we please forget she came by?"

Mum pulled back. "Absolutely. Whatever you need, and whenever you want to talk…"

I nodded. I wouldn't go to her. She'd had enough shit to deal with, and I didn't want to lay any more problems on her shoulders.

"I need a drink," I said.

Cole handed me a bottle of Jack Daniels.

I heard two things a second apart, Mum shouting, "Jasper, what on earth happened in my living room!" and Everleigh screaming, "My cocktail sausages!"

I winced.

"What did you do?" Oakley asked.

"I threw the platter of sausages."

She pursed her lips. "Because?"

"I was pissed off."

"I'll help Mum clean up. You relax and get a drink."

I did just that.

CHAPTER
Twelve

Jasper

Sighing into my coffee, I looked down at Everleigh. At least she was one girl that would never screw me over. My eyes stung from the three hours of sleep I'd had last night. Every time I closed my eyes I saw Max's face staring back at me. Abby's betrayal reminded me of his. I wished it was her face I saw.

"Uncle Jasper, why are you sad?" She asked, looking up at me with her big baby blue eyes.

"That's what happens when uncles find out their wives are cheating hos."

"Auntie Abby's a cheating hos?" My eyes flew open. Shit! "What's a hos?"

Damn it, I'm a fucking idiot!

"Err, home. I said Abby's at home."

She frowned and bit her lip, trying to understand. *I don't want you to understand!*

"It doesn't matter. Why don't you eat your sausages up and I'll let you have ice cream."

"Okay," she replied and popped a cocktail sausage in her mouth. "Uncle Jasper?"

"Yeah?"

"Can we go see Mummy?"

"Yeah. Hurry up and finish that then." She grinned and quickly shovelled more in her mouth.

Oakley worked at The Centre three days a week, and I worked there Monday to Thursday and Saturday mornings. On a Friday, I had Everleigh while Oakley worked one of her days. They would never trust their daughter with anyone other than Cole's parents, Mum and Miles, me and Abby, and Mia.

"Everleigh, don't ever take anyone back that betrays you."

She frowned again, deeper, but replied, "Okay, Uncle Jasper."

I loved how she just responded as if she had a clue what I was going on about.

"Are you and Auntie Abby still loving each other?"

I gulped down sand. "Yes, but sometimes it just doesn't work out. It's okay because Uncle Jasper and Auntie Abby will be happy again – just not together."

I wanted to exclude myself from that. I didn't want a life and happiness with someone, anyone else but I didn't want to tell Everleigh that. She still deserved to believe in happy-ever-after.

"So you won't be married anymore?"

"No, sweetheart. We're going to get a divorce and not be married."

"Oh. Who will you marry now?"

I laughed at her thinking, as if every grown up had to be married.

"No one for a little while."

She bit her lip, trying to make sense of what I'd told her.

"It's okay. I'm happy hanging out with you for now."

"I'll help you find a new princess, Uncle Jasper."

I ruffled her hair, earning a breath-taking smile.

"Thanks, kiddo. Hey, what do you want to do after we go see Mummy?" I asked her, draining the last of my coffee.

"Um." She sucked her lips in as she thought. "Disneyland!"

"We'll need more time than just today for that."

"Um," she hummed, thinking again. "I don't know. What do you want to do, Uncle Jasper?"

"Egg my house." Abby's house. My old house. Not ours anymore. I sighed and clenched my fists. She was living there until it sold. I wanted it gone as soon as possible, so I had no link to her at all. The divorce couldn't come soon enough. I needed to move on, but all this house stuff, dividing shit up, and the legal end of our marriage was making that impossible.

"What's that? Egging?"

"It's when you throw eggs at someone's house. Probably not the best thing to teach you though."

Everleigh burst into a fit of giggles. "I want to do that," she announced and laughed again.

"Alright. We will." *Bad idea. Bad, bad idea.* "Come on."

I got up and held her hands as she jumped down from the stool. She gripped my hand in her own tiny one as we walked to my car.

"When we do this you have to throw and then run really fast, okay?"

Why am I doing this? Because I was hurt and angry, and I couldn't get drunk when I had Everleigh, so something childish and petty seemed like the next best thing.

She nodded her head rather enthusiastically, her hair flying all over the place.

"I can run faster than Daddy," she boasted, her eyes widening in pride. *Because Daddy lets you win.*

"Wow, that is fast!" She grinned, proud of herself. "Now, we're not allowed to tell Mummy or Daddy that we've egged the house, alright?"

"I know." She would tell them; she could never keep anything in. I was thankful for that, even though it got me into a lot of trouble. "Uncle Jasper?"

"Yeah?"

"Do you still love Auntie Abby?"

I felt like someone had stabbed me through the chest. "Yeah, I do."

"But she's a hos now."

Fuck.

"Are you going to marry someone else soon?" She asked, still not grasping the fact that you didn't have to be married.

"No. I'm done with relationships now. From now on I'm gonna do whatever I want."

"Oh," she replied, frowning in confusion again. "Mummy and Daddy got married, didn't they?"

"Yep, but they'll last forever."

"Like Cinderella and Prince Charming?"

"Exactly like them," I confirmed, and opened the car to put her in her seat. She sat down and held her arms up while I buckled her in. "Right, let's go egging, then to see Mummy."

Everleigh swung her legs, hitting them against the seat. "Yeah!"

"This is naughty, isn't it?" Everleigh asked as we stood in

front of my house holding two eggs each.

"It's an okay naughty. This is my house, isn't it?"

She nodded.

"And I want to throw eggs at it so we can." I then realised I'd pretty much given her permission to do whatever the hell she wanted with her own things. "But only adults are allowed to do things like this."

"Why?"

"Because we're bigger and we pay for it."

"Oh," she replied, and nodded as if it was perfectly acceptable.

"Are you ready?"

"Yeah!" she cheered.

"Alright. On three."

"One," she said. "Two. Three!"

We both launched our eggs at the house. Mine hit the front door and cracked. Runny, sticky egg dribbled down the blue painted wood. Everleigh's hit the plant pot beside the door and the stone path. Both cracked, creating a mess, so I was satisfied with that.

She giggled. "That was fun."

"Yeah it was." I didn't feel that much better, probably because I wasn't fifteen anymore, but Abby would have to clean it up, so that gave me something. "Now we run," I said and grabbed her little hand.

Her deep giggles made me laugh. Maybe it wasn't a waste of time after all.

I sat in front of Carol, wondering what the hell I was doing here.

"Jasper, what brings you here?"

Thank God, she'd said something. We'd been sitting in silence since I walked in five minutes ago.

"I don't know. My marriage is over."

Her perfectly plucked but too thin brows arched. "Oh? Why is that?"

"Because she was sleeping with a guy from work." I shook my head. "I knew it too. There was something off. She was distant and kept meeting this Brett for 'work' related reasons. I'm so stupid; I wanted to believe her."

"That doesn't make you stupid. Nobody wants to believe the worst in someone they love."

I still felt like an idiot.

"I don't really know what to say in here," I admitted.

"Sometimes just talking helps. I don't have the miracle cure that'll fix every problem you've ever had. You're the only person that can change your life."

"No miracle cure, huh?"

"I'm afraid that doesn't exist. Unless you put the work in and deal with your problems, everything else you try is just masking it."

I felt like she was saying 'so don't think a baby will be what fixes everything'. I wasn't that stupid; I knew babies were huge amounts of stress, work and worry bundled into a tiny little person.

"I was so close to getting everything I've wanted, and now…" I closed my eyes. "Now I've got nothing."

"When did you know you wanted a family?"

Weird question. Where was she going with this? "When we moved back to England."

When Oakley spoke out about the abuse when she was sixteen, me and Mum took her away to Australia to live with our uncle. We'd returned four years later when the long, complicated court case started. Max got locked away, as did many others in the paedophile ring, including the bastard that abused Oakley. When it was over we returned to Australia briefly to pack up our things so we could move back.

"After your father's court case."

"Yeah. You still think I only want that because I missed out, don't you?"

"I think that you started wanting a family the way most people do. I think you've put everything into it because the idea of a wife and children filled something you've missed out on." She sat forward in her chair. "When you think of your childhood, what comes to mind?"

"That it was one big fat lie. Everything I thought I had wasn't real."

"One part of it wasn't. The good memories you have did happen. Oakley's spoken about this a few times before. From the age of five, she knew your father was someone else, but he didn't stop being the person he was to you until you were in your late teens."

"You don't think I feel guilty about that?"

"I understand that, but you have nothing to feel guilty about, you didn't know. You're allowed to have good memories of him. Oakley does."

"He fucked all that."

She shook her head. "I don't believe that."

I shrugged. "You don't have to."

"What is your earliest memory of your father?"

"I remember him dressing up as Father Christmas. I must've only been three and Oakley was a baby, walking along furniture, I used to help hold her hands sometimes."

Carol smiled. "You know you divert back to Oakley a lot."

I did?

"She does the same thing. It always comes back to you and your mum. She worries how you're doing the most."

"Because she doesn't feel like I've dealt with it," I said.

"That's correct. Do you feel like you've dealt with it?"

"I dunno. I'm not sure how."

"So your father dressed up for Christmas?"

Going back. "Yeah. He did a crap job of masking his voice; I knew it was him straight away. I was so excited when he walked through the door though. He had a sack with a helicopter for me and a teddy bear for Oakley. She chewed on its ear, and I broke the propeller of mine after five minutes. Dad glued it back, but it was slightly bent."

"It sounds like you had a good childhood."

"I thought I did."

She said nothing else but I could tell she wanted to say that I had because I still had good memories. They may be good, but they were ruined. The bad far outweighed the good.

"I got a flat," I said, trying to direct the conversation away from Max.

"That's good."

"Yeah a mate is letting me crash in the place he's doing up to rent. I've got two months to find somewhere else in exchange for painting the place and putting new coving up."

"You seem happier now. You didn't like staying at Oakley's?"

"It's not that. I feel better that I'm not drifting now, you know? It's not home, and I won't get that until my place is sold and I can buy another house but it's a start. I felt like a loser for believing I had a future with Abby and an even bigger one for crashing at my sister's."

"Highs and lows are a part of life, Jasper. There's not one

person that hasn't had to have help of some sort at some point. There's no reason to feel like a 'loser' about it."

I shrugged. "I can't help how I feel."

"Of course. You've spent the last eight years being the strong one that your mum and sister relied upon. You feel you should just be able to deal with this and move on quickly. But you can't, very understandably, so you feel worse about yourself."

I blinked a few times, and she smiled, knowing she'd hit the bullseye.

"I will get over it," I said.

"I have no doubt that you will, but I think it'll go a lot faster, and a lot smoother if you allow yourself to go through it."

Shuffling on the sofa, I nodded. "I'll try."

I went to get something for dinner and crate of beer after therapy. Parking outside the supermarket, I spotted Brett walking to his car with a full trolley. My hand fisted around the door handle. His life hadn't been screwed up by his affair with my wife. Nothing had changed for him.

Shoving the door open, I ran at a dead speed and collided with his back. He shouted out, air leaving his lungs. His eyes widened as he spun around and saw who'd slammed into him.

"Jasper," he gasped. "I'm so sorry. We didn't plan it. It just happened."

"Right, of course, you just fell inside her. Was that how it happened, *Brett*?"

He shook his head. "I am sorry. I've got to go."

I laughed. "Yeah, say hi to my wife for me."

As he walked away, he muttered, "I'm not seeing her."

I couldn't give a flying fuck if he was. I walked into the supermarket, heart pounding and hands shaking, and picked up two bottles of Bourbon.

CHAPTER
Thirteen

Jasper

Rubbing my tired, stinging eyes, I tried to make sense of what was on the computer screen. I'd had about four hours of sleep after downing a bottle of Bourbon and crashing on the sofa. I felt like shit, but at seven in the morning, I woke up needing the toilet and something popped into my head: I'd taken Abby's name.

Now I wished I'd changed my surname to my mum's maiden name and not worried that I would have a different one to my wife. I couldn't stay a Farrell and have anything related to my father, but I should have thought more about what would happen if me and Abby broke up. At the time that seemed impossible though. We were never going to hurt each other. We were going to be one of the couples that made it.

I was lost with no last name to claim that didn't hurt like hell. There was no name I could now take that related me to anyone. Mum had Miles' and Oakley had Cole's. A name shouldn't matter, but when you had nothing it was oddly important.

I dialled Mum's number, and she picked up right when I was about to give up. "Hello?" She said down the line.

Shit, I'd woken her up. "Mum, sorry, I'll call back later."

"No! I'm awake. Are you okay, love?"

"I need a surname."

Silence.

"Sorry?" She finally said.

"I don't want Abby's anymore. I definitely don't want Max's. What surnames are in the family?"

"Um. Are you sure you want to do this?"

"Yeah, I don't want anything to do with her anymore."

"Alright. Well there's my maiden name or your nan's."

"What's nan's?" I should probably know that, but I didn't. I bet Oakley did.

"Scofield."

"Jasper Scofield," I said.

"Sounds good," Mum said. "And I think it would mean a lot to Nan. Are you sure you don't just want to go back to Farrell?"

I ground my teeth. "I'd rather have no name than his."

"I understand, but I'd also understand if you wanted to. It was your name, too, what you were born with and supposed to pass on."

"Well, now it'll die with him and that suits me just fine."

She sighed. "Okay. What did you do last night?"

"Nothing."

"Stayed in and drank?"

"Why'd you ask if you knew?"

"Jasper, sweetheart. You can do better than this. Don't you dare let that woman break you. I know it's devastating to find out someone you love is a different person than you thought, but you can get through it. Pick yourself up, love, you're better than this."

I felt like crap. She'd been through the ultimate betrayal. My wife had cheated; her husband was a paedophile that allowed another man to abuse her daughter. My issues paled in comparison.

"God I'm sorry, Mum."

"Don't you do that either. You've been hurt, and you're allowed to feel hurt. I just want my happy-go-lucky son back. I've missed him this last six months."

"Six months?" It had just been over a month since Abby and I broke up.

"You've not been yourself for a while."

Right. I had hoped they didn't notice how unhappy I was being stuck standing still. I wanted to move forward with my life and with Abby, but for a while we'd been floating, watching our lives pass us by. Or rather I had. She was sailing off without me.

"You're right, Mum." I wanted to be the old Jasper again.

"What are you going to do?"

"I'm going to spend the day sanding down the wall in the hallway ready to paint, then I'm going out."

"Okay," she said, and I knew she didn't understand how that was going to help, besides the decorating part – that was instead of paying rent. The old Jasper would go out whenever possible. I had no kids and no responsibilities so I should be out there living it up.

"I'll speak to you later. Love you."

"Love you, too," she replied and hung up.

"Fancy seeing you here," I said, leaning next to Holly at the bar. "You're drinking. You don't really drink."

"Harry," she said.

"Oh. What's the dick done?"

"He keeps blowing hot and cold, and when I confronted him about it he broke up with me. Now he wants to get back together."

Blind idiot.

"And what do you want?"

"I don't like people playing games in relationships. I like to know where I am and where I stand. When I'm with him, I never know if he's going to go off on one about me liking my ex's status on Facebook. I'm friends with my ex, nothing more."

I shrugged. "Told you he was a dick."

"Thank you for that."

"So you're drowning your sorrows, huh?"

"Thought I'd give it a go. Works for Brad. And you."

"Yeah, but me and Brad are…"

Her eyes widened, the blue brighter with the spotlights above the bar glaring down on them. "If you say guys I'm going to smash this glass over your head."

I laughed, sitting down on a stool. "Not where I was going. We're… I don't know how to put it without offending you."

"Just say it," she said, frowning.

"You're good." That probably wasn't the best word to use. "Me and Brad do the getting smashed and sleeping around thing, but that's not you, Holly. You don't seem like the type that can do casual. And I don't mean because you're female, because I know women that can have no strings sex just as well as I can."

She stared at me for a long minute, and I paid extra attention to her hand wrapped around her glass.

Finally, she sighed. "You're right. I've always been Good Girl Holly, getting high grades and coming home on time. I've never done anything impulsive. I've slept with two people, both of which I was in a relationship with, albeit a short one with Harry, but I thought we were going somewhere. I'm boring, aren't I?"

Oh, dear God, what have I done?

"You're not boring, Holly. There's nothing wrong with not

sleeping around!"

She waved her hand at me. "You think there is."

"When did I say that? Why do women make something else out of what you say?"

"What do you think when you look at me?"

Now, that was a dangerous question.

"I see a woman that has no idea how sexy she really is. You hide behind dark clothes and long jumpers. You put on a lot of that eyeliner stuff to distract people from who you are."

She gulped. "And what if I don't know who I am?"

"I think you do, but you don't have the confidence to be it."

I'd had enough alcohol to tell me that hitting on a mate's sister was a good idea. "You're beautiful and smart and funny and there's a handful of guys in here that would love to chat you up right now. You know if you didn't look a bit scary drinking alone like you're plotting ex revenge."

"Huh?"

"Trust me, when you down shots like that and scowl at nothing you look like a woman scorned."

She pushed an empty shot glass away and blushed. "Oh."

"Hey, don't worry about it. I happen to think the scorned look is hot."

"Of course you do," she muttered dryly. "But thank you for what you said. It was sweet. Sort of."

I meant it. There was something about Holly that drew you in. Her adult innocence was refreshing and a big turn on.

She hopped down off her stool and stood between my legs. "What are you doing?" I asked, stunned.

Her eyes widened, and she shook her head. "Nothing. I need the toilet." Ducking around me, she hightailed it to the bathroom.

What was that? Did she want me as much as I wanted her

right now?

"Can I get you something?" The bartender asked.

"Two shots of tequila, a beer and a…" I picked up Holly's other empty glass and smelt it, "vodka and lemonade please."

He nodded. "Coming up."

Holly got back to the bar just as I paid. Her cheeks were the same pink as when she left. "Do a shot with me, then we'll have a drink. Then I'm taking you back to my flat."

Her eyebrows shot up in surprise. "Excuse me?"

"Holly, babe, you want this, but you're not confident enough – yet – to make the first move. If I'm wrong, tell me and after we've had a drink, I'll make sure you get home safely." She looked down; avoiding my gaze and that told me I was right. "You don't have to be embarrassed to admit you want something or someone. We're adults. You can tell me."

Biting her lip, she sat on the stool and picked up a shot. "I want you," she whispered and downed the tequila.

I cupped her chin and lifted her head. "No more being shy. You can tell me whatever you want. Whatever you want me to do."

Her breath sucked in through her teeth. "What do you want to do to me?"

I smiled and downed my shot. "Come on." Taking her hand, I pulled her off the stool. She stepped into my chest, looking up at me through her lashes. The way she looked at me made the hairs on the back of my neck stand up.

"Are we really doing this?" She asked, pressing her petite body to mine.

I pulled her closer, running my hands up her back. "Only if you want to. Say the word at any point and I'll take you home. No pressure, I swear."

"I know. I trust you. Take me to your place, Jasper."

I fisted her hair, slamming my lips down on hers as my blood sizzled in my veins. She whimpered, her fingernails digging into my flesh. I wanted her, badly. I pulled away and pressed my forehead to hers. "God. How can you think you're plain, Holly?"

She shrugged.

"I'm taking you home now. I want you more than I want to breathe right now which I know sounds crazy, but that's the effect you have on me," I said, running my hand up her back, "so when we walk through my door there's no hiding or being shy. I want to see all of you. There's no limit to what we can do in the bedroom. Ask for whatever you want and don't hold back. You got that?"

Gulping, she nodded. "I've never told anyone what I want before."

"I know. Tonight you will." I sealed my lips over hers, holding her body against mine as the urge to just take her against the fucking bar doubled.

We burst through my front door, attacking each other like animals. What I'd said to her in the bar seemed to work. I wanted her comfortable with me, and I wanted her to be open enough to let me make her come over and over again.

"What do you want me to do, Holly?" I murmured against her mouth.

"My clothes, take them off."

I didn't need asking twice. With my lips still firmly, almost aggressively, against hers, I reached down and pulled her top off. She kissed me again as soon as it had cleared her head. I gripped her firm arse, and she wrapped her legs around my waist as I carried her to the sofa.

Laying her down first, I stripped her leggings off and undressed myself. She looked up at me with wide eyes, breathing heavily. In a matching plain black bra and thong she looked perfect and sexy. It was hard to believe she had such little confidence.

My clothes dropped to the floor the same way hers had. "What now, Holly?"

"You choose."

I shook my head and dropped to my knees, running my finger between her bra-covered breasts and down her belly. "Oh, no. This is what you want. We'll go with my choice next."

Her eyes widened further. "Next."

"There's going to be a lot of nexts tonight." I traced my finger along the top of her thong, and my throat went dry. I wanted her so much. Waiting for her to tell me to touch her properly, to lick her and to fuck her was painful. "Tell me what you want right now?"

"Okay," she whispered. "I want you to kiss me and…"

I smirked when her cheeks turned fire engine red. "And?"

"You're going to make me say it, aren't you?"

I nodded, lips parting in anticipation. "Yes," I replied, completely unembarrassed by how desperate for her I sounded. Why her?

"I want you to touch me." She pointed to her thong. "Here."

"Your wish…" I said, gently sliding her thong down. She lifted her hips to help me. I threw them over my shoulder and climbed on top of her, lips finding hers and hands exploring.

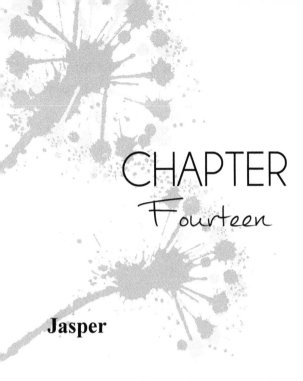

CHAPTER
Fourteen

Jasper

I ran my fingers through my hair and rubbed my exhausted eyes awake before opening the front door. I'd half hoped it was Holly. Since Thursday night, Friday morning and Saturday afternoon all I could think about was how her skin felt against mine, and how she tasted…

But it wasn't the woman I most wanted it to be – it was the last.

Abby stood in front of me. I looked and felt like crap.

"Whadda you want?" I asked, inwardly wincing at the slur in my tired, still half-drunk voice.

"Jasper, are you okay?" She stepped in my flat to get a closer look. "Did you sleep at all last night?"

"A bit. Did you come here to discuss my sleeping habits, or do you want something?"

"Please, don't be like that, Jasper, I'm worried."

"What do you want, Abby?" I asked a little more harshly than

I'd intended, but I was tired and on the verge of a hangover if I didn't start drinking again and she was the second last person in the world I wanted to see.

"Can we sit? I really need to talk to you about something."

Smiling sarcastically, I waved my hand towards my living room. The coffee table was covered in plates, glasses and bottles, but I didn't care what she thought of me anymore.

She ignored the mess and sat down.

"Please, sit with me," she said, looking up at me.

I rolled my eyes and sat. "This'd better be good. You're keeping me from something important."

"Like getting drunk?"

"Yep." And calling one of the women on my new booty call list.

"Jasper, this isn't you. You don't drink things away."

"You don't sleep with co-workers, but people change."

She dropped her eyes, and I sighed, running my hands over my face roughly.

"Just spit it out, Abby, please."

"I'm pregnant." I froze. Time stood still.

"Pregnant," I whispered, and all the air left my lungs.

She nodded. "Yes."

"Mine?"

"Of course!" She looked offended, and I laughed. "Don't, Jasper. Brett and I used a condom. *We* stopped using them years ago."

"Jesus! How?"

I ran my hands through my hair. No. Not now.

"I know you don't need me to explain how."

"Actually, I do. We haven't slept together in a while."

"I know things had been off towards the… end. I've calculated that I'm about eight weeks."

Wow, she was pregnant for over two months, and we didn't know. While she was telling me she wanted to put baby making on hold while she was sleeping with someone else, she was carrying my child.

This was so fucked up.

In seven months, we were going to have a child, and it couldn't be at a worse time. I could barely look at Abby, and every time I did, her betrayal slammed me in the face. It hurt. I wanted to be able to see her without feeling like shit, and having a baby was only going to make that worse. We'd have to have regular contact. She was the mother of my child and no matter how much she hurt me that meant something.

How was I supposed to stop loving her now?

"Look, I understand that this isn't the best timing, and we have a lot of things to get past, but we can. This is us, Jasper."

She had a tiny, innocent baby growing inside her, and I couldn't let my son or daughter down. For the baby's sake, I would be civil.

"Okay. How is this going to work then? Have you seen a midwife yet?"

Shit.

"Yes, I had my first visit today. She's booking me in for a scan because I'm not sure exactly how far along I am."

One of the last times we slept together we'd created another person. God, I wished it could be under different circumstances because all I wanted was my wife and a child. Now I was looking at joint custody and passing the baby back and forth.

"When's the scan?" I asked, looking at her still flat stomach. How long until she had a bump?

"I'm not sure. I'll get a letter in a day or so, apparently. Will you come?"

"You know I will."

A thought struck me. She wanted a career.

"So how does this work? What about school?"

She shrugged. "I don't have a choice now. I'm going to be a mum, so I'll have to work it all around the baby. There are plenty of good nursery schools around for when we're both working."

My face fell. No. You didn't know who was working in those things. The thought of leaving my child with a stranger made me feel sick.

"Not with someone else. We'll sort something out."

"Jasper, I can't rely on my parents and your mum to look after our child."

"They'd love to do it. Isn't it better that he or she is with family rather than strangers?"

She held her hands up.

"Let's not fight about this. We'll talk to them and see."

We'd make it work because I'd rather work nights when Abby could take over with the baby than have it with someone we didn't know. If your own family could hurt you, what was stopping strangers? That was something I was going to have to talk seriously about with Abby.

She already knew how nervous Oakley was letting Everleigh go anywhere – not that she did let her unless it was with me, Cole or Mum – so she knew I'd have a hard time, too.

It wasn't healthy; I understood that, but if unhealthy kept my kid safe, then it was fine by me.

"We're really having a baby," I said, dragging my hands through my hair. *I'm going to be a dad.*

She smiled.

"Yes. I thought you'd be happier I have to say. This is what you've wanted for years now."

"My wife to cheat on me then drop the baby bomb? Not exactly how I saw it play out."

She looked down, ashamed.

"Jasper, I'm sorry. You know I am. It was a mistake. I don't know how many times I can apologise."

"You don't have to apologise at all. Sorry, but you could say it a million times and it'll change nothing. Now I'll be there every step of the way. I'll do everything I can for the baby. I'll be there and provide, but that's it."

"We're having a child."

"And we'll be civil. I'll push my feelings aside and pretend like every time I look at you it doesn't feel like being stabbed in the back and we'll play nice. I want our kid to think we're friends – and maybe we can be one day."

"Friends," she said quietly.

"You can't be surprised by that, Abby. Shit, you honestly thought I'd take you, didn't you? Were you even going to tell me?"

"I don't know. I wasn't thinking."

"Don't give me that cliché bullshit. You must have thought something when you showered between being with him and me."

I hated when people said that after having an affair. It wasn't even one night – not that one time would've been okay. You didn't carry on with someone behind your husband or wife's back without thinking about what you're doing. When you hide things and lie, you're thinking alright. No one had a thoughtless affair. No one just falls into the arms of someone else. It was a conscious choice.

"I was ashamed. I still am. Jasper, I love you, and I made a mistake. The attention was flattering at a time where I didn't feel close to you."

Cop-out. "See, that's what I don't get. If you felt distant why didn't you talk to me? I've gone out of my way to suggest doing things and spending time together. You're the one that pulled away, so don't blame me for that."

"I'm not blaming you."

"Sounds like you are. We've always been able to talk. I've told you things no one else knows. You're the only one I've talked about Max to. After that night in the car where I broke down a month after the trial, I thought we could discuss anything. That was my lowest point, up until now, and you were there. You were the only one I could talk to. It was all you, Abby."

I turned my head and saw her close her eyes. A single tear slid down her face. "Why am I not someone you can talk to?" I asked.

"Telling your husband you're feeling lost and distant isn't an easy conversation to have."

"Spilling your feelings about your father ripping apart your family and allowing his friend to rape his daughter wasn't an easy conversation either. I trusted you above everyone else."

She flinched.

I rubbed the spot above my eyebrows where I was getting a headache.

"This is getting so off topic now."

We couldn't even talk for more than five minutes without it turning into an argument, so how the hell were we going to raise a child together?

"We need to not be around each other right now," I said. "Let's talk tomorrow when we've both calmed down and won't say things we may or may not regret," I said.

"Fine," she huffed. "Call me when you're ready. I love you, Jasper."

I watched her leave, filled with love, hate, anger and excitement all rolled into one. I started to feel panic building inside. I wanted my baby, but I didn't want it to be with Abby.

Oakley opened the door. "You okay?" She asked, stepping to the side to let me in.

"Um. Is Everleigh here?"

"She's with Cole's parents making cookies with Leona, why?" Christ, she had a better social life than me.

"I need to talk to you and don't want her to hear."

"Okay, come through to the kitchen. Cole's making coffee. You okay to talk with him there, too, or do you want to go out?"

"It's fine."

I walked into the kitchen, and Cole turned around. "Hey, man, you okay?"

"I think so," I replied. "You?"

He nodded. "What's up? Coffee?"

"Yeah, thanks. And what's up is that Abby's pregnant."

I didn't have to turn around to know Oakley's jaw probably hit the floor.

"She's pregnant?"

"Yep," I said and sat down.

"Err, forgive me for asking…" Cole said.

"Yep, it's mine," I replied. "And I had to ask, too, so don't worry."

Oakley sat down.

"Wow," she whispered. "I did not see that coming."

I laughed. "You're not the only one."

"Coffee or whisky?" Cole asked.

"I want whisky, but I should have coffee."

"So what are you going to do? Has she decided?"

I frowned. "She's keeping the baby."

God, I don't know what I would have done if she wasn't. It would kill me.

"We've got to bring a kid up together, and I don't know how to stop loving and hating her. I need to be neutral. How do I get my feelings for her to just caring about the mother of my child."

"Jasper, it's not even been two months since you broke up. It's going to take time for you to get over what happened."

"Cole, got any better advice than your wife's?"

"You could get smashed and sleep around…"

"Arsehole," I muttered, making him laugh. That was all I'd been doing though. Since the split, I'd put another fifteen notches on my bedpost.

"Seriously, man, Oakley's right. Stop putting so much pressure on yourself. There's no quick fix for anything, so you're going to have to go with it and get over her the old fashioned way."

"I was kinda hoping you'd be more help than this."

He raised his eyebrows. "Why? I pined over Oakley for four bloody years!"

My sister smiled lovingly at her husband.

"Yeah, why did I come to you two? Neither of you have any experience in moving on. You were both pathetic messes."

"Thank you," Oakley replied dryly.

I held my hand up. "No offence."

"Anyway, less about me and Cole. What are you going to do? Have you discussed what will happen when the baby," she said, stopping for a second to smile, "my niece or nephew, is here? When's the due date?"

"I don't know. We could barely talk about anything without arguing. I'll be there as much as possible. I want joint custody, and I don't think she'll fight it too much, she still wants a career, so only having the baby half the time will allow her to do that. I might need to rework my hours at The Centre."

Oakley waved her hand. "We'll sort it out."

I knew she'd say that. Family was her main priority, too.

"Yesterday I thought I'd lost everything," I whispered. "I can't believe I'm going to be a dad."

"You're going to be a great dad."

"Damn straight, I will. I'll do everything for that kid."

Leaning over, she gave me a hug and whispered, "Congratulations."

CHAPTER
Fifteen

Jasper

"**M**orning," I said to Holly as I walked into work, and again revelled in a blush that I knew meant she was thinking about the sex we'd had.

"Morning, Jasper. You look happy today."

I stopped by her chair and sat on the spot on the desk we'd christened. Her lame attempt at fighting a smile told me she knew exactly what I was doing.

"That's because I am."

"Good. It's nice to see you smiling again."

"Hey, I've smiled since Abby. You should know that better than anyone."

"Shh," she hissed, looking around the empty room.

My smile widened. "There's no one around but you and me, Holly. Now what could we do on this desk with no one around…"

She glared.

"I'm kidding. We should at least wait until I lock up tonight."

Her cheeks turned scarlet.

"Want to tell me why you're so happy rather than making me squirm at work?"

I was momentarily stunned into silence. That I hadn't expected to come from her mouth. She admitted I made her squirm. I could live with that.

"I'm going to be a dad."

Her mouth fell open so wide I could see all of her teeth.

"That was pretty much my reaction, too," I said.

"Oh. Um, congratulations then, I guess."

The light went from her eyes.

"So are you moving back into your old house?"

"What? No. Hey, when I said I never wanted Abby back I meant it. We're having a baby together, but that's it."

'That's it' was a strange phrase to use when talking about raising a tiny person, but that was it, that was as far as my relationship with Abby was ever going to go again. We'd share a child. End of story.

"I see. No offence, but I'm glad you're not going back there. You can do better."

"Anyone can do better than being with a cheater."

She nodded. "You're going to be a great dad."

"I hope so."

Smiling distantly, she spun her chair to face the monitor. "Oakley asked if you'd sign off the wages as she ran out of time. She left a note, I think, but asked me to mention it, too."

Holly had gone from squirming and blushing to ice cold at the mention of me being a dad.

"You okay?" I asked her.

"Yeah, fine." She looked up. "Why?"

I leant over, resting my hand on the desk and completely blocking her view of the screen.

"What're you doing, Jasper?" She asked a little breathlessly. At least she wasn't completely put off.

"What're you doing? There something wrong with me now I'm going to be a dad?"

"Of course not. It's just weird. I feel wrong for..." she shrugged.

"For what?"

"Flirting with you when your ex is carrying your child. I don't know; I shouldn't, because you're single and can do what the hell you like, but..."

"But you're a good girl – most of the time – and you have all these weird morals."

She laughed. "Weird?"

"Yeah, weird."

"If I was having a baby with someone else would you be here right now?"

"At work?"

She deadpanned.

"Alright, fine. Yes, I'd want you, but I don't have any morals."

"That's rubbish. You do."

"Fine, I have some. I think I'd still hit on you though, unless you were with this other guy."

Rolling her eyes, she pushed me back up so I was sitting straight.

"Of course you would because you just can't get enough of me."

Something like that. I'd rather be with Holly than all those other women.

"Why are we even having this discussion?" She asked.

"Alright, sorry." Frowning, I stood up and walked into the office. What the hell was her problem? We'd only slept together a few times, and I wasn't even with Abby. She couldn't be jealous, could she?

"Holly," I said, poking my head around the door. She looked up. "Is there something you want to talk about? Baby wise?"

"No. Why?"

"It's just that you seem off since I told you about Abby being pregnant."

"Look, I don't mean to be off or anything, it's just sudden, and I thought that you were finally starting to get your life back on track. Then this."

Wow, she really had no idea how many nights a week I went out getting smashed. Did she think I'd only slept with her since the break-up? I wanted her to think that rather than knowing the truth – that I woke up with women beside me I couldn't remember going home with a couple times a week.

I wanted to protect that secret and not have her be disappointed in me. In a very short space of time, she'd become someone that I cared about. I didn't want to lose her friendship or make her feel like a random woman I'd fucked since my wife cheated. Holly deserved better.

"As long as you're good."

"I am," she replied.

"Want a coffee?"

"Please."

I went into the kitchen, feeling a lot better for talking to her rather than leaving it. Now if I could only do that with Abby, things would be so much easier.

I wanted nothing to do with Abby, but she was carrying our baby; therefore, I was going to push everything else to the back of my mind and be the best dad-to-be I could.

"Uncle Jasper, where are we going?"

"The petting zoo," I replied, looking over at her to see her reaction.

Her bright, baby blue eyes lit up, and she smiled a full, toothy smile.

"Yay!" she chanted. "Can I cuddle a goat?"

I laughed. "If you want."

Since Cole and Oakley took her there a few months ago, she'd been obsessed with goats. Apparently, she threw a tantrum when she was told she couldn't have one. A day out with her was exactly what I needed to take my mind off everything for a while.

Tomorrow was scan day. I was buzzing at the thought of seeing my son or daughter, but I was also shit scared. Seeing it would make it real. I wanted to forget Abby, but this was going to tie us together for the rest of our lives. Every time I saw her I felt like I was being punched. I just hoped it would get better before the baby arrived.

"Are Mummy and Daddy coming too?"

"No, they're at work. You're okay just going with me, aren't you?"

She nodded. "Can I have ice cream and chocolate?"

"If you promise me you'll brush your teeth extra good tonight?"

"Okay. I don't want my teeth to go black and fall out." Her eyes widened, and she scrunched her nose up.

"That's right, you don't."

"Are we nearly there yet?" She asked, practically bouncing in her seat.

"Almost," I replied. Soon Everleigh would have a younger cousin to nag about timings and hurrying up. I couldn't wait to take my own kid out, too. Weekends and my days off. That was probably when I'd have the baby. I wanted joint custody and the baby spending an equal amount of time with us both.

I felt like I was already being pushed out. Not that Abby had done anything intentionally but her talk of nurseries and pre-school without consulting me made me think she felt she had the most rights and could decide these things on her own. She'd never been like that before. Every decision we made was a joint one. I felt like the dad that was being replaced by a step-dad.

My blood turned cold. Brett. If Abby really was with Brett now would he be the one discussing what to do with my child? I was sickened by the thought of him in my child's life more than me, but there was nothing I could do to stop it if Kerry was right and they were together. She'd seen them together in town.

"Uncle Jasper?" Everleigh said, bringing me back to reality.

"Yeah?"

"Can I have a goat at your house?"

I laughed. "Everleigh, I live in a flat. I don't even have the space for a dog. Where would I keep a goat?"

"In my room. I don't mind sharing."

Things were so simple to kids. I loved it, the innocence and naivety. Just put the goat in the bedroom. If she'd picked an animal that wouldn't eat my flat, then I probably would have bought it for her. I sucked at telling her no.

I got in after dropping Everleigh off home and dialled Abby's number. Speaking to her hurt but I'd have to ignore that. There was no getting away with not seeing her anymore.

"Jasper, hi," she breathed down the phone.

I tried to ignore the pang of heartbreak at hearing her say my name like that.

"How are you?" I asked, working harder than I should to keep my voice even.

"I'm good, just a little tired. Are you okay?"

"Fine. Just wanted to sort out tomorrow."

"Do you want to meet at the hospital or take one car?"

I closed my eyes. Taking one car was something we did as a couple. I'd always call her if we were going out and ask if she wanted to meet at the place we were going, or if we should meet at home and go together. So many times we'd opted for going together, even though it wasn't the easiest thing to do. We did it just to be together.

"I'll meet you there," I replied.

"Alright," she whispered. Even though it was her fault we broke up I still felt guilty every time she sounded unhappy. That needed to pass soon because I resented her for ending our marriage and for making me feel like the bad guy.

CHAPTER
Sixteen

Jasper

We sat in the waiting room in silence. Usually, we'd be chatting or flirting. I hated that it was so different now. *When will I stop loving her?* She'd broken my heart, and I couldn't get myself to stop wanting her. Shouldn't I have automatically stopped the second I caught her all over Brett?

"Jasper," she said, lowering her voice so the couple across the room from us couldn't hear.

"What?"

"Do you think you can get past what I did so we can at least see where things go? We're having a baby now. That's so much bigger than my feelings of insecurity."

"What feelings of insecurity?"

She'd never mentioned that before, not once.

Abby shrugged and rolled her lips inwards.

"I guess recently I'd been feeling like I wasn't good enough.

I kept letting you down because you wanted a child and I didn't feel ready."

"Are you trying to justify what you did?"

"No," she said and frowned. "Of course not, I'm just trying to make you understand why I did it. With Brett, there were no expectations so I couldn't let him down. I'm not trying to make it okay, it wasn't okay. What I did was stupid and selfish, and I'm ashamed of myself. But we're having a child."

"Let's not do this here."

"Why not? We're about to see our child for the first time. I think now is perfect."

She asked for it.

"Fine. Look, I'll be there for you as the father of our baby. I'll do everything I can for that child, but I won't take you back. You knew this was the last chance. We've done this too many times, and I don't want to have this discussion again. Drop it."

I turned away, feeling like shit. How many times was I going to have to say no before she realised I was serious? Just because I'd forgiven her before, didn't mean I was going to again – ever.

"Mrs Dane," someone called from behind us.

"Okay, are you ready to meet your baby?"

I grinned again, so wide the muscles in my cheeks burned. "Hell yeah, I am!"

The sonographer squirted some questionable looking stuff on Abby's stomach, and I looked at the screen. Soon enough something appeared in front of me – but what? It kind of looked like a bean.

"Is that it?" I asked. It was the cutest bean I'd ever seen, and I fell in love right then.

"Yes, that's it."

"Wow," I whispered.

"I'll just calculate how far along you are," the sonographer said, tapping away at her keyboard and looking at the screen. "Okay, so you're five weeks and your due date is March 29th."

The world came to an abrupt stop. That couldn't be right. We were expecting sometime in February. That meant she got pregnant in late June, *after* the last time we'd broken up. I knew what that meant but at the same time my brain refused to process it.

"March," I repeated.

On the table, Abby froze, staring at the screen, eyes wide and mouth open. She looked shocked but how could she be? She knew who she'd slept with. She knew that there was a chance it could be someone else's – Brett's.

Oh, fucking hell, the baby isn't mine.

I stood up in a daze. No. This couldn't be happening.

"Abby," I whispered. She said there had been no one since me. I wanted to have it out with her, but this wasn't the place, so like a dick, I stood there as my heart broke all over again.

When I should have bolted from the room, I stood still, unable to move an inch. The air thickened and tension radiated from both of us. She didn't say anything, didn't look at me, and just laid still, staring at the screen and gripping the edge of the bed.

I felt sick watching another man's baby inside my wife, but my legs had failed me.

Run.

The sonographer reeled off some information, and I briefly caught her saying everything looked fine, but my ears were ringing. Why couldn't I just leave? My body, still rooted to the floor, was punishing me in the most painful way imaginable.

Abby and a baby was all I'd wanted, and I just lost both.

Her belly was wiped and she sat up, taking the photographs.

"Thank you," she said quietly.

She turned around, and my heart slammed against my chest. It was over. All of it. Our marriage and our future, completely gone. She wasn't mine anymore. Her baby wasn't mine. We were done. My eyes stung. I spun around and sprinted from the room.

I ran towards the exit and could hear her hot on my heel. She was running to catch up with me, to say what? There was nothing that could ever make this better. She'd assured me the baby was mine, and her and Brett used contraception. They obviously fucking hadn't. Or there was another man in the frame.

"Jasper, please!" she shouted as I jogged to the car park.

I ignored her.

"Jasper, I'm sorry," she said, running faster to catch up with me. Thank God, I'd insisted on taking two cars.

I slammed against my car, fumbling in my pocket to find my keys. I opened the door, gripping the handle. "How could you not tell me there was a chance the baby wasn't mine? What the fuck are you trying to do to me?" I bellowed.

"I didn't know, okay. I thought it was yours. I'm sorry. My periods have been light, but my midwife said when the baby implants some women can bleed and that didn't mean I wasn't pregnant before they stopped completely."

"So fucking tell me that to begin with, so I don't get my hopes up. Jesus, I've been so happy these past couple days. I bought a motherfucking toy penguin!"

"I'm sorry. I honestly didn't think it could be anyone else's."

"You're always sorry these days. Is it Brett's?"

She dropped her eyes.

"Well, isn't that fantastic. Have a nice life, Abby."

Gasping, her head shot up. "No! Please. I don't want to leave it like this. We have to talk. I need you to believe that I didn't do this to hurt you. I thought you were the dad, I swear."

I got in the car. Slamming the door, I shoved the key in the ignition and got the hell out of there.

It took less time than usual to get home. Much of the journey was a blur. The kid with Abby's eyes and my smile slowly disappeared from my head. She knew. If there was even a chance, she should have said.

I shoved my front door open and kicked it shut. "Fuck it!" I shouted, punching the wall. Pain shot through my hand, so I shook it off. Everything was falling to shit. I felt like I'd just lost my chance to have a family and I was completely lost.

If she'd have at least told me she's slept with him around the same time, I wouldn't have put everything into it. I wouldn't have made plans in my head, and I wouldn't have thought about the first time he or she called me Daddy or peed on me when I was changing a nappy.

Heading straight to the alcohol cupboard in the kitchen, I ignored the dragging feeling weighing me down. I just wanted to get blind drunk, get lost in another woman and sleep. Then I wanted to wake up and have this all be just a shitty dream.

Holly would know what to do. She was having a hard time getting over the library dick who kept trying to get hold of her through her friends and family, so at the very least we could drown our sorrows together. I already felt pathetic but somehow drinking alone took it to a whole new level.

I called her, and she picked up almost right away.

"How did it go?" She asked. "When's the baby due?"

I closed my eyes.

"I can't remember." I'd zoned out by that stage, frozen in shock as the news that I wasn't the dad sunk in.

"The baby isn't mine."

She gasped. "What? Not yours?"

"Abby lied. She's probably been seeing Brett this whole time. She thought the baby was mine, but missed out the part where she was sleeping with someone else. God, Holly, I thought I was having a kid."

"Are you at home? I'll come over."

"Yeah, I'm here."

"Okay, give me ten minutes."

"Thanks," I breathed and hung up.

Less than ten minutes later, Holly knocked on the door.

"It's open," I shouted, not being bothered to get up from the sofa.

She walked in just as I took another swig of Southern Comfort.

"What the hell happened to the wall? Show me your hand!"

"It's fine," I replied, taking another swig.

"Stop that." She snatched the bottle from my hands. "You're not drinking this away."

"I thought I was gonna be a dad, Hol."

"I know," she said and sat beside me, putting the bottle down on the table. "I'm so sorry you got hurt again. She's such a bitch for allowing you to believe you were the father."

"I don't think I've ever heard you say bitch before."

She smiled, blushing lightly.

"Say it again."

"No."

"You're no fun."

She nodded at my bloodstained knuckles. "Do you need me to take care of that?"

"My boner?"

She gasped, her light blush turning lobster red. "Oh my God!

No, that's not what I meant. I didn't even know you had... you know."

"I don't, but you know how I love to make you blush."

"I think we both know I'm not so innocent."

I trace my finger down her neck and along her collarbone.

"I remember."

"Jasper," she whispered breathlessly, "I don't think this is a good idea."

"Wasn't the best idea last time either. You'd just broken up with the library dick."

I expected her to protest or shoot me some smart-arse comeback, but her lips slammed against mine.

Holly taking the lead. That was unexpected. It took all of one second for me to be ready.

I pulled her on my lap, and she curled her arms around my neck. Her lips were soft, but wrestling mine with a needy aggression I didn't know she was capable of. This was petite, shy and sweet Holly - not my usual outgoing type, but right now, I had never wanted anything more.

I pushed my tongue in her mouth. She accepted me instantly, whimpering and pressing her body against mine. My mind was screaming *bad idea*, but I couldn't seem to help myself. There was something about her, something I couldn't stay away from. I'd tried and failed miserably to keep my distance after last time, but I didn't even want to anymore.

"Jasper," she murmured against my lips. "I want you."

I felt a thousand feet tall. My pulse raced. I wrapped my arm under her perfect little butt and stood up. After feeling the lowest I had since Oakley spoke up about what she'd suffered, and finding out Abby was pregnant with another man's child, Holly made it go away - and I couldn't get enough of that feeling. She made it disappear until there was only us.

The six strides it took to reach my bedroom from the sofa felt about a hundred feet, I couldn't wait to have my lips on every inch of her body again. I couldn't wait to feel that incredible feeling as I pushed inside her.

My fingers dug into her skin as she bit my neck and tightened her legs around me. I dropped her on the bed and looked down at her. With no make-up and messy hair fanned out over my pillow she'd never looked so beautiful.

I crawled on the bed and lowered my face to hers.

After the last time, I had silently vowed not to sleep with a mate's sister again. I was going to hell for sure.

CHAPTER
Seventeen

Holly

My eyes fluttered open and I was momentarily disorientated at being in Jasper's bedroom. He slept peacefully beside me with one arm tucked under his pillow. He faced me, breathing evenly. I'd only seen him asleep one other time – the first time we'd slept together – but I could quite happily wake up to his beautiful face every day.

Recently, he'd had so much rubbish thrown at him it was understandable that he drank to forget it, but that wasn't going to do him any good in the long run. I hated seeing him so unhappy. In a very, very short space of time, he'd stolen my heart, tattooing his name across it in permanent ink. I would tell him how I felt if I thought he would give us a chance. But he was going through a marriage breakdown, and yesterday he found out he wasn't the father to his soon-to-be-ex-wife's baby. Now really wasn't the time to drop that on his doorstep, too.

In two months, I was leaving to go back to university anyway and although it was only forty-five minutes away it would be hard to have a relationship with that distance as well as concentrating on my degree. Not to mention the fact that he just wanted to sleep around.

We weren't going to work. Despite how much I wanted him to give us a chance, I understood that this wasn't the time for us. I had faith that if something was meant to happen between us then it would. Perhaps next year when I moved back here – if he wanted.

"I can feel you watching me," he murmured, his voice thick with sleep and a hangover.

My face flamed.

"I'm not," I whispered.

His eyes opened and my breath caught at the pools of light grey staring back at me.

"You're a crap liar, Holly."

I pulled the quilt higher, so it completely covered my breasts.

Jasper's eyebrow arched.

"You're shy after I spent a good three hours with my hands and mouth all over your body."

I flushed again. Why did he have to say stuff so bluntly like that? He wasn't at all shy; we were polar opposites.

"It's light, and you're not drunk now."

He frowned and then sat up faster than I could blink. The quilt was ripped from me, and I used my hands to cover myself as best I could.

"What are you doing?" I hissed, squirming under his gaze. I wasn't body confident. I wasn't anything confident.

"You've got to be kidding me, right? Holly, your body is flawless." He grabbed my wrist, pulling my hand away from my breasts. "Stop hiding."

"Jasper, don't," I whispered, on the brink of tears.

He pulled me up and we were facing each other. I shrank as much as I could and looked up at him. What was he doing?

"You're beautiful. I don't get why you're so shy, especially with me now."

Because I care about you too much, and I care what you think of my body and me.

His eyes darkened as his hand rose, and rested down just above my breast. I stopped breathing as his fingers glided over my skin, leaving a burning path behind them. He held my gaze, trapping me in it as he touched my body all over. I shuddered as he brushed over my hips and down to my thighs.

"Don't ever hide yourself from me. You've got nothing to be ashamed of."

I bit my tongue, desperately trying to prevent myself from crying. It was too intense and too intimate, but as much as I wanted to hide away I loved how he looked at me and how he made me feel wanted.

Feeling a rush of bravery, I reached out and placed my hands on his toned chest, exploring his six pack. He sucked his breath through his teeth and then smiled.

"See, I'm as on show as you are!"

"Yeah but your body is…" I replied, trailing off.

His hand cupped my neck.

"Your body is perfect," he said and leant forwards, capturing my lips in a sweet, slow kiss that made my back arch into him.

Jasper and I made our way into work after he made love to me again. I felt like a woman. Everyone saw me as Brad's shy little sister, but Jasper had given me something that I was sure would stay with me, even if he didn't. I didn't feel quite as afraid of showing a bit of skin off any more. If I wanted to wear a shorter skirt, then I would, because I wasn't the little girl that my friends and family thought I was. He'd given me the confidence to be me. For the first time, someone saw me as a woman.

I felt like going out and buying a whole new wardrobe of 'grown up' clothes and ditching my baggy tops, jeans and leggings. I wanted fitted clothes that made me look twenty. But that also might be because I was wearing my clothes from yesterday, minus the second layer top that I ditched in the hope that no one would notice I hadn't changed.

Oakley was just pulling out of the car park as we arrived. She and Everleigh waved to us as we passed.

"Good, she's already left. That'll save the being late lecture," Jasper said as he pulled into a space.

"Yeah, but she'll be back once she's dropped Everleigh at your mum's. This is only delaying the lecture." My eyes widened. "What are we going to say to her? We didn't think through the whole arriving together thing! What do we do?"

He grinned. "Act normal and tell her you had car trouble maybe?"

"Oh. Yes, we can just do that," I said and opened the car before I slapped him for looking amused by silly Holly.

Every time Jasper had to come to the reception for something – which was more often than usual – he made sure to brush against me, usually with a big smirk on his face. We hadn't spoken about not telling anyone about us, but it was obvious we had to. He wasn't exactly being discreet.

He sat on the reception desk chatting to the ladies of the Over 50s Fit Club. They loved him. It was easy to see why. I tried to ignore their conversation and get on with work, but I could feel

Jasper looking at me and it was very off-putting.

I was on my fourth coffee of the morning; I could barely keep my eyes open. With the stress of my final year starting in a couple of months and my sleepless night last night, I was exhausted. I rubbed my eyes and looked up. Jasper was alone; the Over 50s had gone to their fitness class. He was staring at me.

"What're you doing tonight?" He asked.

"Dinner with an old friend from high school," I replied, wishing I was meeting her another night because if I didn't know any better I'd think he was going to suggest we did something together.

He nodded once, pursing his lips. "Sounds good. You've not seen her in a while then?"

No, so I really can't cancel.

"Not since New Year's Eve."

"Right. Be good to catch up then," he said.

I nodded, getting lost in his eyes again.

"Jasper?" Oakley called from her office behind reception.

His head snapped towards the door and he hopped off the desk as if he'd just been woken from a daydream.

"Coming," he replied and walked off.

I'd never been sure when a guy liked me, so when my exes said they did it was a surprise. It was fair to say I had little experience of reading the signs, but I was getting some pretty big mixed ones from Jasper.

"Amy," I said, giving her a hug before sitting opposite her.

"Hey, sweetie, how're you?" She asked.

I blushed, remembering being in Jasper's arms, his bed, last night.

"I'm good, are you?"

She grabbed the cocktail menu.

"I'm fabulous."

"Good. How's Liam?"

"He's great, too. What's going on with you? Last I heard you were going to dinner with some… Henry?"

"Harry," I corrected. "That's over now though. He was either full on or arctic cold. I don't play games."

She turned her nose up.

"Definitely. No one wants a game-playing boyfriend, too much of a headache. So, you're single."

"Yep," I replied. "But there's this guy."

Her eyes lit up. "Tell me about him, and don't you dare skip on any details."

Where do I start?

"Okay, well he's Brad's friend. Gorgeous, light brown hair, sexy stubble, bit cocky, but he's cheeky with it, so you don't want to punch him. You know what I mean?"

She nodded and waved her hand, telling me to continue.

"We've slept together a few times."

Amy's mouth hit the table. I didn't do one-night stands, and she knew that. I was Holly, the shy, good girl.

"Wow," she breathed. "What was he like?"

"Are we really discussing that?"

"Absolutely! He's good in bed?"

I was sure I blushed again.

"Yes," I replied. "Not that it's surprising, he's had enough practice."

"Ah, a player?"

"Yep. He was when Brad was first hanging out with him, but then he got married."

Her mouth dropped again.

"You're sleeping with a married man?" She squeaked.

"No! Of course I'm not. She cheated, and they broke up."

"When?"

"Um." I bit my tongue. "Almost two months ago."

"Christ, Holly!"

"I know! I don't particularly feel good about it. He's single though, so it's not bad, right? I'm not doing anything wrong, am I?"

"They're definitely separated?"

I nodded. "He's filing for divorce."

"Then you're not doing anything wrong. She cheated on him anyway, what he does now is none of the ex's business."

"Yeah, I just feel bad."

"Of course you do. You're too nice, sweetie. Don't feel bad for having a little fun with a *single* guy."

She had a point. I couldn't help worrying what people would think of me. My family probably still thought I was a virgin, and although I'd had about as much sex with Jasper as I had with my ex and Harry, I didn't want anyone to think I was 'easy'.

"Thanks, Ames, you always did manage to put things into perspective."

"I have to say, in the seven years I've known you, you've never managed to surprise me until now."

"Yeah, well, you ready for one more?"

Her eyes widened. "I'm not sure if I can take it!"

"I think I'm falling for him."

"Oh, no. Babe, don't do that. Bad, bad idea. The guy has just broken up with his wife and is about to go through a divorce. This is the worst time to fall for him. Right now he'll just be wanting to screw the pain away."

I winced. Thinking about Jasper with another woman left a nasty taste in my mouth. My stomach burned with jealousy. I knew it happened, but I didn't ever want to think about it.

"Yep, I know all that, and I agree. Falling for him is probably the worst idea I've ever had, but I don't get a choice. I'd love to stop it, but I can't. There's something about him. At first he was just nice and funny, we got along, and there was nothing more to it." I shrugged. "Well, I was attracted to him, but I'm not blind! Anyway, the more time we spent to together, especially at work-"

"Wait, work?"

"Yeah, his sister owns The Centre, and he co-runs it."

"Oakley Farrell's brother?" She asked.

"Oakley Benson," I corrected. "But, yeah, her brother, Jasper."

"Whoa. Okay, go on."

"We spent more time together, and he was great when Harry broke up with me, and I told him we'd never get back together. Underneath the lad exterior, he is a really nice, caring, loyal guy." I banged my head on the table. "I'm doomed, right?"

Amy flopped back against the booth. "Yeah, I think you are."

"I'm not going to act on my feelings."

"So next time he comes to you you're not opening Hotel Holly and letting him get funky inside you."

I blinked. "What?"

She shook her head.

"My brother and his immature teen mates have been hanging around the house. It would seem their interesting vocabulary is rubbing off on me."

"Right. Well, I'd love to be able to do that. Actually, I wouldn't. I love that he gets to me the way he does. I've never had that before."

"Oh God, Holly."

"I know," I whined. "Why can't I say no to him?"

"Because you're in lurve!"

I glared.

"Not helping." Was I in love already? "Anyway, tell me what's new with you. Take my mind off Jasper."

CHAPTER
Eighteen

Jasper

I pulled my zip up and waved to Courtney or Connie or Cally as I walked out of the stall.

"You're not even going to buy me a drink?" She said.

Oh no, she's a post casual sex drinker. No one wanted to go do anything with someone after they'd just had no strings, one-time-only sex. There were rules about this type of thing that she wasn't following.

"Look…" I trailed off, wincing as she raised her eyebrow.

"Emma!"

"Emma," I repeated. "Shit, I was way off."

And judging by the look on her face her sense of humour was seriously lacking. *Can't think why!* Holding my hands up, I took a step closer to her. Now I was obligated to buy her a drink because even if one-time-only sex meant you could leave, and that be it, it was still common courtesy not to forget their name to the person's face.

"I'm sorry, Emma. I was a dick. Lemme buy you a drink to apologise."

"Oh, so you want to have a drink with me now?"

When did I say *with*?

I smiled. "Of course. I didn't think you'd want to since this was just a bit of fun."

She blinked heavily, and I started to seriously regret my decision to sleep with her. Some people could casual fuck; Emma was not one of them. Either she'd been hurt like me, or she was trying to prove some point to someone – her friends or another guy most likely.

Her bottom lip trembled, and my eyes widened.

"Shit. No, don't cry." *What do I do? What do I do?* "Do you want me to go?"

Shaking her head, she pulled me back in the stall and closed the door.

"I'm sorry," she whispered, fanning her face.

I leant back against the wall I'd just banged her up against and smiled as convincingly as I could. "Are you okay?"

"Yes. I'm embarrassed mostly."

"You've not done this much."

"This is the first one-night stand I've had, and I thought I'd be okay. It's just sex, right?"

Kneeling down as she dropped onto the toilet seat, I replied, "It's not just sex for everyone."

"What's wrong with me?"

"Nothing, Emma. It's fine if you can cut feelings off for sex and if you can't. Now you know, never do it again." I reached out and wiped her tear before it fell. "It's not worth feeling like this over, and waiting for a relationship is nothing to be ashamed of."

"Thank you," she whispered. "I'm glad this mistake was you."

I wasn't sure how to take that.

"Okay," I replied.

"Sorry, that didn't come out right. I just mean that if it was someone else that didn't care I would've felt worse."

"I don't care about anything." Even I didn't believe the words.

She smiled. "Sure you don't."

Standing up, she walked past me.

"Take care, Jasper."

And I felt worse; she'd remembered my name.

Blowing out a deep breath, I left the bathroom. Emma was nowhere around in the bar, so I assumed she'd gone home. I'd had one time fucks go wrong before – the woman that told me she was falling for me five seconds after I'd come and the one that chanted silent words as I did her against the door. To this day, I had no idea what she was mouthing.

I stumbled to the bar and leant my full weight on the wooden top.

"I'll have another SoCo and coke, please," I slurred, pushing my glass towards a hot barmaid.

"Coming up," she replied.

Leaning over the bar, I checked out her arse as she made me a drink. She was slightly slimmer than Abby. I'd always loved Abby's curves. There was something for me to grab onto.

"Ha, Brett loved her curves, too," I said to the person beside me, a bewildered looking fierce redhead.

"Okay," she said.

"My wife is a slut."

"My fiancé is a slut," she replied. "I'm Kate."

"Jasper."

"So your wife cheated."

"With a guy from work, yeah. You?"

"Caught him in my bed with my cousin."

"Shit. Okay, you win." I thought seeing Abby kiss another man was bad enough. I didn't know how the fuck I'd cope with seeing more. "Want a drink?"

"Whatever you're having, please."

"Make that two," I called to the barmaid, and she nodded in reply. "So, Kate, what're you doing with your life since it got fucked up?"

She snorted. "You sound like my family."

"I sound like my family. My sister is always going on about how I have so much more to offer than sleeping around and I should get myself sorted as moving on is the best revenge."

Kate thought for a minute. "Your sister's right about that."

"I prefer getting shit-faced and getting laid."

"The easy option."

I frowned. "Wouldn't call it that."

"Neither would I, but it's easier than facing the fact that your relationship is over, you're alone and somehow have to piece everything back together."

"Well, aren't we the most cheerful fuckers in the bar tonight?"

She laughed. "You need revenge."

"Revenge? What I need is to forget she exists and hope my divorce comes through ASAP."

"Hmm, I prefer revenge."

"How did you do that?"

The bartender put our drinks on the bar, and I paid. Kate ran her long fingernail around the edge of the glass.

"Keyed his precious car and told my aunt, uncle and Bethan's husband that Daniel has Chlamydia so she should get tested."

"Does marriage mean nothing to people these days?"

"Tell me about it," she spat. "I'm off men now. Relationship-wise. It's not worth the hassle and heartbreak."

"I'll drink to that." I picked up my glass, and we clinked.

Me and Kate had another three drinks together; slagging off our exes helped us bond.

"Hmm, worst thing I've done since the break up..." she said, trailing off to think about it. "Oh, I kissed my ex's friend. Not a good move I admit, but it was two days after, and I was feeling shitty. What about you?"

"Well, I've done nothing to Abby." She wasn't worth my energy and I wasn't interested in revenge. Even after hurting me as badly as she did I couldn't do the same to her.

"But I have slept with a mate's sister. More than once."

"Oh, you don't piss on your own doorstep," she said, and I burst out laughing. "Do you like the girl?"

I shrugged. "Sure. She's not the girl I usually go for, but she's cool."

"She's cool?"

"Yeah. Funny, smart, beautiful, easy to get on with, blushes like crazy, has the best reactions-"

"You like her."

I held my hands up. "Whoa, don't start that. I like her as a friend, sure. That's it though. For now, I'm single and having fun."

Fun. That was a word to be used loosely. I was hardly having the time of my fucking life, but after all the shit with Abby it was nice not to care about anything or think of someone else. I could do whatever the hell I wanted, whoever the hell I wanted, whenever the hell I wanted.

"Doesn't mean you don't like her. If she showed up right now and asked you to go home with her what would you do?"

Get my coat.

Kate grinned at my silence. "That's what I thought. It's fine, Jasper. Just because you like her doesn't mean you have to have a relationship, you can just want to sleep with her."

"Thanks," I replied sarcastically.

Holly was great; she really was, but I did not want a relationship with her or any other woman right now. I'd only been separated from Abby for seven and a half fucking weeks. I couldn't even imagine being with someone in the future yet.

"Cards on the table," Kate said. "Are you taking me back to your place or not?"

My eyebrows shot up. Yeah I'd mostly been with women that knew what they wanted, but Kate was on another level. "No feelings. No guilt. No sneaking out the next day. You give me at least six orgasms and cook me bacon in the morning. I'll leave after that, and you'll never see me again."

I blinked in shock. This was my lucky night.

"I'll call a taxi," I said, reaching for my phone.

Kate grabbed her bag and downed her drink and then mine. I grabbed her hand and led her outside as I ordered a car. At half past ten, long before the bars and clubs closed, I had no doubt we'd get one within ten or fifteen minutes.

Kate leant against the brick wall of the bar as I finished the call – ten minutes to kill before we could get out of here. I slipped my phone in my pocket and stepped between her legs.

"So, Kate," I said, running my hands over her hips. "How do you feel about PDAs?"

She hooked her leg around my waist. "I'm all for them," she purred and offered her mouth for a kiss.

My head was being drilled from the inside. I groaned and rolled over, squinting my eyes at the stream of light spilling in through the window.

Something moved at the end of the bed and I sprung up. A woman – Kate, I remembered – laughed and picked up her jacket from the floor.

"I'm going to ignore you forgetting I was here."

"Sorry," I said, wincing.

"It's okay, lover boy, you were quite out of it. I'm impressed you got it up to be honest."

"Thanks." *I think.*

"Well, I had a lovely evening, but I've gotta skip breakfast and run. Good luck with the ex situation, Jasper."

I nodded. "You too."

Kate left, and I dropped back on my pillows.

By the time I was feeling human again, it was almost two in the afternoon, and I'd called Oakley to find out where they were. I missed Everleigh, and I hated that me being a mess was preventing me from spending as much time with her as I wanted to.

"She's at Mum's. Me and Cole are Christmas shopping."

I stilled. "Did I hibernate the summer away? Oakley, it's July!"

"I know, but we need a new ten-foot tall tree for The Centre and Cole found a garden centre that's selling old stock. We figured we'd get some things done. Only decoration shopping, I'm changing the colours this year. I can't think about presents until it's cold."

I couldn't think about any of it until it was December 20th!

"Alright, you freak. I'm gonna head over to Mum's then."

"You okay?"

"Yeah, all sober now. I wouldn't want to be near her if I was drunk."

"That wasn't what I meant."

"Oh, well, I'm fine."

My conversation with my sister ended with me promising to sort my shit out, again, and then I headed to Mum's. At least with Everleigh there I wouldn't get a lecture.

"Hi, love," Mum said, opening the door so I could come in.

"Hey, where's Everleigh?"

"Sleeping on the sofa. Want a hot chocolate?"

I smiled at her over my shoulder.

"Sure."

I sat on the sofa and watched Everleigh sleep. She was so tiny and so innocent. She looked just like Oakley as a kid. Rubbing my forehead roughly, I tried shoving the thoughts and memories away.

Why was it that when all you wanted to do was forget something, it haunted you as much as it could? I just wanted one day when I didn't think about it. When I didn't feel guilt.

"Here," Mum said, putting a mug down on the coffee table.

"Thanks."

"You look tired, honey."

"Wow, thanks," I replied.

"Come on, I didn't mean it like that. Talk to me."

I shrugged. "I don't know what to say."

"You've lost so much in such a short space of time, and it kills me to see you this unhappy. You were happy again when you thought you were having a child, weren't you?"

"Yeah, I was." The baby I thought I was having made my marriage worth something. Even though it ended horribly, I could at least say something amazing came out of our marriage. Now it was just shit.

"You'll be happy again if you open yourself up to a future."

"I don't want anyone."

"Not now. Believe me, I understand not now, but don't dismiss it outright and continue thinking there's nothing out there for you. You will be okay; you will be happy again, and you will find someone to share your life with."

"In that order?"

"Usually. Work on you and the rest will follow."

I didn't say anything else because it would just end up with us bickering. I thought she was wrong, and she thought I was wrong. Neither of us would back down, so it was pointless.

Picking up my hot chocolate, I laid back against the sofa.

"Thanks, Mum."

CHAPTER
Nineteen

Holly

I woke up feeling exhausted again, even after nine straight hours. My stomach was tied in knots. I was four days late with no sign of my period coming and was feeling run down. But not sick. That was a big one, right? If I didn't have sickness then I wasn't pregnant. I laughed at my own naivety.

Looking over at my full-year calendar, I noted the date of my return to university. October 7th. I was looking forward to my final year, but now I wasn't sure if I'd even be able to go back. If I was how could I have a baby at Uni?

This wasn't supposed to happen. I was meant to finish Uni and move almost all the way back home and get a job at the local hospital. Children were supposed to come later. I wasn't the impulsive one. My life was planned out, and I liked my plan.

"Holly," Dad called through the door. "I'm going to work now."

"Okay, see you later."

I heard him grumble about something; no doubt it was because it was his turn to work on Saturday. His reaction was the same every month.

In my bedside table were two pregnancy tests that I'd bought yesterday in the hope that I would come on and could throw them away. Now I didn't even have the slightest cramp, and I knew I was going to have to face this.

As soon as I heard Dad's car start, I got the bag out and went to the bathroom. Putting it off was only driving me crazy. When it read negative it was going to be a huge relief, and I'd wonder why I hadn't just done the stupid thing before.

I locked the door and pulled the stick out of the packet.

Please don't be positive, please.

I'd never done a pregnancy test before. It was terrifying. In high school, I watched one of my friends do it. I sat in her bedroom with Harmony and Amy as Bex peed on a test in her en suite. I remember being so scared for her, but it was nothing compared to how I was feeling right now.

At twenty, I wasn't ready to be a mum. I knew that if I was pregnant, however, I was keeping my baby; there was never any doubt about that.

I sat on the floor, on the bath mat staring at the upside-down test on the floor in front of me.

It's negative; it has to be.

Four days late was nothing. I'd been three days before. But that time I hadn't had unprotected sex.

Taking a deep breath, I turned it over.

The result may as well have been in flashing lights:

Pregnant

I dropped the test and placed my hand on my belly, trying to absorb the enormity of the word. It carried around lifelong responsibility and sacrifice. It was too big for me right now, but carelessly or not, I had created this life. It wasn't the baby's fault it was here, and there wasn't a good enough reason why I couldn't raise it.

I was going to be a mum. I leant back against the bath. And Jasper was going to be a dad. Shit. Jasper! How was he going to react? He already had so much going on with Abby, moving out and pretty much losing himself in drink and women almost every night.

He'd only been separated two months.

Jasper had wanted a baby now with Abby, but I was sure he wouldn't be so happy in this situation. He wouldn't want a baby with a girl he'd slept with on a couple occasions. Who would?

"Holly?" Mum shouted.

I jumped up, alarmed. She wasn't supposed to be back yet.

"Um, in the bathroom. Be down in a second!"

Damn it, why was she home from shopping so early?

"Alright. Brad and Jasper are here."

I gulped, fingers trembling as I shoved the test in the box and put it up my top. My mind was chanting Jasper's name. How could I face him five seconds after learning I was carrying his baby?

After stuffing the test under my pillow, I went downstairs, ready to put my game face on and pretend I wasn't pregnant with the guy I couldn't get out of my head.

"Hey, Hol," Jasper said, grinning up at me from the kitchen table.

Mum was fussing around, putting biscuits and cakes on a

plate for them.

"Hi," I replied weakly, giving him the best I'm-not-carrying-your-child smile I could.

"Tea, sweetheart?" Mum asked.

The word tea set off my gag reflex as I thought about the now disgusting drink. Or was I just thinking that? Was it the shock making me feel ill?

"No, thank you," I replied.

"You okay?" Jasper asked as I sat down beside him. He had a permanent twinkle in his gorgeous grey eyes whenever he spoke to me now. My body went crazy every time I saw him, so it was only fair he had something that gave away what was between us, too.

"I'm fine. Just didn't sleep that well last night."

His eyes flicked to Brad, who was up at the counter deciding which tea to have with Mum.

"I can help you sleep if you want," he muttered, leaning in close.

Yes, I did want, more than anything. But it wasn't real. I was carrying his child; I needed more than casual sex. He'd told me once that I couldn't do casual, and he was right, but with him it was so much more. If it wasn't more to him, then I couldn't sleep with him again.

"I'm okay," I muttered, not committing to anything or leading him on.

"Sure you're okay?" He placed his palm over my forehead, and I tried to ignore the butterflies he gave me. "You don't have a temperature. Are you sick?"

"No, it's not that. I don't feel sick."

Well, I did but not because of a bug.

"Maybe you should have an early night. I'll cover reception

tomorrow. You take it easy."

"Thank you."

Getting over him wasn't going to be easy when he was being sweet and caring. "I should take it easy tomorrow. Hopefully it won't turn into anything then."

And I could get an emergency appointment at the doctor surgery to have this pregnancy confirmed.

"Yeah. If you need anything else…"

I smiled, fighting the urge to kiss him.

"Holly," Dr White said, smiling with affection. She'd been my doctor since I was a baby and was thrilled when I told her I wanted to get into medicine. She'd even suggested applying for a pharmacist position here. I wasn't even sure if that was possible now.

"Hello, Dr White," I said as we walked along the corridor to her surgery.

"How is university?"

I tugged on my top as if she could see a bump. There was no bump and wouldn't be for a while yet.

"It's great. I love it."

"I knew you would." She shut the door behind us, and we sat down. "Now, what can I do for you?"

This shouldn't be so hard, but I opened my mouth, and nothing came out. She was somewhat of a family friend, and I didn't want her to be disappointed in me.

"Holly?" She prompted.

"I… I'm pregnant."

"Oh. Okay. You've done a test, yes?"

I nodded. "Two actually."

I'd done another one when Jasper and Brad left, just to make sure. The same pregnant result stared back at me.

"Alright. Well, congratulations." Congratulations? "When was the first day of your last period?"

"July third," I replied. I remembered because that was the day before I met up with Amy for lunch.

"Let's calculate your due date then." She got out a circle chart and studied it, turning the top layer so casually. "According to this you're due on the 9th of April. But your scans will be able to give you a more accurate date."

"Okay," I replied weakly.

"Are you okay, Holly? Can I assume this wasn't planned?"

"Not planned," I confirmed.

"The father?"

"Is so messed up right now he's going to question if he's the dad."

Dr White frowned, so I told her everything and by the time I'd finished I was sure she would think I was a slut. I'd slept with two men within five weeks of each other, but I'd had a period between breaking up with Harry and sleeping with Jasper.

"Was there anything different about your last period?"

I knew this was it. If I lied and said it was lighter, she would send me for an early scan so we could be sure of my dates. The idea of lying to her made me feel horrible, but I needed something concrete to go to Jasper with or he might, understandably, doubt me.

I pressed my fingernails into the palms of my hands and prayed I didn't look guilty. "It was a lot lighter."

"Hmm," she said. "It is possible to have light bleeding when the embryo implants into the uterus. I think it's best to send you for a scan, and then we can be sure. I don't want to leave you until twelve weeks in case we're a month out."

Licking my dry lips, I nodded. "Thank you."

"It's my pleasure. I'll print out some dos and don'ts, and we'll arrange that scan. I'll request you're seen this week and also book you an appointment with the midwife."

The local midwife was also the one that delivered me. Mum still spoke to her about my 'interesting' birth whenever she saw her. It was times like this I wished I lived in a big town rather than a small village.

"Okay," she said after she'd given me pages of printed-paper and gone over any questions I had. "Make another appointment if there's anything else you need but if not I'm sure I'll see you back here at some point. Perhaps when I check over the baby."

I smiled. "Thank you."

Standing up, I shook her hand and walked out. In the next few days, I would hear when my scan appointment was. A very big part of me hoped it was in a couple weeks time so I could prepare myself.

Armed with my scan picture, proving Jasper was the dad; I knocked on his door and waited. My heart was racing, and I felt nauseous. I had absolutely no idea how he was going to react, not even an inkling.

He opened the door, and before I could chicken out and ask to borrow sugar or something lame like that I walked past him and into his flat.

"What is it, Holly?" He said, grabbing my arm as I rushed through the living room.

"Holly?" someone's voice I didn't recognise came from the kitchen, and I froze.

He had a woman here.

A beautiful brunette with legs up to her armpits appeared

from the kitchen. I was dumbstruck. Here I was, about to announce to Jasper I was having a baby, and he was shacked up with a one-night stand.

"Um, Holly this is Leanne. We met last night," Jasper said.

I managed a weak smile. "Hi, Leanne."

"Holly, hi. Lovely to meet you. Do you want to join us for bacon rolls?"

My stomach turned. "No, thanks."

If I did I would definitely be seeing them again later.

"Everything okay?" Jasper asked. His discomfort was blindingly clear.

I blinked a few times, desperately trying to think of something to say.

"I was just passing on the way to pick up something I left at work. I wanted to know if you need a lift tonight? We're sharing a taxi but couldn't get hold of you to ask and if you want to share we'll book a bigger car," I rambled. "I would've called, but I was driving and your place is on the way so…"

I pinched the scan photo between my fingers in my pocket as I spoke, gripping it for dear life. This was awkward for everyone but Leanne it seemed, she stood leaning against the door frame grinning.

"Sharing a taxi will be great," Jasper replied. "How come Brad didn't call?"

"Ah!" Leanne exclaimed. "Brad, the friend, and Holly, the sister!"

Jasper winced as I glared up at him. He told her that?

"Hey," he said. "I was drunk, and it's not like she's going to tell."

"That's not the point," I hissed. I didn't want him going around telling people our business. The thought of people knowing who I'd slept with filled me with horror.

"All right, sorry," he replied, holding his hands up. "I won't mention it to anyone again, but it wasn't like I was bragging about it. I'm not proud of going behind my mate's back."

I felt like crying. This wasn't how it was supposed to happen. I expected him to rant, tug on his hair and throw the occasional swear word but not this. He slept around; that wasn't a secret, but seeing it with my own eyes hurt like hell. I should've known I couldn't have no strings sex. And he wasn't supposed to regret what happened between us.

"Forget it. It's fine. I'll get Brad to let you know when the taxi is picking you up."

Turning on my heel, I made a quick exit. Jasper called my name, but I ignored him. I couldn't see him with her again. I sprinted out of the door and towards my car, wiping the tears which had started streaming from my eyes.

CHAPTER
Twenty

Jasper

I hopped in the taxi. Cole and Oakley sat in the back of the seven-seater talking to each other with doe eyes. It made me want to gag. Brad was on the middle row of two and Holly the front row of two. Brad's legs hung over where I wanted to sit so it would have to be near Holly.

After the awkward situation earlier, I didn't want to be trapped beside her for twenty minutes. I really had to stop talking about her to the random women I slept with. Not only could it get back to Brad but it annoyed me how much my drunken mind was on her.

"Hi," I said as I sat down.

She looked up briefly. "Hi."

"You okay?"

"Yes. You?" She replied, barely meeting my eye.

And I thought this would be awkward...

"Yep," I replied and lowered my voice to add, "What's wrong?"

"Nothing," she mouthed.

"Bullshit."

"Man, if I can walk at the end of the night, punch me," Brad said, poking his head between the seats.

I forced a laugh. "Yeah, deal. What're you forgetting tonight then?"

"Hmm," he murmured. "I can't decide between the long day at work today or the blonde in the pub that turned me down last week."

"Wow, those are your only problems!" Holly said, rolling her eyes at her brother.

"Oh, and what's your biggest problem right now, Hol? Shall I wear my pink pyjamas tonight or my blue ones," Brad replied in the worst imitation of a woman's voice ever.

She turned back and stared out of the window.

Brad poked her arm. "Are you on or something? You've been moody all day."

"Just fuck off, Brad!" she hissed.

Whoa.

"Ugh, definitely on," he said and retreated back. Holly muttered the word *pig* under her breath.

What the hell was going on?

Right now sitting in the seat beside Cole while his lips were attached to my sister's was more appealing. Whatever was wrong with Holly was seriously going to piss all over the fun tonight.

We arrived at the club, and as there was no queue – not a good sign – we were ushered straight inside.

"We're leaving if it's dead," I said as we walked up the stairs. I was determined not to let anything ruin the night.

"Ladies, sit down and gentlemen, to the bar!" Brad exclaimed, reaching above his head and pointing to the bar.

Holly frowned and headed towards the seating area that was too quiet for this to be a good night.

"Is she okay?" Oakley whispered to me.

"How should I know?" Though I was starting to think I had something to do with her bad mood. Was it about yesterday? We'd agreed that sex between us was casual, she seemed happy with that and had instigated one time herself. I was shit scared that she had changed her mind and things between us would get awkward. I liked Holly, but I was nowhere near the relationship place right now.

She rolled her eyes and followed Holly to an empty table in the corner of the seating area. I helped Brad and Cole carry over the drinks. We must have at least four each.

Brad put the tray of ten shots down "First, we do shots. Two each, one after the other."

Holly shook her head. "I don't want one, Brad."

"I've bought you one now! Drink it, you're not driving." He sat down and pushed two shots towards her.

Hell, if she didn't do it, I would. If I wasn't getting laid, I was getting smashed.

She pursed her lips. "I don't want it."

"Don't make her," Oakley said, looking at Holly with an expression I knew very well – suspicion.

I downed my shot and then almost spat it out. *Fuck, Holly's pregnant!* I choked on nothing and stared at her.

"She's being a baby. It's just a couple shots!" Brad exclaimed.

"Oh, for fuck sake, Brad, *I can't*!"

Holly didn't shout often. Brad sat back, eyes wide. The air got thicker, and I struggled to breathe. My baby or Harry's?

Not again.

"Oh, Jesus, don't tell me you're knocked up? Are you kidding me, Holly! You're only twenty years old! Fuck it, I'm gonna kill Harry!"

"Can you please shut up, people are looking," she hissed.

"Where does he live? Near the church, right?"

"Stop it!"

Not my baby. I should've been relieved, but I couldn't help feeling sick at the thought of her having another man's baby.

"What number, Holly? Never mind, I'll see his car." Brad stood up.

"It's not Harry's!" she blurted out.

Fuck!

I fisted my hands on my knees. Holly didn't look at me. My world shifted again. Just when I was starting to get back on my feet, this happened. I was desperate to know if that was true or if she just said it to get Brad to sit the hell back down. I'd never felt like getting shit-faced so much before.

"What?" Brad said, dropping himself back on the chair. "Well, who the fuck is it then?" He looked appalled. I wanted to punch him for the way he looked at her. She wasn't a slut.

Holly stood up, avoiding eye contact with everyone. "I need to go."

I stood automatically, needing to talk to her. "I'll make sure you get home."

Oakley had her accusing face again. She looked between me and Holly. "Are you sure? I can take her."

I shrugged. "It's fine. You talk some sense into this one," I said, slapping Brad on the back. "You're better at lectures and advice than I am."

"Right," my sister, who blatantly knew the baby was mine,

replied.

Brad said nothing as Holly and I left. He just stared at his drink with a clenched jaw. Oakley also said nothing, and I knew she was waiting for us to get out of the way before she launched into how he shouldn't have spoken to Holly like that. As if he wouldn't be regretting it already.

"He'll cool down," I said as I opened the exit door for her.

She smiled weakly and nodded.

Neither of us said a word the whole way home. I gave the taxi my address, and she didn't ask me to turn around and take her to her parents'. We needed to have this conversation.

I got out and Holly followed closely behind, chewing the inside of her cheek nervously. I tried to look calm but inside my heart was racing. The palms of my hands were damp, and I almost dropped the keys as I unlocked the door.

A baby.

A baby with a woman I'd shagged a few times. It didn't look good. When I had a child, I wanted to be with its mum, living together and fully prepared – or as prepared as you could be.

I stopped in the living room and turned to her. My heart was in my mouth.

"So," I said and realised I didn't know what to say. "You're…" I nodded to her stomach.

She smiled. "Yeah, I'm pregnant."

"Shit."

"That's what I thought when I found out. I had a scan to check when it... happened." She bit her lip. "I kind of lied to the doctor and told her I wasn't sure of my last proper period so she'd book me for an early scan."

Just like Abby.

"I… You're pregnant with *my* baby?"

"Yes."

If she'd told me she used to be a man, I would've been less shocked than this. Fear gripped my throat as she confirmed it. I was going to be a dad.

I ran my hands over my hair. "Shit!" I wanted to believe her so badly, but I'd had this ripped away from me before. I couldn't get excited about having a child if there was a chance I wasn't. "Are you sure?" I asked.

She reached into her bag and pulled out an envelope. "I have my notes and a scan if you'd like to see?"

I held my hand out. My pulse thudded in my ears. The picture was of a little bean thing, just like Abby's. But this one had the outline of a forming head – a big looking head, and what something that resembled a fish tail. It was a different angle though, so I wasn't sure whose bean was older.

"Oh my God," I whispered, staring at it in awe.

"I know." Holly was looking at me anxiously.

"Yeah. She's the most beautiful weird looking little thing I've ever seen."

She laughed quietly, clearly relieved I wasn't angry. "I keep thinking it's a girl, too."

"I bet we'll both be wrong."

"I don't care really," she said.

"Neither do I." I shook my head and reluctantly held the photo out to her. "I can't believe this. It's really mine?"

"Yes," she whispered. "You can keep that picture. I've got a copy, too."

I smiled and gripped the photo hard. My baby.

"Thank you."

"I thought you'd freak out," she said.

"Honestly, me too. I feel like I should, but I know I'd regret it. We did this together, why should I get to go out and wasted when you can't? Plus, I think I'm in shock."

She laughed.

I blew out a deep breath. "Okay, so what happens now?"

Jesus, I was in a rented flat and wasn't even dating Holly. As happy as I was to be a dad, this wasn't how I imagined it would be. It didn't feel real at all.

"I've not thought that far ahead yet." She sighed and sat down on the sofa. "This isn't supposed to happen for a good five years at least. Thankfully, I've finished year three at Uni though; that would've been difficult if it was midyear. I can defer and go back once the baby's here. Mum and Dad are being supportive. Dad even said he'd clear the junk room out for the nursery."

Right, because we didn't live together. My child was going to be somewhere else.

I frowned. "As soon as my old house is sold, I'll buy a new place. You'll let the baby stay over with me too, right?

"We've got plenty of time to figure all that out. This is all so sudden and unexpected; I've not really had time to think through all the details," she said.

"Like how you're going to finish Uni? I know you said you'd defer, but when you go back we'll have a baby. Where would you live then? You're forty-five minutes away. God, Holly, you're not taking the baby there, are you?"

She held her hands up.

"Stop, please. I'm getting a headache. Uni is the last thing on my mind right now; I've recently found out I'm having a baby! Whatever happens, I'll never move away and take the baby with me. You're half responsible for this-" she pointed to her stomach "-so you can bet your arse you're going to be close by to help take care of it!" She sounded nervous. I couldn't blame her. I felt like I was in a dream.

My shoulders relaxed in relief. "Okay. Good. I can't believe we're having a baby."

"Me neither."

"I thought you were on the pill?"

"Hey," she snapped. "You didn't wear a condom so don't-"

"Whoa, whoa, whoa. I wasn't blaming you. I just thought you were. And I always wrap up, it's just with us..." *I was too into you to think straight.*

She nodded. "I was, and I still was up until the day before I took the test. My doctor said the antibiotics they prescribed for an ear infection I had could have interfered with the pill." She bit her lip. "I didn't even think about it."

I wrapped my arms around the now most important person in my life and pressed my forehead against hers.

"It's okay. Happens, right? We're just lucky it's with some-one that isn't freaking out about it."

She melted into my chest.

"Not many men in your situation would class it as lucky. Not many women would either."

"Well, we're not like many men or women. What do you need from me, Holly?"

"I just want you to be there. I want you to attend the appoint-ments, or as many as you can that don't clash with work."

I raised my eyebrow. "Fuck work. I'll sort something out. What do you need?"

"I just answered that," she replied, looking at me like I'd lost it.

"You answered for the baby, me being there is a given. I'm talking about you."

"Oh." Her cheeks reddened. "Um, I guess I need you, too. I may have weird cravings in the middle of the night."

I tightened my arms around her.

"Really, just for midnight craving runs, huh?"

I was flirting with the mother of my baby five minutes after she'd told me we were having a child. Only Holly could get me to do that. She was unlike any girl I'd known or been attracted to. I was quickly becoming addicted to her shy blushes.

Lowering my head, I raised my eyebrow, making my intentions clear and giving her the chance to stop me. She didn't, so I kissed her.

CHAPTER
Twenty-One

Holly

I sat beside Jasper on his sofa. Telling him went a lot easier than I thought it would. I loved that he was happy about it and planned to be there for our baby. My child deserved a dad and Jasper was going to be a fantastic one. It was such a relief that he wasn't running.

I could still feel his lips against mine, kissing me tenderly. Right now I just wanted to kiss him again, but I'd just dropped the baby bomb and we had a lot to talk about.

"I really, really thought you'd freak out," I admitted, pulling my legs up on the sofa.

"Why?"

"Because of everything that's happened recently. I mean eight weeks ago you thought you were a year off having a baby with your wife. Then you thought she was having your baby only to find out it's the man's that she cheated on you with. Now this."

His frown deepened. "Thank you for that lovely summary. And for making me sound like a prick."

Okay, that was a lot. Jasper had crammed about a year's worth of ups and downs, heartbreaks, one-night stands and drama into about seventy days.

"That's not what I meant to do. Your marriage breakdown was Abby's fault. She wrongfully made you believe you were one hundred per cent the father."

"Still, doesn't look that great, does it?"

Well, no.

"It doesn't matter, Jasper. I'd just like to concentrate on the future, not the past."

"This future," he said, biting his lip and running his fingertips over my stomach. I stopped breathing. Why did his touch make me feel like I was floating? He was the wrong person for me. I didn't go for cocky, womanising older guys. He was seven years my senior but sometimes seemed five years my junior!

It was the eyes. Those smouldering, grey eyes that pulled me in. He was painfully good-looking and cheeky too. No wonder he'd had so many women. Would that continue? There was no reason why not; he was single and just because he was a dad didn't mean he couldn't still have a social life.

I didn't like it, but I couldn't do anything about it.

"What're you thinking?" He asked. "Your eyes have glazed over."

"Nothing," I replied a little too quickly. "Just trying to get my head around the fact that I'm going to be a mum."

"You're gonna be a great mum."

"I hope so. Me and Brad had a great childhood, and I really want our child to have the same."

"She will. I'll make sure of it," he replied.

His eyes filled with a passionate determination that broke my heart. He would give our child what he had taken away from him. I couldn't imagine finding out someone I loved so much was a monster and had hurt someone else I loved.

Jasper's relationship with Oakley was so touching. I thought I was fairly close to Brad before I met them. I'd do anything for my brother but actually we weren't really that close at all. So much of Jasper's happiness was directly linked to Oakley's, and I know he'd do anything for her. They had the relationship I hoped my child would have with a sibling – way, way, way into the future.

"This still seems like a dream. Actually, the last two and a half months of my life have."

"I'm sorry, Jasper. I know things have been hard for you recently, and with the divorce still hanging over you, there's a lot you still have to deal with. Guess this isn't helping," I said, placing my hand over our growing baby.

"Hey, this is the one thing keeping me together. I'd planned on getting smashed again tonight. For the past few weeks, I've been drifting from one bottle to the next, one woman to the next just trying to forget. My life was quickly going down the toilet, and I didn't even care."

He placed his hand over mine.

"This is my reason to get my life together. I don't want to be a mess anymore. I want you and the baby to be able to rely on me. I promise you I'll be that man, Holly. I won't let either of you down." *The way your dad let you down.*

"I know you won't," I replied. He was going to be great; I knew that already. He'd be there for us both and do whatever was needed to provide for his baby. I wish we were doing this properly. I wish we were together.

In a very short space of time, he'd made me want a life with him, and I didn't jump into relationships. I was always the careful one that thought things through. My brain seemed to have switched itself off the first time Jasper kissed me, but I didn't ever want it to turn back on because he made me feel complete.

"What about Uni? Seriously?"

"What do you mean, seriously? I said I was going to take a year out."

"I know but is that the best idea? I have no experience with these things, but I think if I took a year out I wouldn't want to go back; I didn't want to go back after the Christmas break at school. You're different to me. I get that. You're smart and know what you want, but that doesn't mean you'll want to finish, especially with a baby, and I don't want you to regret that in the future."

Okay, I could understand that, but he really didn't know me at all if he honestly thought I wouldn't finish my degree.

"Jasper, I'll go back. I just have all this," I gestured to my stomach, "stuff going on and I'm afraid that if I take on too much it'll stress me out."

He frowned, and I knew I'd won him over.

"I don't want you stressed."

"Me neither."

"But we'd make sure you weren't. I'll do whatever I can. Don't let this slip away from you because we're having a surprise baby."

"A surprise baby."

"Well, yeah. No offence, but I didn't exactly expect this."

"No," I said and shook my head. "That's not what I meant. Believe me, I didn't expect this either. I mean that you said surprise and not mistake."

"Our baby isn't a mistake."

"The time and mother is?"

"No. The time and mother is sort of a surprise, too, but a good one."

Something hit me like a truck.

"Jasper, do you mean the mother is a surprise because there could be more out there?"

He laughed and completely inappropriately, I did too. He had a great laugh, deep and sexy. "No, Holly. You're the only one I went bareback with. The others I had more... self-control with. Sorry about that. I shouldn't have put you in this position to begin with. Not that I regret it, or the outcome."

"It's fine. Takes two. I could have refused unless you put a condom on. I guess I didn't have much self-control either."

He flashed me a grin.

"Especially not when you got going."

"Okay, that conversation is over," I said as I felt my cheeks heat. Even after everything we'd done and the confidence he'd given me, I still felt embarrassed when talking about it. I thought that would disappear, but it seemed to be a trait that was sticking.

"Of course it is. Whatever you want I'll support, just let me know, okay?"

"Sure. Thanks, Jasper."

He held his arms out. "Come here."

I climbed on his lap and curled up, closing my eyes. His arms circled my body, and he held me close. I smiled, breathing in his perfect, unique scent.

CHAPTER
Twenty-Two

Jasper

"What the hell is wrong with you?" Oakley snapped, pushing past me. "I know that Abby hurt you and the divorce is hard, and I'm sorry for that, but that doesn't excuse you sleeping with our twenty-year-old employee! And not to mention your friend's sister. What were you thinking?"

"Come on in," I said, with an irony-laden welcome gesture.

She glared.

"I wasn't thinking, okay! That night I was a bit of a mess, and she was upset about that Harry dick. We ended up sleeping together, no big deal." I wasn't going to tell her it had been more than once.

"No big deal," she replied flatly.

"Well, okay, now it's a big deal, but you're making it out like I planned it. Believe me, I was as shocked as you are now when I woke up next to her!"

Holly was gorgeous, don't get me wrong, but she wasn't my type. I didn't go for the shy ones or the dark eye make-up – it just wasn't my thing. Past tense. I wanted her now, badly.

"Well, that's lovely. Bet she felt really special! Nice one, Jasper."

Shit, now I've upset my sister. Sex could just be sex, but not to Oakley, not after what she went through and if she thought anyone was being taken advantage of, she freaked.

"I didn't mean it like that, just that neither of us knew what was going to happen. Holly actually jumped when she woke up and saw me. She was just as surprised. I'm not exactly who she goes for either."

Her type was quiet bookish guys. I think the last thing I read was the back of a pizza box to see how long to cook it for.

"What're you going to do now?"

"We've not got that far yet." I walked into the living room and sat down. "I've gotta get a house. I can't believe this is happening."

She sat beside me. "You're going to be okay, both of you. Is Holly planning to move back when the baby arrives?"

"Yeah, her parents have already marked out a room for the baby. I feel like it's a dream."

"Well, it's not, so you'd better get yourself sorted out, and I don't just mean buying a house."

She meant the alcohol and my promiscuous behaviour.

"I know. I don't want my kid hating me."

Oakley bit her bottom lip, and I knew what she was thinking: *the way I hate our sorry excuse of a dad.* That was the bottom line, as much as I felt like running until I got my head around the news; I would never let my child down like that. I would never put myself before my baby.

"You're going to be a great dad."

Shit. I'd gone from no kid to losing one to another man, to having one again. My head was spinning, and even now I was half waiting for Holly to say there was a mistake, and it wasn't mine.

"I hope so. I'm fucking terrified."

She laughed. "I remember that feeling. You both have a lot of support though."

I didn't want to tell her I was terrified of someone hurting the baby. I didn't stop her getting hurt. Who's to say I'd even know if anything was going on again? I trusted my friends and family, but I'd trusted my father at one point, too.

"Does Brad know?"

"Do I look dead?" Holly wanted to wait a while. I liked the idea, but the longer we left it the harder it'd be.

"Make sure you tell him. He'll be even angrier if he finds out from someone else. I'm sure he'll be fine about it eventually; you and Holly are both adults."

She stood up.

"Lecture over?" I asked.

"Yes. I just came here to shout at you before meeting Cole and Everleigh at the diner."

"Lucky me."

"Are you going out tonight?"

"No, I have Everleigh tomorrow morning. That kid plus a hangover..." I shuddered. "And I guess I should start that sorting-myself-out thing now."

"Yes, you should. Call if you need me. Love you."

"You too," I replied as she left.

"Hey," I said as Holly walked in the door to work.

She stopped in her tracks and checked her watch. "You're

early."

"Funny," I replied dryly. "How're you feeling? Had any morning sickness?"

"Not really. I feel a little more tired than usual but apart from that I don't feel any different."

"Okay, good. You want a coffee? I picked up decaf on the way."

She smiled and put her handbag down on the desk.

"That was sweet. Coffee would be nice, thanks."

At that moment, Oakley walked through the door and did the exact same thing as Holly had, only she looked at the clock on the wall rather than her watch.

"I'm not always late," I said defensively and walked away.

The kitchen being beside reception meant I could hear their conversation. It helped that I poked my head around the door.

"How are you?" Oakley asked Holly.

"Good, thanks. You?"

"I'm good. Jasper told me."

Holly blew out a big breath. "Thank God! I hate keeping things in, but I wasn't sure, and he should be the one to tell you. I'm sorry."

Oakley laughed. "You don't have to be sorry." She suddenly hugged a surprised Holly. "You're having my niece or nephew! Welcome to the family."

My eyes widened, mirroring Holly's, but I suppose she was now part of the family. She was the mother of my child, Oakley's niece and Mum's grandchild. Holly was going to be in our lives forever. I didn't mind that. In fact, a part of me liked it. Me and Holly got along – out of bed too – and if I had to be 'stuck' to someone else for the rest of my life then I was glad it was her. There was something about her that I trusted. Perhaps it was just because she was having my baby and that meant we had to get along and not piss each other off.

"Thank you," Holly replied, smiling shyly as they broke the hug. "It's all kind of sudden but Jasper's been great. He makes me worry less."

"Good! And if you need anything, just ask, okay?"

"Well, I have an appointment."

Oakley nodded. "Put your appointments in my diary, so I know when you'll be out and that'll save you asking every time."

Holly visibly relaxed. "Thank you. I'll try to schedule them when I'm not here, but I think Jasper wants to come, too."

"Stop worrying. Go whenever you have to. I remember all the appointments I had, but luckily I was here so I could take off when I needed."

"Think you'll be doing that again one day?"

"If Cole has his own way, definitely."

"You don't want more."

"No, I do. Not yet though."

She was still dealing with the stress of worrying about something happening to Everleigh. I could relate to that. I felt it every day, too.

"Jasper, less earwigging and more kettle boiling," Oakley said and turned her head.

Damn. Busted. I smiled too wide. "Coming up!"

Ducking back into the kitchen, I made our drinks, listening to Oakley and Holly laugh at Marcus chatting about Everleigh's latest gymnastic mishap. The kid just did her own thing.

Marcus adored her and her I'll-jump-off-whatever-the-hell-I-like attitude, even more now he'd given up hoping she'd follow in Oakley's footsteps and be Olympic material. Oakley was very disciplined, but now I knew it was because she'd needed something else to focus on through the abuse.

I carried our coffees through to the reception.

"Hey, man," I said to Marcus. "Want a drink?"

"No, thanks. I've got a class in five."

Holly hadn't told him. He definitely would have said something.

I put the drinks down on the desk and wrapped my arm around Holly's shoulders.

"Me and this one are having a baby," I said, earning an elbow in the ribs. She stared at me with her jaw hanging open.

Marcus looked between us, silently taking in our news.

"What?" He exploded. "When? How? I didn't even know you were together."

I winced. Everyone was going to assume we were together, and it never made me feel any better when we had to tell them our child was the result of a few no-strings nights.

"Oh," Marcus muttered, noticing our sudden awkwardness and catching on. "Wow, Holly, I didn't know you had it in you, girl!"

"What, to have random, meaningless sex," she said, blushing and scowling at the same time.

"Meaningless," I repeated.

I'd had meaningless sex too many times to count in the years between me and Abby first breaking up, and this last – and final – separation and never before had the word made me feel lousy. *What the hell is wrong with me?*

She shrugged, squirming under my arm. "Sorry, I didn't mean it like that, just that we're not together or anything."

"Well, as interesting as this conversation is," Oakley said, grabbing her coffee, "I should check my emails."

She walked into her office, and I turned my attention back to the woman that just called sex with me meaningless.

"As fun as this domestic is I've got to set up for class." Marcus left too, and we were alone.

I raised my eyebrow. "So it was meaningless."

She sighed. "No. I just explained, and you know what I mean. It was hardly our wedding night, Jasper."

"That's not the point. I just didn't think that was how you saw it."

"We used each other. That's what casual sex is."

"Yeah, I know it is, but I didn't think..."

"You're bloody impossible, you know that?" She pulled away and walked around to her desk. *What have I done now?*

"Holly?"

"Don't. All you want is no-strings sex, so don't complain when that's exactly what you get."

"I'd hardly call this no strings. You're fucking pregnant!"

Her head whipped back as if I'd slapped her, and I groaned. "I didn't mean it like that. I don't resent you or this situation. I want our baby, but let's face it, neither of us planned it, did we."

I slowly stepped closer to her, weary that she might be mad. My choice of words was not my greatest. She didn't move, so I wrapped my arms around her back.

"That came out wrong. Can we just forget the last few minutes happened, please?"

"Sure," she replied, and I knew I was forgiven because she hugged me back. "This is going to take work, you know?"

"Yeah, I know." We were still practically strangers, and we were having a baby together. There were many disagreements to come, but we'd get there – we didn't have a choice.

CHAPTER
Twenty-Three

Jasper

"**H**e's gonna hate me," I said, sitting in Holly's living room as we prepared to tell Brad that I was the father of Holly's baby.

"He might be angry, but he won't hate you."

"Of course he's going to hate me and 'might be angry' is the-"

"Alright," she snapped. "I was trying to help and calm your nerves, but fine, he's going to want to castrate you. Happy?"

I threw my hands up. "No!"

"Jasper, get a grip."

I stood up. This was going to go badly. There was an unwritten rule about mates' sisters and not only had I crossed that line – more than once – but I'd also got her pregnant. I didn't regret what happened with Holly. I'd never wanted anything as strongly as I'd wanted to be with her those nights, but I should have spoke to Brad about it so it wouldn't affect our friendship.

"Why have you started pacing?" She asked.

"Are you kidding? I'm about to tell a mate I knocked up his sister!"

"*We* did this. You didn't do anything on your own."

I pointed at her. "Let's open with that."

The front door opened.

"Holly?" Brad called out.

"We're in the living room."

"We're?" Brad said as he walked in and spotted me. "Jasper, hey, man, how's it going?"

Oh shit. My throat closed up. This was Brad, a mate. I wasn't supposed to have a baby with his sister, especially not when we weren't in a relationship.

"Good. Look, there's something we need to talk to you about."

He looked at Holly who stood up.

"You okay? Is everything alright with the baby?"

"Yeah, fine," she replied.

His attention then turned to me, frowning.

"What do you both need to talk to me about?"

"I'm the baby's dad," I said.

Holly gawped at me. We had discussed that we were going to explain a little better than that. Blurting it out was stupid, but there was no easy way of softening a punch like that. It just needed to be out there.

He blinked heavily. "I'm sorry, you're what?"

I wrapped my arm around Holly, and she leant into me. Her petite body fit against me as if she'd been made for me. I liked it way more than I should have.

"I'm the dad."

He looked between us for a long time, and I had no idea what was going through his head. Different ways to castrate me, probably.

"I don't understand. Are you together?"

"Um no," Holly said. "It happened... about eight weeks ago now."

He ignored Holly. "You slept with my sister."

"Yes."

"What the fuck is wrong with you?" He growled.

"Hey!" Holly shouted. "Don't even start that sexist bullshit, Brad. I chose to go to bed with him. A few times."

It was my turn to gawp at her. You don't tell him that!

"Look, man, I get that you're pissed with me-"

"Pissed with you? You used my sister and got her pregnant."

"Oh my God, I just said drop the sexist stuff!" Holly threw her arms up in frustration. "Don't blame him for something I entered into willingly. Hell, I even instigated one of those times."

I turned to her. "Seriously, why do you do it?"

"How many times has it happened?" Brad snapped.

Holly blushed. "That doesn't matter. All you need to know is that Jasper and I are having a baby together, and we're both happy about it."

Brad shoved his hands through his hair. "What the hell is wrong with you, man? I knew you were struggling with the breakup, but I had no idea you'd completely lost it. You're not in the right place to have a kid. You've been separated from your wife for five minutes!"

"I've been in a place to have a kid for the last two years. My divorce won't interfere with being a dad."

"What about Holly?"

"What about her?"

He clenched his jaw. "You've screwed her life up and you-"

"Hey!" Holly snapped. "He hasn't screwed anything up and when are you going to open your eyes and realise I'm not some helpless child? I'm twenty, almost twenty-one, Brad. I've been living away from home for the last three years. I'm a grown-up."

"You're grown up enough to have a baby?" Brad asked, almost sneering.

"Is anyone ever one hundred per cent ready? I'm going to be fine. I'm not doing this on my own." She looked at me, although she hardly needed confirmation.

"I get why you're worried. I've not exactly been the most mature person since I split with Abby, but I would never walk out and leave Holly to do this by herself. I'm going to be there every step of the way." I looked down at Holly. "I'm here for whatever you need."

She smiled up at me. "I know that."

Brad cleared his throat, and we both looked at him.

"Is there something between you two?"

"Just a baby," I replied.

The indecision in Brad's eyes was clear. He didn't want there to be more to it, but he also did. No one wanted to think their sister wasn't wanted by the man who got her pregnant.

"Just a baby," he repeated.

"Mate, like you said, I've only been separated from my wife for five minutes. I'd turn down Katy Perry at the minute."

"And I'm not desperate for a relationship," Holly said. "Women are fine to be by themselves these days, you know!"

Brad rolled his eyes. "I wasn't being sexist. I want to know if my little sister is going to be okay."

"I will be."

"Uni?"

"Taking a year out."

Brad was too calm. If we were alone, I'd have a black eye by now.

"Yeah," I said. "I've been thinking about that."

She looked up at me with an I-dare-you-to-disagree-with-me expression.

"Hear me out." I sat down, pulling her with me. "The baby is due in April when you'll already be halfway through your final year. If you go back and take a few weeks off after the birth, we'll figure out childcare.

"Jasper, missing a few weeks is huge."

"I know." Well, I didn't. I had no clue about university really, only what I'd looked up on her Uni's website to see if we could work it, so she didn't have to miss a year. "But you could catch up, you're the smartest person I know. I'll have the baby as much as I can so you can study, and I know my mum and your parents will, too."

"Listen to him, Hol," Brad said.

The front door opened, and we all froze. Their parents were home. Time to tell them, too.

"Alright?" Their mum, Sylvie, said. "Oh, hi, Jasper."

"Hey."

My pulse raced. I didn't want them to hate me for having a baby with their daughter. A daughter that everyone still seemed to think of as a young girl. She was anything but a child.

"What're you two up to then?" Their dad, Carl, asked, referring to me and Brad of course.

Holly licked her bottom lip. "Um. Well, actually Jasper was here with me."

They both cocked their head to the side, perfectly in tune with each other.

"Oh?" Sylvie asked.

"Not like that exactly." Holly took a deep breath. "Jasper is the baby's dad."

In tune again, their mouths dropped open, and I was sure Carl stopped breathing.

Okay, so she was going in for the kill, too.

"What?" Carl asked, staring at us dumbfounded. "How is Jasper the father?"

"We're happy about it," she said, hoping to diffuse the situation. "I know it's sudden and I'm still young, but we can do this. It's going to be fine."

"Fine! You're going into your last year of university soon and now pregnant by a twenty-seven-year-old man that's not even divorced from his wife yet! How is that fine?"

Holly glared. "I understand you're upset, Dad, but I'm an adult."

His eyes teared up, and she leapt to her feet, hugging his waist tightly.

"I know I've always been the youngest, and everyone has treated me differently because of that, but I'm a grown woman now, and I can make my own decisions. And I can have a baby."

They pulled away.

"When's the wedding?"

My eyes practically fell out of their sockets.

"Very funny, Dad."

"I'm not happy with you," he said, his eyes tightening as he looked at me.

"I understand that. But you know I'll be here for them both," I reassured him.

He shook his head. "This is…"

Holly shrugged. "I know. Jasper was probably the last guy

you suspected."

Sylvie came out of the daze she'd seemed to slip into, and she hugged Holly.

"You're not too disappointed in me, Mum, are you?"

"No, sweetheart. Can't lie; I wish the circumstances were different, but I think you'll both make wonderful parents. And at least we know where Jasper lives."

"So I'm not getting kneecapped?" I asked, grinning.

Holly slapped my shoulder. "You have to ruin it!"

I laughed. "Seriously, though, you don't have to worry about an absent dad, I'll be here so much you'll be sick of me." I needed her to know I would never let her down.

"I know," she whispered, smiling.

CHAPTER
Twenty-Four

Holly

"What do you want, sweetheart?" Mum asked. We'd been going over university and work and baby arrangements for the last half an hour, and I was starting to get a headache. There were so many things to consider.

I shrugged. "I don't know. I used to want a career, but now I'm pregnant I couldn't imagine leaving the baby all day. Don't get me wrong, I want to do something, and I'll need to, but maybe part-time. Until she's school age anyway."

Mum frowned. "What part-time career do you want?"

"I don't know."

"You need to think about that. I know you want to be a good mum but being a good mum means providing, too. You also need to think about what *you* want. Just because you're having a baby, doesn't mean you have to give up your dreams."

"Yeah, I guess. I want to be a pharmacist, but maybe when

the baby starts school I should be looking at pharmacy in a doctor's surgery rather than a hospital: The hours are more family friendly."

"And until then?"

"I'll see if I can stay at The Centre part-time."

"Okay." She looked away.

"What?"

"Nothing, love." She hugged her mug of tea with her hands. "Look, I'm not saying being a receptionist is beneath you – it's not. A job is a job, and you'll be providing, which is the main thing."

"So what are you saying?"

"It's just hard to watch your child who has worked towards her dream career have to put it on hold. That's all."

"I know it's going to be hard, and I still have a year left to study, but I can defer for a year."

"You don't want to work full-time until the baby is in school, but you think you'll have time for a full-time course when the baby is just a year old?"

I bit my lip, feeling the weight of the world on my shoulders.

"Oh, I'm sorry, love", she said, clearly seeing me sag. "I'm not trying to bring you down. I'm just concerned. Holly, we will do everything in our power to get you that degree, but it's not going to be easy."

"I get that. Uni is full on, but at least I don't have classes all day five days a week. I'm sure between me and Jasper we can work something out. You know how keen he is to be a dad."

She smiled. "Yes, he is. And I think you mean between your father and I, yourself and Jasper, and Jasper's parents we can work something out."

"Thanks, Mum."

"What has Jasper said about it?"

"That I should go back in October and take a few weeks off after the birth."

"Well, that does make sense. Uni is almost starting again, and you still have just over seven months left. The year will be almost over by the time the baby comes; you'll only have a few months left."

"Yeah, I see his point, but I don't want to be stressed out with studying when I'm pregnant. And definitely not taking my final exams when I've got a newborn..."

"Honey, it's going to be a lot more stressful trying to do a whole year with a baby crawling around and demanding your full attention."

I wanted to bang my head on the table. It would be easier to do it all now.

"I'd need to take three weeks off after the birth at least." Two weeks was the legal requirement, but I knew I'd want and need longer.

"Of course. But you could catch up the things you've missed, and we'll all help."

I narrowed my eyes.

"You've been talking to Jasper." He'd said the same thing to me just a few days ago.

She held her hands up.

"Yes. Don't be angry though, we're only trying to help. It's a well known fact that not everyone who takes a year out goes back."

"I would go back. But you're right; it'd be crazy of me not to struggle past the final few months and finish my course with a new baby rather than deferring and having to do a whole year with a young child."

Just then we were interrupted, and my head was spinning so much it was a relief.

"Look who I found wandering around outside," Dad said, walking into the kitchen with Jasper trailing behind.

"I wasn't wandering around, I was walking to the door," he said. "Wandering makes me sound like a stalker."

Dad turned to him. "You got my daughter pregnant, you're whatever I say you are."

"Fair enough," Jasper replied and sidestepped him. Deep down, Dad liked him but he was stubborn, so it would be a while before he admitted it again.

He sat beside me, and his aftershave filled my lungs. I tried to act cool as if he had no effect on me at all, but I couldn't help leaning just that little bit closer to him.

"How's my baby doing?" He asked, placing his hand on my stomach.

"She's fine."

He looked up at me with the biggest grin I'd ever seen.

"Good. I wonder when we'll feel her kicking around in there."

I shrugged. "A while yet."

"I can't wait."

"Me neither. Although, apparently the kicks to the ribs really hurt. Oh, but something you'll be happy to hear, I decided to go back to Uni next month."

"That's great, Holly." Jasper beamed, and so did my parents. "What about living arrangements?"

I looked at Mum and Dad.

"Think I can move back here just before the birth?"

The drive to and from university every day would take about forty-five minutes each way so that would be too much for me to do each day. But I needed to be close when I was near to my due date because I had very little idea of what it was going to be like.

"As if we're going to say no!" Dad said, sitting down beside Mum.

"Thanks."

Jasper leant back, placing his arm on the back of my chair.

"And if he did you could just stay with me."

Dad barked a laugh. "I don't think so."

Wow, living with Jasper. Recently, that fantasy had filled my head more times than it should, and I didn't know if it was because I had real feelings for him or because I was carrying his baby. Who was I kidding, they were real feelings!

"She's carrying my baby," Jasper said, trying to keep a straight face. He and Dad had a weird relationship; they teased each other a lot, and it was sometimes hard to tell if it was in jest or not. At first I was worried Dad would hate Jasper, but he was very quickly coming around, probably because Jasper had been perfect.

"Anyway," I said, pulling Jasper up with me. "We need to talk about some stuff so we'll see you later."

"Leave your door open, Holly," Dad said. I could hear the humour in his voice, but I didn't look back because him trying to be a 'cool dad' was annoying. Jasper, however, laughed as we walked up to my room.

"We should actually have sex and call your dad's bluff," he joked. I noticed he waited until I'd closed my door before he said it though.

"Hmm, I'll pass, but thanks for the offer."

He gripped his heart.

"You wound me. I thought I was irresistible." Giving me his big puppy dog eyes, he pouted his lip and cocked his head, giving the full effect. My heart pounded.

"You're not that irresistible."

"Then why're we up here?"

I rolled my eyes. "To talk about how this is all going to work. Do you think your mum will be able to help with childcare for the few months the baby's here before university finishes?"

"You're kidding, right? Try taking her off my mum! We're all going to help, Holly. I'm so glad you decided to stick at Uni."

"Me too. My friend Li is coming to visit on Friday. I'd like you to meet her. You don't have to or anything-"

"I'd love to meet her."

I sighed in relief. We weren't together so why would he want to meet my friends? I was glad that he took an interest. He probably just wanted to check her out because she would eventually have contact with our baby.

"We need godparents!" I said.

"Alright, moving on. What made you think about that?"

"I don't know. There's just so much to do, and you only get nine tiny months. Hell, by the time you find out it's only eight months!"

"Calm down," he said, holding his hands up. "Why don't you think of two and I'll think of two."

"Who's your two?" I asked.

"Cole and Oakley."

I could've guessed that.

"Brad and Amy."

"There. Tick that off your list. Stop stressing, Hol. Hey, we agree on things easily. I've never had that before. Ha, I should've married you and not Abby."

I laughed, pretending to take it as a joke when something deep inside me wondered what it'd be like to be Mrs Scofield. If he decided to keep his new surname, you never knew with him.

CHAPTER
Twenty-Five

Holly

"When is Li getting here?" Jasper asked, eyeing my still flat belly. I was sure he was keeping an eye on it so he could be the first to see the bump.

"In about an hour."

"And she definitely speaks English?"

"Jasper!"

He looked up and raised his hands. "Hey, don't go getting all defensive. I'm not being an arse or anything, but you met her in on your exchange thing, and you speak Chinese."

Okay, he had a fair point.

"Yes, she speaks English. Better than you actually."

He smiled teasingly.

"Why didn't you want to go to China when she invited you? I thought you wanted to go back."

"I do, and I would've, but if I get a bump while over there…"

Jasper couldn't wait to see the bump first.

"You stayed because of me?"

I did a lot of things because of him. Like getting butterflies, blushing fits and heart palpitations.

"I can't miss anything – not that I'd want to – but you can so I don't think it's fair if I go off and risk you missing seeing my belly stick out or my squealing over the first kick."

"Thank you," he whispered.

My heart skipped at the low rawness and sincerity in his voice. I was lusting after the man I was having a baby with, a man that pledged his allegiance to the No-Strings Attached Club. I was doomed.

"So, we've got time before she arrives," he said, wiggling his eyebrows.

"Jasper!" I whacked his upper arm.

He pouted. "I don't even get a kiss?"

I tried to stare coldly, but he could probably sense my eagerness. And I was sure he could hear my heart beating.

Lowering his head he said in a very low and seductive tone, "You want to kiss me."

Yes, but it's a bad idea. I liked him way too much to not get hurt when he ended our casual physical relationship. I had everything pinned on him falling for me when his heart was healed again, and I didn't want to like him even more in case he didn't. If he ended up with someone else – even the thought made me feel sick – we'd still have to get along for our child's sake.

I bit my lip and his pupils dilated.

He inched closer, and I gripped his arms, both eager and resistant. Smiling briefly, he closed his eyes and then he was kissing me. The tips of my fingers dug into his flesh, making him groan. His hand gripped the back of my hair, and the kiss turned wild.

He lifted me, and I wrapped my legs around his waist, clawing at his back to get him closer. I wasn't sure if it was my overactive hormones, but the sexual tension between us had spiked.

Jasper laid us on my bed and kissed his way down my neck. Something inside my head was telling me this was a bad idea, but it had been seriously muffled as every nerve ending in my body burst to life. I gripped the bottom of his t-shirt and pulled it over his head. My hands greedily gliding over his muscular six-pack.

Biting his way down my neck, he pinned me to the bed with his arms and legs. I gasped as his lips trailed over my skin, his hot breath giving me goose bumps.

"Jasper," I whispered, arching my body into his.

He was up in a shot, pushing off me. I gasped, eyes widening. "What?"

I was about to freak out when he reached for the top of my leggings, yanking them down as quickly as he could. I lifted my butt to help, but they were off in a flash. Sitting up, I helped him get my top off and then unbuttoned his jeans with shaky hands. We hadn't been together in what felt like months, and I missed how I felt with him.

His steely, heavily lidded eyes pierced into mine, showing me how much he wanted me. I unhooked my bra and with my newly found confidence, whipped my thong off too. Jasper made me feel wanted and sexy.

Looking up, I said, "What?"

His mouth parted, and he sucked in a deep breath.

"You're so beautiful," he said, running his fingers over the skin between my breasts.

He got off the bed and took off his jeans, keeping his lust-filled eyes on me. He slipped on a condom I handed him and crawled back on the bed slowly. I squirmed under his gaze, my body on fire for him.

"Jasper," I whispered.

His body covered mine, and he lowered his lips to my jaw.

"I know. I've got you."

He entered me at a maddeningly slow pace.

"Holly," he groaned and kissed me.

"Li!" I shouted, running out of the door to greet my friend. I'd missed her. We hadn't seen each other since we were eighteen, but we wrote all the time.

"Holly!" she replied with the same enthusiasm and ran at me. We collided, hugging like long lost sisters.

"Whoa, whoa, whoa, whoa! Break it up, you'll squish my kid!" Jasper shouted from behind us.

Pulling back, I rolled my eyes. "Li, this is Jasper. Jasper, Li."

"So you're the one that got my friend pregnant," Li said, shoving her hands on her hips.

Jasper did a bow. "That's me."

I felt the floor whip away beneath me. Li was beautiful, smart, confident and outgoing. How could I not have seen before that she was his type? I swallowed my jealously. She wasn't here long, and I wanted us both to enjoy seeing each other again.

"Come inside! We've got so much to catch up on," I said, pulling her towards the door.

She made a quiet squeal and bound into the house behind me.

"I missed you. And we *do* have a lot to catch up on, *mum*!"

"I know," I said as we sat down on the sofa. "Crazy, isn't it?"

"Super crazy! That was the last thing I ever thought would come out of your mouth."

Li and I spent the next two hours gossiping and catching up.

Jasper joined in the conversation when needed and kept us supplied with drinks and chocolate. He'd won Li over immediately and had her laughing at some of the things he got up to as a teenager. When the doorbell rang he went to answer it.

"He's very cute," she whispered.

I grinned. "I know! I hope the baby gets those good-looking genes."

"Please, with you as its mum and hottie out there as its dad, there's no doubt!"

Jasper walked back in the living room with Amy trailing behind.

"I approve," Amy announced, nodding to Jasper.

He frowned. "Of course you do."

"She said you were cocky."

"Charmingly cocky," he corrected, making her laugh.

The uneasy feeling settled in the pit of my stomach again. I knew Amy would never let anything happen with Jasper, but the thought of him wanting her hurt.

"Anyway," Amy said. "You need to leave. This is girl talk time."

Japer turned to me. "I know when I'm not wanted." Beside him, Amy raised her eyebrows at me, and I tried to not react. "Call if you need anything," he said, leaning down and kissing the top of my head. "Keep that baby safe. And you two ladies, keep that one safe." He nodded to me and then walked out.

"Bye, Jasper," Amy shouted in a singsong voice. I threw a cushion at her.

"Are you joining us for dinner?" I asked Amy.

She sat down and gave Li a hug. "No, unfortunately I have plans, so I thought I'd come over now and catch up. I won't be around much this weekend."

"Oh?" Li said.

"Me and Liam have a make-or-break weekend planned."

"What? Things are really that bad? Why didn't you tell me when we went out, or the other hundred times we've spoken on the phone?" I asked.

She grimaced. "Well, you've got a lot going on and-"

"I don't care what I have going on, I want to help you too."

Amy smiled and sat back.

"Right, no baby or Jasper talk. I want to know everything that's going on with you and Liam."

"Okay," she said. "But quickly before we start, I think he likes you, too."

"Definitely," Li agreed.

"Sure, we're friends, and I'm carrying his child." I deliberately left out the part where we'd had sex in my bedroom only an hour ago. They both opened their mouth to say something else. I held my hand up. "No more. We're moving on. What's going on, Amy?"

She sighed, shoulders slumping.

"Things have been strained for a while. I'm ambitious and working towards my degree, I know the career I want and what I have to do to get there. He's the opposite. He's bored at work, hates being shut inside a warehouse all day but does nothing about it. I hate people that complain about a situation but don't change it. It's like he's waiting for his dream job to miraculously land in his lap."

"What is his dream job?"

"Spray painting cars. Custom stuff, not accident touch-ups. When I suggested he changed jobs and worked for a mechanics while doing a course, he looked at me like I was crazy. Now surely if you're advertising for a job and someone has experience working with cars and the other one has been working in a factory you're going to go with the mechanic."

"It's okay, stay calm," I said as her voice got louder the more frustrated she got.

"Sorry. I just hate seeing him drift like this."

I could relate to that. I'd hated watching Jasper get drunk almost every night and walk around like he'd checked out long ago.

"He gets frustrated at me getting frustrated. I think he resents that I know what I'm doing and what I want, and I resent that he makes me feel bad for it. I worked really hard to get where I am, and I'll continue doing that. We're just so different."

"I think he'll be the same when he gets a job he likes," Li said.

Amy threw her hands up.

"Me too! He talks about it with such enthusiasm. I seriously fall in love with him all over again when he gets that passionate; it's really cute. But then, nothing. I don't want to push but at the same time I do because his moods are driving a wedge between us."

"You need to be sneaky about this. If you suggest something, he won't listen, or it'll be a bad idea. You need to plan it, so he thinks he thought of it all along," I said.

"That what you do with Jasper?"

"No, he's usually a step ahead of me anyway," I replied and frowned. "He thinks everything through to death."

Amy sighed dreamily. "Ah, that would be nice."

"You'll be fine. Hey, why don't you do a bit of research and see what's around the area where you're going? Maybe you'll find some inspiration," Li said.

"That's actually a good idea," Amy replied. "Right, this weekend we're getting things sorted out."

I nodded, wishing I could be that decisive so quickly.

"Now that's done. Tell us about lover boy!"

Groaning, I threw my arm over my head and laid back in the sofa. "There's nothing to tell. We're friends, and we're having a baby."

"And you're in love with him," Li said.

I dropped my arm. "Not love. I just like him an unhealthy amount."

Amy laughed. "Li's right. You love him."

My heart leapt. "Oh. I do, don't I?"

The both nodded, laughing.

"Damn."

CHAPTER
Twenty-Six

Holly

"**Y**our next scan is October 11th at eleven, right?" Jasper asked for the millionth time. He was panicking about being so far away from us now I was back at Uni. All the way in the car as he prepared to drop me off he'd been memorising dates, or trying to, he'd get stressed and muddle them up.

"Yes. I'll be home Thursday evening though. You know this, stop stressing."

He gave me a tight smile. "What time are you getting back Thursday?"

"I'll leave as soon as I'm done so I'll be back around five or six."

"Want to get dinner when you're back then? I mean; I wouldn't have seen my bump in a couple weeks," he said, running his hand over my flat belly.

I loved him even more knowing how much he loved our

child.

"Sure," I whispered, finding it hard to resist the urge to push up on my feet and kiss him. "Nothing spicy though. She doesn't like spicy."

"We're so going to be screwed if we have a boy," he said, shaking his head and smiling.

"Why? You don't want a boy?"

"No, I don't care what it is, but we always say she. You've only ever looked at girl stuff or thought of girl names. The poor boy will be called Annie."

"I'm not sure I like Annie so much now."

"Okay, well, whatever we decide. Where do you want these?" He asked, holding up one of my thongs.

I gasped and grabbed it from his hand. "I hate you! God, if I wasn't pregnant I'd jump on you right now."

"Hey, you can still do that," he replied, laughing and dodging my hand as I tried to slap him. "The midwife said sex in pregnancy is perfectly safe."

"I didn't mean that kind of jumping on you!"

He sighed. "Oh, well, we're almost at the horny month."

He'd been going on about this for a while. Apparently, he'd seen on TV that month four was when your hormones went crazy, and you were turned on a lot.

"Hmm, but you'll be back home, and I'll be here, surrounded by plenty of good-looking men," I teased.

He froze on the spot, face falling.

"Hey! As if I'm going to sleep with anyone else while I'm carrying your baby. I'm not that kind of girl," I said. That hurt.

"I know you're not."

"Then why the face?"

"Nothing. You want me to move that wardrobe over?"

He walked to the end of my room and looked either side of the wardrobe. The look wasn't 'nothing'. I didn't want to even say it in my head in case I'd got the wrong idea but… jealousy? The idea that he could be jealous over me gave me a thrill. But I still wasn't going to push it. I wanted us to be together, but I wanted him to make the first move, so I was sure it was what he really wanted.

"Sure. I'd do it myself but…" I rubbed my belly.

Jasper smirked. "But you're a weakling girl?"

I knew he'd only said that for a reaction, so I didn't give him one.

"When you've finished that you can buy me lunch. The baby is hungry." I could tell him the baby wanted its mum to have a diamond necklace, and he'd buy it. He was obsessed with doing things right and controlling everything – because he'd had no control over what his dad had done to them.

Jasper bought me lunch and then, later on, dinner. He was hanging around, not wanting to leave. As time went on his posture changed dramatically. He was tense and uneasy.

"I'll be fine, Jasper," I said as the clock ticked closer to ten p.m.

He forced a smile. "I know that. Promise you'll call if you need anything."

"I will. Please, stop worrying, we'll be alright."

His jaw flexed, but he said nothing.

"We'll be fine," I repeated. I watched his eyes darken in what looked like fear. He was scared to be away from us in case something happened.

"Jasper," I whispered, my heart breaking for him and how much he was still suffering after what his dad did to him.

"Don't," he said and covered his lips over mine. I was

shocked at first, but by the time I knew what was happening, I responded to his desperate kiss.

My final class of the day was over, and I couldn't wait to get home. I'd completed two weeks back at university and knowing I had a baby coming made me miss my family even more. I wanted to be around them while I was pregnant and over-emotional. I'd ventured into the crying-over-the-stupidest-things realm and needed my mum.

"So glad this week is over," Yasmin said as we walked back towards our shared flat. "I thought it was never going to end."

"Me too. It feels like the end of the year rather than the beginning. I have no idea how I'm going to get through the rest of it." I had six months of my pregnancy left and eight months of Uni.

With all the work of the final year already starting to pile up, I was having major second thoughts. Studying for final exams with a newborn was going to be a nightmare. At least if the baby was already here when I started my final year I'd be able to get childcare. It was okay for everyone else to be positive about it when they weren't the ones that had to do it.

"You'll be fine, Hol, you've aced every test and assignment so far."

"That's because I have time to study. What am I going to do when I have a screaming baby needing my attention?"

"Don't they sleep like sixteen hours a day at first?"

"Ha, where'd you read that? I'll be up every few hours, exhausted and stressed. And that's just from taking care of the baby. This all seemed like a good idea a month ago, now the more I think about it the more I want to leave."

"Hey," she said, grabbing my arm, bringing us both to a halt. "You can do this. Hell, you'd pass with flying colours right now.

Stop stressing, you've got this."

I didn't feel like I had it. Nothing was under my control any more, not even my own body.

"Yeah. Thanks, Yas," I said. We started walking again, and she linked her arm through mine. "What're you doing this weekend?"

She paused before answering.

"Out with the girls. Shame you can't make it."

"Next weekend maybe."

"You're here next weekend. Cool. Jasper coming?"

"He's not said anything. Think I need a weekend with you guys anyway. I've barely had any girl time since I've been back."

I'd been home the last two weeks. Some girl time was definitely in order, and they'd make me relax and see things more clearly.

As soon as we got back to the flat, I started packing to make my way home and Yasmin hopped in the shower to start her night-out preparations. She went all out, glamorous make-up, nails, classy fake tan, natural-looking false eyelashes and killer dresses. If I was to do the same I would look ridiculous, but Yasmin always looked flawless. She was Jasper's type, definitely.

"I'm heading out now," I called as I pulled my small suitcase on wheels behind me.

She looked up from where she was painting her toe nails hot pink.

"Okay, babe. Safe trip back and I'll see you Sunday night."

"You will. Have fun and be careful." I kissed her cheek and left the flat.

When I arrived home Jasper's car was in the drive. I made my way in, butterflies in my stomach as I made my way to see him.

"I'm home!" I shouted, closing the door behind me.

Mum came rushing out of the living room and gave me a bear hug.

"Hi, sweetheart. How are you and the little one?"

"We're good." She pulled me into the living room and Jasper sat on the sofa next to Brad laughing about something. My heart skipped a beat at how beautiful he was. He looked up, and a smile slowly crept on his face.

CHAPTER
Twenty-Seven

Jasper

"Uncle Jasper, can I feel Auntie Holly's belly, too?" Auntie Holly?

"Um," I said, taken aback by her new name for Holly. How could I tell her she's not really her aunt?

Holly took Everleigh's hand and placed it on her small stomach. She wasn't freaking out about just been called aunt at all. I should be freaking out, but I wasn't.

"Of course you can. Can you feel that? That's the baby kicking."

I stared at Holly. Why wasn't the idea of her being Everleigh's aunt suffocating? Yes, we were having a child together, but that didn't mean we had to be together.

I swallowed what felt like sand. Holly beamed down at my niece, and something inside me stirred. Holly. I liked Holly. A lot. The realisation hit me like a fucking freight train. How the hell could I have let that happen? I didn't want to want anyone.

Everleigh squealed and pulled her hand away, and then put it back. "It feels funny!"

"Tell me about it," Holly said.

"Where's my granddaughter," Mum said, bursting into the room with her arms full of presents. Miles followed behind her, carrying a large pink gift bag and another three presents in the other hand.

"Mum, I told you not to spoil her," Oakley scolded.

"Hey, I cut down a lot!" she replied. Everleigh turned around, and her eyes almost popped out of her head. She lit up and ran towards her nan, and I stood still, rooted to the floor.

I was falling in love with my baby's mum.

"You okay?" Holly asked. "You look pale."

I'm finding it hard to breathe right now.

"Fine," I replied. "Drink?"

Her forehead creased, probably concerned that I was finally having a breakdown.

"Sure. You really okay?"

She stepped closer, and I could smell her Charles Worthington shampoo. I only knew what it was because I checked the ingredients to make sure there was no funky stuff in there that could make the baby come out green or have five heads. It didn't.

I stepped back, needing to put some distance between us before I did something stupid like kiss her.

"Orange juice?"

Turning around, I walked to the kitchen not waiting for a reply. I knew that was what she'd have. Idiot. *I'm a massive idiot.* My divorce wasn't even close to being final and here I was falling in love with someone else.

"Hey, man," Brad said, standing up straighter.

Well, at least it wasn't 'hey, fucker' anymore. "Hey," I replied. "You alright?"

"Yep. You?"

"Yeah, just getting Holly a drink."

His lips thinned.

"Look, mate, can we get past this?"

"If I'd got Oakley pregnant?"

"Cole would kill you."

He sighed sharply. "You know what I mean."

"Alright. I get it; I'd be pissed, too, but I didn't do this on my own."

"I don't care if she threw herself at you, you should've said no. I've never put much thought into my little sister having kids, but I assumed it'd be after she's finished Uni and with someone that she's with. Not a one-night stand."

"Isn't that what most of us want? Doesn't always happen like that. Life's not that perfect, mate. I can promise that she'll never be alone in this."

I could stand there and tell him I was falling for her and that everything I wanted was within my reach, but I was scared that if I admitted it out loud I'd lose it. And I was scared that she didn't want anything to happen between us.

"I need something stronger than this," he said, holding up a cup of what must've been Coke.

"Me too, but it's a four-year-old's party."

He smiled. "Right. Better wait for the after party then."

"Am I forgiven?"

"I reserve the right to hold it over you if I want the last slice of pizza, first call on who to chat up or who's paying for the last round."

I held my hands up. "Deal. And if you're a dick to me I can

use the I've-slept-with-your-sister line to shut you up."

"I fucking hate you, Jasper," he said, shaking his head and holding his hand out. I shook it, glad to have my friend back.

"You've made up," Holly said from the doorway.

"Er, yeah. Suppose it could be worse, could've been a guy that did a runner."

Her jaw tightened. "I don't sleep around, Brad, Jasper was my first."

I spun my body to face her. *I'm her first?*

Holly registered the shock in my eyes and added, "First one-night stand! Not my first first."

"First or only?" I asked.

She blushed scarlet. "Only."

Good.

I mentally calculated her sexual past. Her first boyfriend, Harry The Boring, and me. Only three.

Good.

"Can we talk about something, no, anything else?" Brad asked.

"Cocktail sausages," Holly said, eyeing the two stacked bowls on the counter. And I was pretty sure I saw another plate in the dining room with the rest of the food too. When I asked Oakley to grab another bag because they were what Holly was craving I had no idea she'd go that crazy.

I still couldn't even eat them after lobbing the full plate at the wall when I was arguing with Abby.

"What?" Brad asked, looking at Holly like she was crazy.

"Her craving," I said. "Cocktail sausages dipped in chocolate milkshake."

Brad turned his nose up. "Holly, that's disgusting!"

She held her hands up. "Hey, it's not my fault. It's what Jasper's child wants."

The baby was my child whenever it made her hormones freak out, made her pee extra, turned her ankles into 'cankles', or wanted weird things to eat. I was pretty sure it was going to be all mine when she was in labour, too.

"I think this one is going to be just like his or her cousin," she said.

Christ, two Everleighs!

I passed her one of the bowls. "Maybe not. Oakley didn't like them when she was pregnant. Actually, she didn't really eat any meat because at the time she was absolutely not going to 'eat any fucking defenceless animals'." I tried to imitate her voice, but even I knew I'd failed.

Holly laughed. "That's probably for the best. Think I'm going to be sick of them by the time she's here," she replied, popping two in her mouth.

"Are you two together?" Brad asked out of nowhere.

"No," I said.

"This is messed."

"It's not. We're happy. Right, Holly?"

She nodded.

"Yeah. Honestly, Brad, everything's fine. This is working for us so please can you just be happy for us and excited to be an uncle?"

"Hey, I am. I just don't know how you do the 'best buds having a baby' thing."

"Man, you should've just said. You're still my bestest bud."

He stuck his middle finger up.

"You're both adults so do what you want. Just can't help thinking this is all going to go horribly wrong." He stopped and smirked as I put my arm around Holly. "Or horribly right."

I stuck my middle finger up.

Neither of us wanted that. We'd known each other five months and were already having a baby. There was no need to rush anything else. The more I thought about my future the more I saw Holly beside me but as much as I wanted her I still didn't feel ready for a new relationship.

Holly bit her lip and looked away. There was something she wanted to say. "Hol, spit it out."

"Okay, this is no big deal but my aunt is getting married next Saturday, and she asked if I wanted a plus one. Fancy going with me? Free food and alcohol."

"Love to," I replied. But not because of the free food and booze. The more time I spent with her the more I wanted. It was ridiculous and annoying and not only because she was carrying my child.

"Pass the parcel time!" Everleigh shouted.

I grabbed Holly's hand. "Come on."

"We're playing?" She asked.

"For the baby, yeah."

"Jasper!" Holly said and laughed, squeezing my hand.

CHAPTER
Twenty-Eight

Holly

"So this is husband number…?" Jasper asked, trailing off.

"Five."

"Wow, I've given up after wife number one. How does she still believe in marriage?"

I looked down, playing with my fingers under my small baby bump. He never wanted to be married again. Half the time it didn't even seem like he'd ever want a relationship again.

"Not every woman is going to cheat on you, Jasper," I said quietly.

He turned his head, and I avoided eye contact in case he could see through what I said.

"Maybe not, but how do I know who will and who won't?"

I won't.

"You can't know that, no one can. You just have to find someone you trust."

"The only women I trust are my mum, sister and you."

And me.

If he trusted me, why was he still ruling out a relationship? I curled my arms around my belly. Because he doesn't want a relationship with me. He doesn't feel that way about me.

Tears sprang to my eyes, so I picked up the Order of Service and pretended to read it. I wasn't ready to hear that and have my little family fantasy ripped away. The baby and I were going to be alone. He'd be there, of course, but it wasn't the same as us being together.

I was spared; the music started playing, signalling my aunt's entrance. I stood with the rest of the guests and plastered a smile on my face, pretending my heart wasn't breaking.

Inviting Jasper was a mistake. When he agreed immediately I was elated, but now I felt lower than I had in a long time. I was almost at the point of finding myself, and had a clear image in my head of what I wanted, but now that was gone and a part was missing.

Tammy walked down the aisle for the fifth time, arm through her dad's, beaming as if it was the first. For her, I hoped it was the last. I wanted to be that happy to be with someone. I didn't need Jasper to achieve what I wanted career wise, but I felt like I did for what I wanted in my family life.

Tammy passed us, keeping her eyes on an equally thrilled Toby. Jasper's arm wound around my waist, and his hand rested on my hip. I wanted to push him away. If we were going to have a strictly friendly relationship, then I didn't want the physical contact that made warmth spread through my entire body. But I didn't push him away because I loved the feeling too much.

We sat down once Tammy reached the front and the music came to an end. Jasper's arm stayed around me.

"They look so happy," I whispered, leaning into him because I was too damn weak to pull away.

Get a hold of yourself, Holly! And I would, tomorrow. Right now I wanted to enjoy today with my family and my baby's dad.

"They do," he agreed stiffly as if he was adding in his head 'For now'.

Why I thought bringing Mr Negative to a wedding was a good idea I'd never know.

Once the ceremony was over we went into another large, high ceiling room that gave the place a grand feel for drinks and canapés while the photographer did his thing. Since I wasn't a bridesmaid I didn't have to pose for many photos, which suited me just fine.

"Orange juice?" Jasper asked.

"Please."

"You want the Pimms fruit on top?"

I shook my head. "No, thanks, that's way too tragic."

He pursed his lips.

"If you weren't pregnant you probably still would have had the OJ."

"I wouldn't. At weddings, I get drunk."

He gave a crooked grin.

"Well, as soon as this one," he cupped my belly, stroking it with his thumb, "is out, I'm taking you to a wedding. I'd love to see you drunk again."

"I'll hold you to that."

"Holly, darling, you look beautiful," Tammy said. "Oh, you've got that pregnancy glow."

That glow was because my temperature was running higher than usual. I wasn't glowing, I was a fat, hot mess. I'd only just started looking pregnant – even though I was five months – and not like I'd had too many pies.

"Thank you. You look gorgeous. Congratulations!"

"Thank you, love. Where's your date? He's very yummy," she said, wiggling her eyebrow.

I looked over to see Jasper at the drinks table, talking to Brad and his date, Casey.

"Over there," I replied, nodding my head towards him.

"And this is baby daddy?"

"Yes."

"Hmm, you've done well there!"

I nudged her arm. "You've just got married!"

"Hey, I can still look. What's the story there anyway? Your mum said you're not together, but then you turn up here…"

"We're just friends. He doesn't want a relationship."

"Bad experience?"

"His ex cheated on him. He's in the middle of a divorce."

"I know how that feels." Her eyes narrowed. "You love him."

I blinked in shock. "I… No."

"You do. You're in love with him; it's written all over your face."

It was written all over my face? Did he notice it? Was that why he was blowing hot and cold?

"You look like a deer in the headlights right now, Hol. If he's in the middle of a divorce, the last thing he's going to see is another woman in love with him. If I can recall, you're less than warm towards members of the opposite sex."

"Can we stop talking about me now, please? This is your wedding."

"Yes, so we should talk about whatever I want."

I groaned, making her laugh.

"Okay, point taken. I'll drop the subject, just be careful. I don't want you getting hurt. Give the boy time, he's not in the place to even think about a future relationship at the minute."

Don't I know it.

"So where're you going on honeymoon?" I asked, changing the subject.

"Jamaica!"

"Wow."

Jasper walked back over to us, awkwardly holding two glasses of orange juice and a glass of champagne. Now I knew they said you should eat for two – although you shouldn't – but this was ridiculous.

"Congratulations," Jasper said, handing Tammy the champagne. He gave me an orange after and kept one for himself. What?

"Thank you and thank you," Tammy replied, taking a sip and then kissing Jasper on the cheek.

"You're not drinking?" I asked.

"No, I'm taking you home tonight."

"Oh. Right, well, I'm sure we can get a lift with Mum and Dad or Brad if you want to drink. We can pick your car up tomorrow." I'd assumed we were going to do that anyway. "Or I can drive."

He laughed. "You're not driving my baby. I don't mind not drinking. Gotta look after you anyway, so I need to be sober."

"How much trouble do you think I'm going to get into?"

He looked me up and down, and I blushed. My aunt was right there!

"In that dress…"

"He's right, you look stunning, sweetheart," Tammy said and winked. "Anyway, I'd better move on." She glided across the floor elegantly with the train of the dress following. I wanted that one day. With Jasper.

"I look fat."

He snorted. "You don't look fat. You look pregnant and so beautiful I can barely keep my eyes off you." He took my hand and caught my breath.

Why say things like that if you don't want anything to happen between us?

"I love it when you blush."

I didn't. It was embarrassing. "You make me do it a lot."

He smiled. "I know. Think we're gonna get fed soon?"

I laughed, shaking my head. Moment over.

When it was time to go through for the meal Jasper and I took our seats along with my parents, Brad, and Casey.

I fell into conversation with Mum and Casey while Dad, Jasper, and Brad chatted about football. My cheeks ached from smiling so much, especially when Jasper's hand found mine under the table. It was so easy to pretend that we were together, or that he was open to it in the future at least.

The evening reception kicked off with Britney Spears and the top tier of the wedding cake falling off the stand. The bride and groom shrugged it off, too happy to care that their six-tier cake was now a five. I'd dragged Jasper around, introducing him to more family and then we used the excuse that my feet were hurting to escape and sit back at our table.

Brad and Jasper held a conversation about some car part for a full ten minutes, and I sat there wishing I was anywhere else. I laid back in my seat, looking around, bored. Poor Casey, it looked like they weren't getting on. She had been texting for a while.

"Okay?" Brad asked.

"Yep," I replied.

"Dance with me," Jasper said, standing up and holding his hand out.

Brad turned to his date. I could tell he still wasn't completely happy with me and Jasper having a baby together. At first I thought it was because I was his sister, but now I think it's because Jasper was his friend. They spent a lot of time together, even when Jasper was with Abby, but now he comes to see me a couple times a week and most weekends.

I took Jasper's hand, and we walked to the dance floor. Thankfully, it was quite full so we wouldn't have the embarrassment of being the only ones. He wrapped his arms around me and pressed his body to mine as much as he could.

My small, five-month bump poked him in the stomach, and his eyes lit up. "I hope she kicks," he said, and started swaying us to the music.

"You wouldn't say that if you were getting the kicks from inside."

"It really hurts?"

"When she gets my ribs it does but only for a second. But I'd rather she was active, so I don't worry about not feeling her move."

She was small for five months; below average, but not below the smallest size she should be. Still, my midwife was keeping a close eye on her growth, and I was possibly going to have another scan next month.

I expected him to say something, but he just continued to stare at me. The air between us thickened, and I gripped his shoulders. He was going to kiss me, I think. My body heated, and I felt a little lightheaded.

"Holly, if you don't like PDAs in front of your family, walk away now."

Walk away? Like I could even if I wanted to, and I definitely didn't want to.

I stayed, and he lowered his mouth until his lips brushed so lightly against mine it tickled. There really was no need for him to tease.

"Are you going to kiss me or not?" I breathed. As I spoke, he lowered his face to mine and kissed me.

CHAPTER
Twenty-Nine

Holly

Jasper sat on my bed reading the pregnancy book as if he was being tested on it. Since I'd got home for the Christmas break, we'd been together pretty much every minute he wasn't working. I'd even done a few shifts at The Centre, offering my help because I knew they were busy when really I just wanted to be around him for longer. I was getting pathetic.

He was determined to know everything that was going on with the baby and my body. It was sweet that he took so much interest, but there was something else to it. He was obsessed with knowing everything and planning for every eventuality.

He knew three different routes to the hospital, had my doctor and midwife on speed dial and a first aid kit – complete with towels and baby clothes – in his boot. It was over the top, and I wasn't sure how to tell him to relax and enjoy watching our baby grow without stressing over every detail. He just couldn't seem to accept that he couldn't control everything.

"Jasper, you've read that a million times already," I said, "and the birth will probably go differently to those books anyway."

He looked up over the book. "You don't know that. We need to be prepared, Holly."

"There's prepared, and then there's what you're doing. You're going to either go crazy by the time she arrives or be exhausted."

Ignoring me, he stuck his head back in the book.

"Do you think they'll let me stay in the hospital with you?"

I shook my head. "No, they don't allow dads or partners to stay. You can visit all day and until the evening though."

The book dropped to his lap. "We need to speak to them about that. Maybe we can get a private room – you can hire those – and see if I can stay there, too, it might be different if we're not on the main ward."

"It'll be fine. I'm sure I can manage for a few hours between you leaving at night and coming back in the morning." I know I hadn't been around babies much, but I was confident I could do it. The midwives were there to help and guide me. Surely all I'd be doing was breastfeeding and changing nappies anyway.

"I don't want you two on your own."

"We won't be."

His beautiful face was marred with a frown.

"Holly, the midwives don't count. They don't care enough."

"What?"

"Will one stay in your room all night?"

"No, of course not, but if I need them they'll come in."

"Then I need to be there. What if something happens?"

Oh. That's what this was about. He was scared because of what happened to Oakley. I felt awful that he worried about us to the point where he didn't feel he could leave us for one night, but it was unhealthy. We were going to be apart from him, so he had to get used to it and realise we were okay.

"Jasper, nothing is going to happen to us. We'll be fine in the hospital for a night or two."

"Something might happen."

"If you don't trust me to look after our child-"

"I do!"

I threw my hands up. "It doesn't sound like it. What happened to Oakley-"

"Shut up," he snapped.

My heart ached. It was still so hard for him to talk about, but he couldn't see that it was why he was feeling so anxious. How could you get someone to seek help when they wouldn't even admit there was a problem?

"For all our sakes, the baby's included, you're going to have to talk about it."

"No," he replied and shut down.

It was so hard to talk to him once he was done with something, but I wasn't about to give up. If he continued trying to control everything, I was going to be suffocated. I couldn't live with him constantly calling or texting, telling me what I could or couldn't do or where I could go. His fear was real and I understood, but I wouldn't let it rule my life.

"Please, Jasper."

He snapped his teeth together. "This is my baby, too, Holly. You don't get to make all of the decisions. I won't leave my child with strangers."

"Strangers? She'll be with me – her mum! Do you think I'm going to leave her on the ward while I go see a movie or something?"

He gave me an exasperated look.

"I'm perfectly capable of protecting my baby."

I could see in his now dark grey eyes that he was thinking 'My mum thought that, too'.

"I want to be there," he said

"No," I said. "I'm not going to kick up a fuss at the hospital over this. We will be fine. The ward is secure. No one will hurt her. You need to talk to someone because worrying yourself sick isn't going to help the baby."

"I'll be fine."

Sighing, I ran my hands through my hair.

"I won't be, Jasper. We can't live like this."

"We don't have to. There's no need for you to worry."

Right, because we weren't together and he had no interest in me romantically. I was fine as a friend he occasionally slept with, but that was where it ended. I knew I shouldn't take it too personally; he didn't want a relationship with anyone, but it did hurt.

The more it hurt, the angrier I got with him and with myself. It was too much on top of having an unplanned pregnancy, worrying about being a good mum and finishing university.

"I think you should go," I said. "I can't do this, Jasper. It's too hard."

"Do what?"

I threw my hands up. "This. Us."

"What us?"

Exactly.

"We're having a baby, Holly, nothing is going to change that now. You can't just order me out of your life because you're pissed off with me."

"I'm not. I'm ordering you out of my house."

"Is this how it's going to be? We disagree on something and you make me leave? You can't do that. This is my baby, too."

I groaned. No one got to me as much as him. I could feel my temper boiling below the surface, ready to explode.

"Stop looking at me like that," he said. "I'm not arguing with you. When you're home it'll be different, but I'm staying at the hospital."

"We both make decisions, so why should I just pander to your every fucking demand?" I shouted.

"You're being unreasonable."

My eyes widened. "Me?"

I was not the unreasonable one.

"Why don't you want me there? I thought you'd like the help after giving birth."

"I don't like why you want to do it."

He shook his head. "You're the most confusing and frustrating woman I've ever met, Holly."

"And you're the most stubborn man I've ever met! I can't believe we're arguing over this; it's ridiculous. You can be at the hospital for dad's visiting like everyone else."

"Now who's being stubborn," he muttered.

"Alright, get out. I'm serious, Jasper. You're being stupid and I know you don't mean it personally, but that's how I'm taking it. I need time away from you because when you're in front of me I can barely think straight."

I shouldn't have said that. Dropping my eyes to the floor, I bit my lip.

"Holly," he said, and I could tell he'd regretted pushing me. His voice was low, deep and intense, and it sent a shiver down my spine. He got to me so much because I was completely in love with him.

"Please. I need you to give me some space to think."

He stepped forwards, pressing his lips to my forehead and

rubbing his thumb over my belly. "Okay," he murmured against my skin. "Call if you need me."

"I will. I just need some time."

Stepping back, he nodded.

"I get it. These last few months have been pretty intense."

He turned and walked away.

I sat down when I heard the front door close behind him. I thought I'd feel better once he was gone, but I didn't. He worried, and I wasn't helping by sending him away rather than trying harder to talk to him.

If we couldn't find a way to communicate and resolve our issues then we were going to have a tense relationship, and our relationship was now going to have to last forever – as parents, if nothing else. I swung my feet up on the sofa and laid down.

"Morning," Oakley said.

"Hi. How come you're in on your day off?" I asked her.

She smiled sympathetically, and I knew straight away – Jasper.

"He called me last night," she said, "and told me what happened. Then he asked if we could swap days."

"I'm sorry."

"Don't be. I know how he is, and it can be pretty intense. He's scared, Holly, and he doesn't do feeling scared well. For the last eight years, he's been the strong one, and although he worried himself sick about us all I think it's really hitting him hard now that he's going to be a dad."

"I feel awful for sending him home last night."

"No, you were right to. It's not healthy, and you can't just go along with it because you're afraid of upsetting him. You've got to be honest about how you feel, or you're going to end up resenting him."

Being honest about how I felt about him would not do me any favours right now.

"Yeah. I don't want to lie to him, and we've both said we need to talk openly. It's hard to tell him he's not staying at the hospital when I know why he wants to."

"I know," she said and smiled. "He'll be fine though, and he wouldn't be allowed to stay anyway. Don't let it get you down. He'll come around when he's had time to think it through."

"Has he been to see Dr Hales again?"

"Not recently. He went a few times after he split up with Abby but not recently. I'll be talking to him about that because I really think Carol can help him get some perspective and realise what he needs to do to move on."

"What do you think he needs to do?" I asked, eager to hear her thoughts.

"I think he needs a conversation with our dad."

That I did not expect. I thought she was just going to tell me he needs regular therapy and to talk to Dr Hales about what happened and how it affected him.

"Really?" I must have sounded as surprised as I felt.

She shrugged.

"He hasn't talked to Dad since he was arrested. He's had no closure and none of the questions he has have been answered. Up until now he could deal with that enough for it not to affect his everyday life too much but now he's faced with bringing an innocent baby into this world, and I'll put a lot of money on it eating away at him."

"You think he'll be okay?"

"I won't let him not be," she said.

Neither will I.

CHAPTER
Thirty

Holly

Jasper smiled sheepishly at me as I opened the door. "Hey," he said.

I stood back so he could come in. "Hi."

"Are you parent's home?" He asked and walked inside.

"No, everyone's at work."

"Good."

"Hol, I'm sorry. These last couple of days have sucked. I hate arguing with you."

"I hate arguing with you, too." But I still didn't know how we were going to resolve anything properly.

"Can we stop worrying about everything that might happen in the future and concentrate on getting ready for this one?" He asked, glancing at my belly.

I knew that didn't include him stopping to worry about the

baby's safety. It had to, and he had to want it, but he wouldn't face his demons.

"Sure," I replied, knowing if I brought it up again we'd just fall straight back into the same argument. I knew Sarah and Oakley had been through it with him a few times, too. "I'm about to watch a birth video, want to join me?"

He frowned. "Do I?"

"Probably not but if I'm watching it you are, too."

"Why did you ask, then?" He said, wrapping his arm around my waist as we walked into the living room. It was so nice to have things back to normal between us. It had only been a couple days, but I hated arguing and not talking.

"Sit," I ordered and went to put the DVD on.

He got comfortable and raised his arm as I walked back to the sofa. A thrill ran through me that he wanted to snuggle up as we watched probably the most gross DVD we ever would. I wanted to know what my body was going to go through, but at the same time a part of me wanted to go into it naïve and utterly unprepared. If I didn't know how bad it was, then I wouldn't be able to freak out about it.

"You ready?" Jasper asked as I pressed play on the remote.

I curled into his side and shook my head. "Not at all."

"You'll be fine when it's our turn." He pressed his lips to my temple and whispered, "I'll never let anything happen to either of you."

I closed my eyes and squeezed my arm around his waist as my heartbeat went crazy. I hated Abby for what she'd done to him and wished she'd broken up with him before she slept with Brett so he wouldn't have been as hurt and closed off to future relationships.

The DVD started, and the excitement from the parents was

infectious.

"Maybe this won't be that bad," I said.

Twenty minutes later and I realised I'd jinxed it. Big time.

I stared at the screen in horror as the baby pushed its way out of its mother.

"Jesus. Fuck! That's not natural," Jasper said with wide eyes and looking traumatised.

"Well, it's alright for you!"

"I can't look away," he whined. "Why can't I look away?"

"I'm having the epidural."

"Holly, make me look away!"

"Can you stop now? You don't have to worry about this, I do!"

The mother screamed as the baby's head popped out and then there was definite tearing.

Jasper heaved, and for a second I thought he was going to be sick on my mum's new sofa. He pressed his fist to his mouth and squeezed his eyes closed.

I wanted to look away too, but whatever was preventing him earlier was now stopping me. Women did this more than once? What on earth was wrong with them? My own mum did this twice. How could she not hate us?

"I'm scared," I whispered, wishing I'd never agreed to watch it. Oakley was wrong; this wasn't helping me understand what was going to happen to my body during birth, this was making me wish I could opt for a caesarean.

"Me too," Jasper replied. "Is it over yet?"

"I'm not talking about the video! I'm talking about the fact that I'm going to have to do this in three month's time."

He gulped and turned his body to face mine.

"I'm so sorry, Holly." His eyes dropped to between my legs,

and I hit him. "You're tight so I don't even know how it's going to happen."

My face burst into flames. "Shut up!"

"I can't believe you're still a prude after we had sex in the back of my car, at The Centre, in the bath-"

"Okay! Please can you stop now?" I didn't need him to list all our indiscretions.

He grinned. "Alright. Seriously though, what the hell are you gonna do?"

I shrugged. "Lots of drugs. Remember me saying this now; I want everything. Don't let them try to push me into having a natural birth."

On the screen, the mum gave one last, long scream that didn't sound human, and the baby slid into the midwife's arms. My mouth fell open. Wow. The camera zoomed out to the two crying parents as they shared a quick kiss, and then their child – which was announced a boy – was placed on his mum's chest.

Jasper fell silent. His hand found mine, and he weaved our fingers together.

Oh, that's why women do it more than once.

The little baby boy who had a good set of lungs on him wailed, but his parents stared down at him in wonder, amazement and love.

"I can't wait for that part," Jasper said. "I'd go through that for what they're feeling right now."

"I wish you could," I replied, and he laughed. He let go of my hand, and I felt colder. But only for a second as he wrapped his arm around my back and drew me closer to him. I laid my head against his shoulder, and when his hand rested on my bump, I almost cried. This was what I wanted. Me and him and our baby.

"I can't wait until he or she is here now."

"Me neither," I said. "It's going to be amazing. And exhausting."

"I'll be here as much as I can."

"I know you will. You're going to be a fantastic dad, and you know you're welcome here anytime you like. I'll never say no to you seeing the baby."

He shifted slightly, and I looked up. He was nervous.

"I've been meaning to talk to you about that."

"About what?"

"About me staying here some nights. Or you two staying at my place. It's not fair that you do every night feed; I want to be equally as exhausted."

"Where would you sleep here?"

"On the floor in the baby's room? I don't care where I sleep; I just want to be here where I can look after her."

We were both still so confident it was a girl.

"We can sort something out, I'm sure. The baby will be in my room for the first few months anyway."

He nodded once. "Well, maybe I can stay in your room, too?"

"Unlikely," Dad said, flicking the switch on the wall. Light flooded the room, and I groaned. *Thanks for ruining the moment, Dad!* We had only just got back on track, and I really didn't want to fall out with him again. I hated us not being friendly, and I missed the flirting too.

"Ah, come on, Carl, after what I've just seen you have nothing to worry about."

I elbowed him in the side and he laughed, flashing me his million-dollar smile. He was joking; I could tell by the glint in his eye and the way his fingers dug into my lower hip ever so slightly. Heck, after what I'd just seen I wasn't sure if I ever wanted that again!

When it was time for Jasper to leave and go home to his flat, I walked him to the door, wanting nothing more than for him to stay or for me to go, too. "I'll see you tomorrow?" He asked.

"Definitely," I replied. Thank God, Uni was over for Christmas break, I hated missing him and weekend visits weren't enough anymore.

"Good. You'll come to Cole and Oakley's for dinner, too, right?"

"Yes." I'd already said I would, but I loved that he wanted to confirm, like he wanted to make double sure I was definitely going with him. Like I'd say no.

Jasper kept his hand on my bump, waiting to be kicked again. He wanted to feel the baby move almost all the time, so his hand was practically glued to me. Not that I minded, I loved his touch. He was already head over heels in love with our little one; it was so touching to watch.

After the scan they said that although my bump was measuring a few weeks behind, the development was on target, so they put it down to my petite size and, 'some are just smaller, that's how we get averages'. It made sense, but I still worried. They estimated she would be around five, and a half to six pounds when she was born, I hoped she stayed inside me a week or so longer, just to get her up to a more 'average' weight.

Cole and Oakley had just taken Everleigh upstairs to get her pyjamas on ready for bed, so I made small talk with Jasper and Oakley's parents and Cole and his sister, Mia's parents.

"Why are we here then?" Sarah said to Cole's mum, Jenna, and his sister, Mia.

As soon as Cole and Oakley stepped out of the room they'd been gossiping about why we were really here. It was as if we didn't all get together regularly.

"She kicked!" Jasper exclaimed, grinning so wide I thought his face would split.

Sarah and Jenna were over in a flash, laying their hand on my stomach. They'd asked me the first time and now just assumed they had free reign. I didn't mind though; they were family. It was strangers that I didn't like touching without permission.

"And it might be a he," Sarah said.

"You only want that because you've already got a grand-daughter," Jasper replied.

"I don't care as long as we get healthy."

I didn't care either, but I still thought girl. I could just see me and Jasper with a fair-haired daughter, hopefully with Jasper's gorgeous, grey eyes.

"You feel that?" Jasper said, smiling at me.

"You're kidding, right?" I felt every movement!

He laughed and for a second I though he was going to kiss me, but he looked away, startled by Leona's giggle as she placed her little hand on my bump, too. Cole's niece was so cute and such a big sister figure for Everleigh. I had no doubt that even though she wasn't related to my baby, she'd be just as protective and caring.

Sarah beamed, obviously picking up on our almost kiss, too. She'd never said anything to me about my relationship with Jasper, but I could tell she knew I wanted to be with him. I suspected she never mentioned it because she knew he wasn't ready for anything new yet and didn't want to hurt my feelings. I understood the situation, and I could wait. Jasper was the person I wanted to spend the rest of my life with, so what was a few months or a year in exchange for a lifetime? Or what I hoped would turn into a lifetime.

"Does it hurt?" Leona asked.

I shook my head. "Not really. It just feels weird."

"I miss that," Cole's mum, Jenna, said. "Feeling your baby moving around inside you is incredible."

"Have another one," Sarah joked, making Jenna laugh.

"Oh, I don't think so. I'll settle for more grandkids." She looked at Mia who shook her head, determined that Leona was going to be her only child. "All down to Cole then, I guess."

Jasper scowled.

Suddenly Everleigh squealed. We all looked up, but no one moved because as I'd come to understand – from a few almost-heart attacks – that was her excited squeal.

"Nanna! Grandma!" she screamed, running into the room. Cole and Oakley were right behind her, arm around each other, laughing. In the hand that she was waving around was a scan picture. "I'm going to be a big sister!"

Everyone immediately leapt up to congratulate all three of them. Oakley had said they wanted more children but weren't trying just yet. Perhaps her pill didn't work either. A chorus of 'Congratulations' and 'I'm so excited' echoed through the room.

"How far along are you?" Sarah asked, gripping Oakley's hand once we all sat down again.

"Fourteen weeks. I'm due on the 14th of June."

"You've known all this time, and you didn't tell me?" Jasper said, frowning.

Oakley sighed. "We wanted to wait for the twelve-week scan."

"You're *fourteen* weeks."

She leant into Cole's side, and he kissed the top of her head. They were so sweet together. I wanted that, too. "I know, but the scan was closer to thirteen weeks and then we wanted to keep it to ourselves for a while. Plus, we were worried how Eveleigh would take it. Turns out she loves the idea of a brother or sister."

"Fine," he replied, grumpy, and I elbowed him in the side. "I'm happy for you both."

The side of Oakley's mouth pulled into a smirk as she noticed what I'd done.

"Thank you, Jasper."

He gave Oakley a hug and then it was my turn.

I smiled; excited to share this experience with Jasper's sister and excited the baby would be my child's cousin.

Christmas morning in my house was always hectic. We opened presents, played Christmas songs, danced around the living room, picked at chocolates and cooked the dinner as a family, messing around as we went.

I'd just finished moving my presents up to my room to clear space for later, when my aunt, uncle, cousins, and grandparents arrived in the afternoon, when my bedroom door was pushed open.

"Hello?" I said, and took a step towards it, and then jumped as Jasper sprang through the doorway in an elf costume. I burst out laughing.

"What are you doing?"

"Merry Christmas!" he exclaimed, wrapping his arms around me in a tight hug.

"Again, what are you doing?" I asked, still laughing.

He pulled away and jingled the bell on the end of his green hat.

"I promised Eveleigh I'd be an elf months ago. I hoped she'd forget but..."

"Well, I'm very glad she didn't."

"I'm on my way there now so don't think I'm crashing your

Christmas."

As if I'd think that.

"I just wanted to stop by and let you laugh at me – and to give you this." He pulled a red velvet pouch out of his pocket, and that was when I saw the red and white striped tights.

I bit my lip to stop myself laughing, and focused on what he was giving me.

"Hold up your hand," he said.

I held my hand out, palm up and he tipped a necklace out. It was a simple oval-shaped white gold necklace with tiny diamonds framing the edge.

"Wow," I whispered, holding it up. "It's beautiful."

He took it off me and opened it up. Inside was a picture of me.

"It's from the baby, too. I thought when she's here we can put her picture in there and have mother and daughter. Or son. I keep forgetting we don't know, and it could be a boy."

I suddenly felt choked up.

"You like it?" He asked.

"It's gorgeous. Thank you so much."

"You're welcome."

"I feel bad now. We agreed no presents."

With the baby coming, we were saving to buy all the things that she needed!

"I know, but I saw it in the jewellers when me and Oakley were deciding on earrings for Mum and I really wanted to get it for you."

Gripping the necklace in my hand, I surged up on my tiptoes and kissed him. This was officially the best Christmas yet.

CHAPTER
Thirty-One

Jasper

"**O**h, for goodness sake, Jasper, none of these pushchairs are going to shoot out knives and stab the baby! They're all fucking safe, now pick one!" Holly growled.

My mouth dropped. It wasn't often that she surprised me. Coming on to me, and telling me she was pregnant were about the only other times. We'd decided to get the big baby items in the January sales, and I was seriously regretting it because Holly's hormones were on fire today.

"It's an important decision."

"No, it's not. Naming the baby is an important decision, so why don't you think more about that and I'll pick the sodding pushchair."

So, hormonal Holly wasn't much fun. I never knew if I was getting normal Holly or the version of her that seemed to hate me above anyone else in the world.

I held my hands up. "Okay. Those four have the best safety features."

"I figured that since they're the only ones still in front of us!"

I was scared to suggest names.

"What about Ebony?"

She stared at me as if I were crazy. "Do you hate our baby?"

"What? No, of course not."

"Ebony was my great nan's dog's name. I can't name my baby after poor Eb."

Well, how the fuck was I supposed to know that?

"Okay, not Ebony."

She shook her head and went back to the pushchairs. I should get her mum to list all the names of her relatives back as far as she could remember, and their pets, just in case.

On the side of the room was a long shelf full of books for pregnancy, birth and babies. I swiped a baby name book and opened it up randomly. "Frankie?"

"No."

I flicked over pages, landing on another one. "Libby?"

"No."

"Natalie."

"Oh, for goodness sake, if you're not going to suggest seriously, don't bother."

I did with Ebony.

"Daisy?"

She paused. "That's pretty."

Good, no pets named Daisy.

"That can go on the maybe list."

"Sophia."

This time I got a smile. Wow. "On the maybe list, too."

I was on a roll now. I flicked back a chunk of the book.

"Maud."

Her face fell. *And we're back to Jasper's a bastard.*

"Boys now?" I asked, trying to go for that smile she'd called cute before I turned into public enemy number one.

"If it's a boy I'd like to call him Oliver, after my grandad. Do you like that?"

"Yeah, I like it." Not that I'd say right now if I didn't!

Her face warmed, and she put her hand on my favoured push-chair.

"This one for little Oliver or either Alice, Daisy, Sophia, Ella, Annie or Jessa."

I laughed. But I thought we'd crossed Annie off the list a while ago. I wasn't going to question her.

"Lunch now? We've got an hour before you wanted to leave for Uni."

"Sounds good. Should we get this now?"

"Yeah, I'll just go pay. Why don't you take my keys and meet me in the car."

She arched her eyebrow. "Why? Want to chat up the lady behind the till?"

"No, you said your feet hurt half an hour ago."

She flushed and muttered, "Oh. Thank you."

I handed her my keys, biting back a sarcastic comment because she was pretty damn scary of late. I'd learnt quickly when not to tease her.

Once I'd paid for the pushchair and arranged for it to be delivered to my place, I joined Holly in the car.

"I feel bad," she said.

"Why? Do you have pains? Should I call the midwife?"

She laughed. "It's not physical. You need to calm down, or

you're going to have a heart attack."

My shoulders sagged, and I started the car.

"Why do you feel bad?"

"You're buying all the big things. The pushchair, the cot, the car seat. All I've bought is clothes, nappies, and toiletries."

"Holly, it's my child, too."

"I know, but we should share the expense."

"Well, you're a poor student. I have plenty of money saved since the house sold."

"That's for a new house!"

"I'll cope. Don't feel bad. I want to buy all this stuff, and I work full-time. Now, what do you fancy to eat?" She gave me a guilty smile, and I rolled my eyes. "Let me guess, you want to go to a supermarket and get picnic type food to eat back at mine because you want cocktail sausages?"

Her smile stretched. "You're the best."

I stood between my soon-to-be ex-wife and the woman that was having my baby. Both faced each other, bumps almost touching. Abby's was a lot bigger. She was only a few weeks ahead, but it looked like months. My little girl really was small.

"How're you getting on?" Abby asked, giving me an accusing look that screamed see-I-knew-you-wanted-to-sleep-with-her. Back when I was with Abby, I genuinely hadn't wanted anything from Holly. That wasn't the type of guy I was.

"Good, thanks. You?" I replied.

"Fine. How's your pregnancy going, Holly?"

Holly took a subtle step closer to me, and I hated that she felt uncomfortable or vulnerable. I wrapped my arm around her waist, not caring what Abby thought. Holly was the important one, and I didn't want her to think I was going to run back to my ex and leave her to go through the pregnancy alone – or whatever she was thinking that made her so uncomfortable.

"It's going well. Yours? You look really good."

Abby smiled, but it was bitter.

"Thanks, mine's going well, too. I've not even been sick."

"No, I've not had much sickness either."

But she's made up for that with hormones.

"How's Brett?" I asked and felt Holly tense.

Abby's eyebrows twitched and she suddenly stood taller.

"He's fine, too, excited for the baby's arrival. We're not together though."

Same situation as us. I watched Abby smile up at me the way she used to, and I was relieved to notice I felt nothing for her anymore. She wasn't the person I thought she was. It didn't bother me whether she was with Brett or not.

"We're excited, too, aren't we, Hol?"

"Can't wait," she replied, pressing her side against mine.

"I heard you were back at university, Holly. That must be stressful."

"Not really. I love my course and my pregnancy is going just fine. I'm more focused because I have to get as much as I can done before she comes."

"She? You know what you're having?"

"No, but we always say she," Holly explained.

"Oh, well that's cute," Abby said in a tone I knew all too well. She'd used it when I told her I wanted to work at The Centre. Abby thought I could do more with my life but after watching my sister build it up and change peoples' lives I realised there was nothing I'd rather do than be a part of something that gave so much back. The day a four-year-old girl called Georgie came for her first ballet class was the day I was sure I'd done the right thing by working there. She'd had her legs amputated after contract-ing meningitis when she was just six months old, and The Centre raised money for her to have new prosthetic legs that allowed her to move around like any other child. Being part of that wasn't a waste.

"What about you? Do you know?"

"No, we decided to wait. Although Brett is desperate to find out."

I gritted my teeth at her mentioning his name. He had the life I thought I was going to have, and I hated him for it. I didn't want Abby back, but I hated how we ended. Me and Holly being parents wasn't a mistake, but a baby born out of casual sex was not what I thought was going to happen.

"How's work going?" I asked.

"Good. Busy, so the days fly by. I'm looking forward to being off with the little one, but I'm also anxious to get back and not miss any opportunities."

Her career still came first. Though I couldn't blame her for making it a priority – kids grew up, and you still had to have a life – but I would've thought returning to work wouldn't be something you looked forward to before your baby was even born. Surely, you'd want to enjoy the time at home with your family before you worried about going back?

"Glad it's going well. Anyway, we should get going. Some-one's got a craving I need to see to." Holly smiled, trying not to laugh. Yeah, that might have sounded a little wrong. "Take care, Abby," I said, not bothering to correct it because it really didn't matter what she thought we were doing.

Holly and I walked away and turned down the next aisle.

"If you do have any of *those* cravings, let me know," I whis-pered in her ear, making her laugh. The air changed – charged. We both wanted it. But we were in the middle of the supermarket. It would have to wait.

CHAPTER
Thirty-Two

Holly

I rubbed stretchmark cream over my bump and pulled my pyjama top down. So far the cream was working, but that might just be because the baby was small, and I still had two months of stretching to do yet.

A Happy Valentine's Day card – tragically from my Mum – sat on my dresser, laughing at me. The only proper card I'd got before was one from my ex, but that was years ago. Not that I expected to get one. Who would be lusting after a pregnant hippo!

Picking up my phone, I dialled Jasper's number for his routinely morning we're-fine call. "Morning," he said. "You got anything in for breakfast or want me to pick something up?"

"What?" I said. "You're here? I thought you were coming next weekend."

"Changed my mind. That okay?"

"Yeah. Where are you?"

"Just coming through town. Be there in five. Food?" *God, I need to get dressed!*

"Can you pick something up?"

"Bagels? I'm almost outside that deli place."

"Egg and bacon please."

"See you in a few."

I hung up the phone and pulled my wardrobe open, scanning my maternity tops. Thank heavens for leggings; they were a pregnant woman's best friend.

Just as I'd finished putting some mascara on, there was a knock on the door. I fluffed my hair and tried to stop smiling quite so broadly before I let Jasper in.

Leaning casually against the door frame in a pair of ripped jeans, grey t-shirt and black leather jacket, he took my breath away.

"Hey," he said, giving me one of those heart-stopping smiles where his eyes light up.

"Hey, come in."

From behind his back he pulled out a bunch of red roses and did a little bow.

"For you."

"Thank you, they're gorgeous." It was the first time I'd got roses. My ex bought me a cheesy teddy holding a heart – not that I was ungrateful; I loved it until he broke up with me. "You didn't have to get me flowers."

He shrugged. "They were half price from the garage."

I laughed and rolled my eyes. I could tell they weren't, they were too large, and there was fancy red-and-white crepe paper around them. I grabbed a vase, filled it with water and popped them in.

He walked past me and grabbed two plastic plates from my wardrobe. He handed me one and sat on the bed with his.

"Thanks, I really needed this. Your child is making me doubly hungry."

"You're supposed to be eating for two."

"Myth," I said. "But it would be nice."

As we ate, my eyes wandered to the roses sitting in the vase by the sink. I would have to arrange them properly later. Without even knowing it, he made me feel special and wanted. I held on to the hope that it wouldn't be too long before he was ready for a relationship again and that he'd want one with me. The image of us together with our baby was one that I clung to. It was the reason that I didn't give up and just plan for a friendship between us, but I knew I was risking getting hurt.

"How's everyone back home?"

"Good," he replied with a full mouth.

"You're gross, Jasper."

"Hey, don't ask me questions until I've finished eating and I won't reply with a-"

"Alright!" I waited until he'd finished, which took about three bites with the amount he shovelled in. "House hunting going okay?"

He shrugged. "It's alright. Thankfully, the flat has enough room for tons of baby stuff so even if I'm still renting when she arrives I'll have the space for her."

"And the space for me?" I asked, chewing on my lip. I didn't want to ask, but I wasn't comfortable being away from my baby. It was selfish, I knew that, he would have to spend nights away from her, but I couldn't help it.

"Are you asking to move in with me?"

I elbowed his arm. "No. I'd just feel more comfortable if I

was there, too."

He frowned.

"Not because I don't think you could handle it, please, don't think that. It's just being away from my newborn makes me feel panicky already. Plus, she'll need my milk. When she's older you can have her overnight without me but to start with I'd like to be there."

He nodded slowly. "I understand that feeling. There's room for three. Always will be."

I wasn't sure if that covered forever the way I wanted it to.

"You want to get some more stuff this weekend? I can take it back to your parents for you when I go. You said you wanted one of those vibrating, music playing, all-singing, all-dancing chairs."

"Sounds good to me."

"Cool. Then I'll take you out to dinner. It is the card company's day after all."

"Someone's bitter."

"Catching your wife with another man will do that."

I winced. "Crap. Jasper, I'm sorry, I didn't think."

"Forget it. It's fine."

"How are you about all that now?" I asked, not entirely sure I wanted to hear the answer.

"Alright, I guess. Still hurts, the way it all happened, you know? I could live with her leaving me a lot easier than I can knowing she'd been sleeping with someone then coming home to me. I thought she wanted to wait to have a baby because of her career, and that's it. Guess shagging Brett put her off too." He laughed, but it was bitter. "Then she went and got pregnant by the fucker. It's like a double slap in the face."

"I'm sorry."

He snapped out of his mood and smiled at me.

"Doesn't matter now. We've got this one on the way," he said, covering my little bump with his hand. "And I couldn't be happier about that. Plus, my lawyer said the divorce should be finalised in the end of next month or so. I'll be able to finally put it all behind me."

"Good," I replied, meaning putting everything behind him and because of the divorce. As soon as he had no more ties to her there would be no more talk that involved Abigail Dane, and hopefully he would start looking to the future. I wanted him to be happy and have nothing dragging him down.

"How are the therapy sessions going?"

He never liked talking about them; it was as if he was ashamed to admit he needed help. Everyone did at some point. I saw facing your problems as a strength rather than a weakness.

"Fine," he replied.

"You can tell me about it if you want, you know."

"No offence, Holly, but you're the woman carrying my child. I don't want to dump my crap on you when I'm the one that's supposed to take care of you."

But he wasn't supposed to take care of me, just the baby. He was too hard on himself all the time, thinking that he needs to do more and be stronger.

"You do and you still can. You tell me to unload on you, so you can do the same."

I rolled my eyes as he fought a smile, knowing he'd turned my words dirty.

"Thanks, Hol, you always know how to cheer me up."

He was in need of cheering up?

"Talk to me. Please."

He sighed. "It's going well, I guess. She makes me look at things differently, and I'm starting to believe some of what she says. I'll be fine. Please, don't worry."

Well, that gave me absolutely nothing to go on. Could he have been any more vague? He wasn't going to give me anything else, so I let it go, hoping he'd open up properly when he was ready – if he ever would be.

"Alright," I said as I took his plate with mine to wash up. "I'll just sort out the flowers and then we can go. Oh, I need to do my make-up properly first."

"No, you don't. You're perfect as you are."

That was probably a lie, but he made me feel beautiful enough to push my make-up bag aside. If anyone ran screaming though, I was never going to trust him again!

"Thank you," I said.

"No need to thank me, just being honest."

It wasn't just the words that he said; it was how his words made me feel. He was the first person to really see me as a woman. Being the youngest in my family and the youngest amongst my friends meant I had always been treated as a child, people had gone out of their way to look after me just that little bit more. I appreciated that they cared, but I didn't want to be Little Holly in my twenties.

Jasper took me shopping, spoiling our unborn baby with clothes and cuddly toys and spoiling me with lunch out, a movie, and then dinner in the evening. When we got back to my empty flat, we laid on the sofa chatting about whatever popped into our heads. I realised that the last seven months had been the best of my life, and a lot of that was because of him.

CHAPTER
Thirty-Three

Jasper

"Jasper!" Holly's voice pierced through the bathroom door. Something was wrong.

I leapt up out of my seat and sprinted to the door. She'd locked it. I banged my fist on the door. "Holly, what's wrong? Open up!"

"My water just broke!" she shouted.

Shit! It was too soon. We had another three weeks to go. "What? Open the door and let me in!"

"I'll be out in a second. Call the hospital."

"What's happening?" Mum said behind me.

I spun around, ripping my phone from my pocket.

"Holly's water broke," I said, dialling the hospital with shaking hands.

Thirty-seven weeks was when you were considered 'safe' but the baby was smaller than average already. I wanted her to stay inside her mum for as long as possible until we knew she'd definitely be safe.

"It's too soon, Mum," I said, willing them to pick the damn phone up.

"It's going to be fine. The baby is old enough now."

She stepped past me, leaning towards the door.

"Holly, sweetheart, are you okay?"

The midwife picked up and I spoke in a rush, stumbling over my words. Holly finally opened the door just as I was told to bring her straight in.

She smiled, but I could tell by the tension in her shoulders that she was worried.

"You get straight to the hospital," Mum said. "I'll call your parents, and we'll make our way there whenever you want us to."

I knew she'd want to come with us, but she was giving us time alone.

Holly gulped and replied in a small voice, "Okay, thanks. You can all come soon if you'd like."

That wasn't what we'd said we'd do, but it was understandable that she'd want her mum there, too.

"We'll wait to hear from Jasper, give you a chance to get checked out and wrap your heads around it happening now, and then we'll be there," Mum said.

"Come on, Holly, let's go." I offered her my hand and she took it, gripping hard. "Are you okay? In any pain?"

"No, not yet," she replied as we walked out towards the car. "Lucky you're such a control freak over this and packed the hospital bags two weeks ago, huh?"

I flashed her a smile, hoping she couldn't see through mine, too. Inside I was terrified. "See, it is paying off."

If something happened to either one of them, I don't know

what I'd do.

"Yeah, only nothing is going to fit the baby."

I opened her door and helped her in.

"I'll pick up some early baby nappies and get Oakley to buy and wash some clothes," Mum said.

I hadn't realised she was following us out, but of course she was. Miles was right behind her, looking lost and concerned.

"Thank you, Sarah," Holly said.

Mum leant down and kissed her cheek, whispering something.

"Let us know if you need anything else," Miles said.

"Thanks," I replied and hopped in the driver's seat.

As soon as Mum had closed Holly's door, we were gone. The drive to the hospital would only take twenty minutes, but I kept having visions of Holly giving birth in a lay-by. Since we'd watched the birth video, she said she wanted all the drugs available to her. I hated the thought of her in pain so I wanted to make sure she was near as many options for pain relief as possible.

She bit her lip, tensing.

"Contraction?" I asked, pressing down on the accelerator.

Her body relaxed.

"Yeah, but it wasn't bad." She laughed. "I expected it to be awful, but it was no more than period pain. I know I'm jinxing the hell out of this right now, and it'll be unbearable soon though!"

"You'll be fine. We'll soon be where they have epidural."

"I want four," she said, making me laugh.

I grabbed her hand. "You can have anything you want."

When we reached the delivery ward we were whisked straight into a room and two midwives followed us in. By the time we'd arrived she was in so much pain she could barely walk. I hated seeing her like that.

"Okay, if you'd like to lie down on the bed, Holly, we'll assess how far along you are," the older midwife, Annette, said.

I helped Holly on the bed, and her face reddened as she pushed her leggings down.

"Okay?" I asked her, keeping my eyes on her face as the midwives did their thing. I think the shyness was because I was in the room. She nodded, gritting her teeth and reached for my hand.

"Don't leave me," she said, sounding so vulnerable I was instantly scared.

"Not going anywhere. I promise."

"Wow, looks like you're eight centimetres already," Annette said looking up and smiling.

Holly pushed herself up on her elbows, releasing my hand.

"What? How is that possible? I thought I had about twelve hours!"

Shit!

"That's the average. You're thirty-seven weeks and four days?"

"Yeah," she replied. "The baby's small."

The midwife who was flicking through Holly's pregnancy notes, Jen, looked up.

"You're full term and although the baby is on the small side there's nothing to suggest he or she isn't perfectly healthy."

"Aghhh!" Holly cried suddenly.

"I can see the head," Annette said. "Not long now, and I'll need you to start pushing."

"Oh my God, this isn't happening," she sobbed. "It's too early, too quick, Jasper!"

I stroked her hair. "Shh, sweetheart, it's going to be fine. Hey, you'd rather it was over quickly than be in pain for half a day, right?"

"I guess. I just thought we'd have more time but-" She stopped abruptly, hissing through her teeth. "I want to push. Should I push? Am I fully dilated?"

That quick?

"Absolutely, chicken," Jen said. "That's your body's way of saying you're ready. On the next contraction give us a good push."

"Oh God, I'm scared," Holly muttered. She flopped back on the bed and reached for my hand.

"Should it happen this quickly?" I asked, kissing the back of Holly's hand to try and calm her down. I was terrified for the next contraction.

Jen smiled. "It can do. That's why you hear stories of people giving birth in cars or lifts."

That wasn't much comfort. I leant over and kissed Holly's temple.

Ten minutes later and Holly was pushing with every contraction, and because it was all happening scarily fast she couldn't have anything for the pain besides gas and air, which she'd tried, but as it didn't work straight away she gave up.

"Push, Holly!" I said.

"Jasper! I swear to God if you tell me to push one more time, I'm going to kill you!" She groaned, and the sound was raw and scary. "You did this to me!"

It was safe to say she hated me when she was in pain. I wanted to point out that we'd done this, but I thought better of it.

"You're doing amazing, Hol. Do you want the gas and air?" I asked.

She collapsed back on the bed as her contraction subsided.

"The gas and air does nothing. I want an epidural."

"It's too late for that, babe."

She glared through slitted eyes and growled, "I fucking know that!"

Perhaps I shouldn't speak until I'm spoken to.

"Holly, the head is right there. One more push," the midwife said.

Gripping my hand and turning my bones to dust, Holly pushed, and her eyes widened.

"Oh God!"

"The head is out!"

I looked up at the midwife with tears in my eyes. Our baby's head was out!

"Well done, Holly. One more big push and we'll be there."

She panted, eyes wide, mouth open. Her hair stuck to her sweaty forehead, and she was starting to get the shadow of dark circles under her eyes, but she looked absolutely perfect to me.

Holly's guttural cry sent a shudder through my whole body; she squeezed her eyes closed, pushing hard, and then she slumped back on the bed, panting. The room was silent for a second before a piercing scream stopped my heart.

"You have a beautiful baby girl!" the midwife said, holding our tiny gunk-covered baby up.

Holly burst into tears, and I stared at our little girl with fascination. I already loved her more than anyone or anything in the world. She literally stole my heart in a second.

Annette checked her over and less than a minute later, she was placed on Holly's chest, wrapped in a white blanket.

"Wow," I whispered, stroking her soft cheek. She'd been cleaned a little, but the gloopy crap was still in her hair.

"We thought a girl. Hi, baby," Holly said, cradling our daughter close.

Shit. I have a daughter! I gulped, trying to keep it together.

"What're we going to call her?" I asked.

Holly looked up and smiled. "You pick. I love both."

We had two names left on our list and wanted to wait to see which one felt right when she was born. I looked at her, taking in her button nose, puffy lips and light brown eyebrows.

"Sophia."

"Yeah. I think Sophia suits her."

I didn't want to say that she was a puffy, wrinkled little thing, and any name would suit her, but it was true. Sophia felt right.

"Okay, we just need to take her now to weigh her," the midwife said.

My heart leapt into my throat. I didn't want her out of my sight.

"Take her where?"

"Not far," she replied and pointed to the counter on the side. "She'll be in the same room."

I nodded, and Holly handed her over. I could tell she was watching me, wanting to ask if I was okay. There was nothing okay about the depth of my fear for Sophia. Most parents worried, but I literally felt sick about the thought of leaving her. What if something happened to her while I wasn't there? I'd *never* forgive myself.

"How're you feeling?" I asked Holly.

"Tired. Sore. Happy."

Annette cleared her throat. "Holly, you have a small tear. We'll give you an injection to speed up the delivery of the placenta."

My eyes widened, and I shuddered. I did not need to hear that.

"And then we'll give you another injection to numb the area and get it stitched, okay?"

"Alright," she replied, covering her mouth with the back of

her hand as she yawned. She looked at me and grimaced. "Do you want to go outside for this?"

"No." Yes! "I'm not leaving you. Wanna crush my hand while they're doing it?"

Annette laughed. "The injection might sting a little, but after that she'll be fine."

"Yeah, see. Why don't you stay so I can crush your hand while they do this delivering thing and inject me then go out for a few minutes and call everyone? They're going to want to know she's here already."

I grabbed her hand, kissing her knuckles. "Okay, if you want."

Holly squeezed my hand, and flinched as they injected her. She didn't take her eyes off me as if I was somehow helping just by being there.

I love her.

I didn't just have feelings for her – I was fucking in love with her!

"All done. We'll give you a second and then see if we're ready to stitch."

Holly pulled a disgusted face.

"Don't worry, you've not torn too badly, it shouldn't take many."

She grimaced. "Please don't tell me. I'd rather not know."

Jen smiled and took Sophia back from the trainee.

"Five pounds and two ounces," the trainee announced.

I grinned like a fool. I thought I'd lost everything when Abby cheated, and I thought I'd never want to put myself in that position again, but suddenly now I did. I wanted everything, and I wanted it with Holly. But what did she want?

"Jasper, you can go now!" she said.

"Are you embarrassed?" Her cheeks turned pink. "Holly, I've just seen you shove a person through there, and you're embarrassed about me seeing you get a few stitches!"

"My dignity left when the contractions really kicked in. No contractions mean you need to leave. Please."

"This should only take ten minutes. We'll get Sophia to the breast and do the stitches. Why don't you call your loved ones and announce this little one's arrival and by the time you're done we will be, too."

Jen stroked Sophia's cheek and handed her to me.

I'd held a baby before, but suddenly I was petrified. Everleigh I could hand back, but Sophia was all mine and Holly's responsibility. I looked down at my daughter, and she stared right back, even though I probably just looked like a hazy blob to her. She was perfect.

"Hi, sweetheart. I'm your daddy," I said. My voice was thick with emotion. "I promise I'll protect you. I love you, little girl."

I kissed her forehead and reluctantly gave her to Holly.

"I'll be outside. Call if you need anything."

"I will. Thanks, Jasper."

"Thank you," I said, bending over to kiss Sophia again. As I went to stand back up, Holly caught her breath. We were inches apart. I wanted nothing more than to kiss her, and she seemed to want it, too.

I pressed my lips to hers briefly, not wanting to push my luck.

Mum rushed through the door, carrying the biggest bunch of pink balloons I'd ever seen. I'd hoped we'd have a few minutes alone. Holly's mum and dad had just left to get a coffee and give us some time to ourselves, but it seemed that we weren't going to get any.

"Where's my little girl," she said, making a dash for Sophia. Holly smiled and handed her over.

"Well done, Holly, she's beautiful."

Now I knew she was saying well done for giving birth, but Sophia was half my genes, she couldn't have included me in the compliment?

"Congratulations," Oakley and Cole said simultaneously as they followed Mum, holding a balloon, a bunch of flowers and a pink gift bag they must have picked up in the hospital store since this had all happened so early.

I hugged my sister because my mum had bypassed me completely. Looks like I'd just been knocked down her list of favourites! Oakley's baby bump kicked me, and I grinned. Soon it would be them doing this.

"No Everleigh?" I asked.

She pulled away and shook her head.

"She's with Cole's parents. We thought it'd be better if we waited until you're home. Holly's just given birth, the last thing she needs is a four-year-old bounding around the room."

"Oakley, Cole, have a quick hold now because I'm not giving this angel back until the end of visiting." Mum handed Sophia to Oakley who stared down at her niece with a tear in her eye. "Miles will be here soon, he's just parking the car."

"Yeah, we would have parked and all come up together, but Sarah shouted. A lot," Cole said, leaning over Oakley's shoulder to see his niece.

"Hey, it's not every day you get another granddaughter!" She turned away and sat on the bed, facing Holly. "How're you feeling?"

"I'm fine, considering, but it wasn't long ago that I had some pain killers."

"Keep taking them, even if you think you're feeling better. I made the mistake of stopping on the third day after I had Jasper; I soon picked them up again," Mum said.

I watched my mum, stepdad, sister and brother-in-law coo over Sophia and Holly, and I realised that without even knowing it, Holly was well and truly part of our family. Now all I had to do was grow a pair and tell her how I felt.

CHAPTER
Thirty-Four

Jasper

Driving away from the hospital made me sick to my stomach. Holly had promised she would call if she needed anything, but that only reassured me a little. What if something happened?

Five-year-old Oakley silently screamed my name in my head.

The maternity ward was secure, but that didn't mean it was impossible for something to happen. I gripped the steering wheel. I wanted to go back and beg them again to let me stay. I'd sleep under Holly's bed if they were just worried about me taking up space and getting in the way.

What if someone managed to get onto the ward? There were stories of children being snatched from hospitals all over the world. It could be Sophia as easily as any other kid out there.

The thought of someone hurting my innocent baby ripped me apart. It flitted through my mind constantly. I pictured the same scenario, with Oakley, then Everleigh, then Sophia. Then I saw Sophia crying, wailing. And then Oakley's silent scream.

Rubbing my forehead, I tried to concentrate on the road while the images I couldn't shake from my mind threatened to pull me under. My chest felt tight, and I worried I was on the edge of a mental breakdown. *No, I'm the strong one.*

I pulled into Oakley's drive just as the ache in my chest started to make me want to hurl. Before I'd got out of the car the front door opened and Oakley wrapped her cardigan around her, waiting for me.

"Everything okay?" She asked.

"I can't stay with them," I said, walking past her into the house.

"You mean you're not allowed to stay at the hospital or Holly said no?"

"Hospital," I replied.

I was going out of my mind. They were there alone.

"Holly is exhausted and in pain from the stitches. Anything could happen, Oakley."

I gripped my hair as I felt fear consuming me. My lungs tightened to the point where I gasped for breath.

They're alone. Anyone could hurt them.

"Jasper, calm down. Breathe!" Oakley said, rushing to my aid. But she was too late; I slumped to the floor as my legs gave out. What if someone was hurting Sophia?

Oakley dropped to the floor, and I gripped her. She was so young and so innocent. How could they have done that to her?

"I can't..." Breathe.

I could see Oakley age five, scared, hurt, crying. And then Sophia was in her place.

"Jasper!"

Oakley's voice floated away. I gasped for breath, but no air passed to my lungs and I descended into darkness.

I came round to my sister slapping my cheek.

"Jesus, you scared me!" she hissed, wiping her damp eyes.

Groaning, I sat up and clutched my head.

"I swear if you don't get help, Jasper-"

"Alright, alright," I said, cutting her off. "I get it. I'll make another appointment with Carol." I'd had a couple but clearly I needed more because something in my head wasn't working properly, and I needed her to fix it.

"Are you okay? Can you stand?"

"Yeah, stop fussing." I pushed myself to my feet, and she rose, too, holding her hands out, ready to catch me. I'd squash her if I passed out again. I made sure I was steady so I wouldn't risk hurting her or my unborn niece or nephew.

"Stop fussing? You just had a panic attack and fainted!"

"Passed out," I corrected, holding my finger up. Much more macho.

She pursed her lips. "Talk to me."

"I'm not there," I said. "What if something happens and I'm not there to protect them?"

She smiled sadly, her eyes filling with tears.

"I was so scared when Everleigh was born. I panicked, thinking if I wasn't with her something would happen. Well, you know I did. No one is going to hurt them."

"What if they do? What if something does happen and I didn't do anything to stop it?"

"Stop! Calm down, you're going to have another panic attack. Sit."

She pointed to the kitchen table. "I'll make you some tea then we're going to talk."

"I don't want tea, I want to be at the hospital."

She flicked the kettle on and spun around.

"You can't be there 24/7. I know what it feels like, I never wanted to let Everleigh out of my sight. I still don't, if I'm honest. But it's not realistic. You can't always be there. The nurses and midwives are there to help and protect them."

A burst of laughter left my lungs.

"Yeah, so was he. I just don't understand why and how he let it happen."

I hadn't expected that to come out.

"Not everyone is Dad. I know what it's like to focus only on the negative, but most people out there are good."

"So you're okay now?"

She tilted her head to the side.

"Jasper, you, Mum and Jenna have Everleigh when I work because I can't let her go to nursery. I'm starting to talk to Carol about school a whole year in advance because I'm so scared of her being somewhere alone. I'll never be over it, but you have to let go a little."

I rubbed my hands over my face.

"What do I do?"

"Don't freak, but I think you should go and see him."

I froze. Had she lost her fucking mind?

"Hear me out, and stop looking at me like I'm crazy."

"Then stop talking crazy," I said.

"You said yourself you don't understand it. Not that I think you ever really will. But I think you need a conversation with him. You never got that."

"I don't want it. I can't sit there and ask him why he did what he did to you."

"Good, because this isn't about me. You need to ask him why

he did it to *you*."

I frowned. "He didn't do anything to me."

"That's crap, and you know it."

"But seeing him…" No. I don't know how I could sit there and not lose it.

"This is about you, no one else. You need closure, too. Jasper, you're still stuck with what he did until you face it. Please, don't let him screw up enjoying having a new baby. He took that from me when I had Everleigh, but not this time." She placed her hand over her perfectly rounded belly. "Cole Junior will have me properly from the start."

"You know you're going to have to think of a better name than that, right?"

She smiled. "We can't agree."

"Jasper's an awesome name."

"Hmm, I don't like it."

I narrowed my eyes.

"I'm kidding! We're swaying towards Bentley."

I nodded once. "Good cars."

"Way to get me off topic. You know what you need to do, don't you?"

"Fuck," I said. "I need to see him."

She smiled, but it wasn't wholly genuine.

"Good. When you've got your answers, you can leave him behind and focus on Holly and Sophia. And for goodness' sake, ask her to move in with you!"

"I will. When I've got myself sorted out. She doesn't need my stress on top of caring for Sophia. And thanks, sis."

"Any time," she replied and grabbed two mugs ready to make us a drink.

As soon as Oakley was settled at the table opposite me I

blurted something else out that I didn't intend to: "I love Holly."

My sister's smile rivalled a Cheshire cat's.

"Finally! I was so hoping you'd realise you're perfect together. And you have a beautiful little girl." She started to cry. "I'm so thrilled for you, Jas, you deserve all the happiness in the world."

"I can't wait to get them home."

"When are you going to tell her?"

"Soon. Not in hospital. I need to find another house ASAP."

"Well, maybe if you'll stop being so bloody picky."

"I want a decent garden for Sophia to play in."

She shook her head, laughing.

"Let's not get into it again. Anyway, now you'll have Holly helping you so it'll go much quicker."

I scratched the back of my neck. "You think she'll want to move in with me?"

"Do you want her to move in?"

"Of course. I want us all under one roof. Might be a little too soon though, don't you think?"

"You've just had a baby together. But anyway, it'd be a few months if you bought a house tomorrow. I'm the wrong person to have this conversation with."

"Right. I should talk to Hol."

"Yeah," she said and did the cat grin again. This time I did it, too. I just hoped Holly felt the same way – I had a suspicion she did.

CHAPTER
Thirty-Five

Holly

Jasper laid Sophia down in the Moses basket and tucked her in. She slept a lot, but the midwife told me that was perfectly normal for a three-day-old baby. I'd felt better ever since we got home this morning. Back at my parents' was where my bed and my things were, so I felt more me.

Since he picked us up at half past eight his morning, Jasper hadn't left our side. He'd taken his two-week paternity leave so he could be here. With Mum, Dad, and Brad at work I was glad that I wasn't alone for the very first day of having her at home. As much as I hate hospitals, having the midwives around was a comfort.

"How long do you think she'll sleep for?" He asked, staring at Sophia. I loved how he looked at her. She already had him around her little finger.

"Probably three or four hours. She's not been waking much

between feeds."

"Lazy baby," he said and smiled.

"Yeah, I'm pretty sure she's storing all that rest up for when she's older."

He looked over and grinned wide. "And then she'll use it to stay awake all night. I can't wait."

"Wow, really? Maybe I'll drop her off at yours at nine at night and pick her up in the morning then."

"Fine by me."

You say that now…

He turned away from Sophia, giving me his full attention. "Do you want anything?"

"Something to eat, but I can make it."

He thrust his hands out to stop me from getting up. "No. You sit and rest, I'll make you something."

"You're taking what the midwife said too seriously, Jasper. I can make myself a sandwich!"

"You've given birth and had stitches. The midwife said to take it easy for the next week, so that's what you're going to do."

He grabbed my blanket, which he had insisted on buying from the hospital shop, and laid it over me.

"Now you chill and watch some TV, and I'll make lunch."

"Jasper?"

He turned around.

"Thank you."

"Any time."

After lunch, my aunt, uncle and cousin turned up to see us. Jasper kept close by and my heart ached at the reason; he was scared of someone hurting Sophia. I hated his dad even more for the anxiety Jasper felt over her safety. I trusted every member of my family around my daughter, but he couldn't do that. New parents had enough to worry about without those sorts of thoughts going through their heads.

"She looks like you, Holly," Uncle Bill said, cradling Sophia in his arms.

I smiled. She didn't look like either of us yet, in my opinion.

Jasper sat beside me; tension radiated from his hunched shoulders. He watched Sophia like a hawk. It looked as if he was seconds from ripping her out of Bill's arms. Uncle Bill lived on a farm, so growing up I spent most of my summer holidays there, running wild in the fields and helping him feed the animals. He'd never hurt anyone. But that's probably what everyone thought about Max until the truth came out.

As much as I hated that he didn't trust my family I had to make allowances for what he'd been through. And Oakley was right; he hadn't dealt with it at all.

"When's her next feed, Holly?" Jasper asked. He knew he was just saying it in the hope they would hand her over to us.

My back stiffened. "Not for another hour," I said. "Aw, lean in further, Mary, that's a lovely picture." I unlocked my phone to take a picture of Sophia with her great aunt and uncle.

"Can we talk about something?" I asked when we were finally alone again.

"Anything," he replied.

"It's about your dad."

"Then no."

"Jasper, come on."

He stood up and fussed around, folding a couple of Sophia's blankets.

"There's nothing to talk about, Holly," he said, avoiding my gaze.

"What's going on? I can tell when you're hiding something, you know."

"I'm visiting him! Okay?"

"Oh."

He dropped the pile of already folded blankets and sat back down.

"I'm visiting him."

That wasn't what I'd expected to come out of his mouth. The few times we'd spoken about it before, he'd got angry and shut down. I'd never have expected him to say he was going to see him.

"You want to?"

"No. I have to. Oakley seems to think facing him will help, and right now I feel like I'm going to have a panic attack, or a heart attack every time someone goes near Sophia, so I'm willing to give it a try. I don't want to feel this shitty whenever someone comes to see her. I don't want to lay awake most of the night worrying that something's happening to her."

"I had no idea you were that scared."

He turned his head, and I saw in his eyes how badly it affected him.

"Holly, I'm terrified," he whispered.

Every night when he'd left the hospital with a smile on his face saying that he'd see us 'first thing' again, he'd been hiding how frightened he was about leaving us.

"Why didn't you tell me this before?" I knew he worried, but not to the extent that he couldn't sleep.

"I didn't want to worry you. Christ, you'd just given birth, you didn't need my shit, too."

"Hey, you can talk to me whenever you need to. I don't want you to think I've ever got too much going on, okay?"

He smiled tightly.

"I mean it, Jasper. Promise you'll talk to me in the future. I can help."

"I wish you could."

"Stay here tonight. Maybe if you see that she's fine it'll be easier."

"Maybe."

"I'd die before I let anyone hurt her," I said.

He wrapped his arm around me and kissed my temple.

"I know you would, but I can't help feeling the way I do. I'm sorry. I'll try harder."

Sighing, I sunk into his side.

"And I'll try harder, too."

"You need anything? I'm going to go to the shop and pick up some more dummies for Soph. We've dropped two already today, and we can't sterilise them quickly enough."

"Good idea."

"So…anything?" He asked and stood up.

I reluctantly let him go and blushed. There was something. "Um, just the dummies."

"What?"

"It's fine. I can get Mum to get it."

"No, I want to. What is it?"

"Honestly, Jasper."

"Tell me. I don't mind getting whatever you need. Tell me, Hol."

Flushing what was probably now a deep red, I replied, "I need more maternity pads."

"Oh." He blinked a few times and then nodded slowly. "I can do that."

How embarrassing.

"It's fine, I'll text Mum now and ask her to pick some up on her way home. I meant to get more at the hospital, but I completely forgot. I have a couple left so I'll be fine until this afternoon."

"It's fine, Holly. It won't take me long. Anything else you need?"

He picked his jacket and key up.

"Are you really getting my maternity pads?"

"Yeah, you need them. What else? Those nipple ones, too? Nipple cream, you got that? The midwife said those bad boys might leak and crack."

I really did not want to have this conversation.

My face felt like it was on fire. "No! I have enough of those, thank you."

His smile grew the more my face heated. "You're embarrassed by this, aren't you?"

How was he not?

"Holly, I watched you stand up and bleed out what looked like the remains of a human sacrifice, I'm pretty comfortable buying you those towel things now."

"Oh, Jesus, please just leave, Jasper."

He laughed and bent down, kissing the top of my head. "Call me if you need anything, okay? I'll be fifteen minutes, tops."

"Thank you."

CHAPTER
Thirty-Six

Jasper

I stared at a long row of sanitary products. How many different types did women bloody need? How the hell was I supposed to choose between them? Taking a quick look either side of me to make sure no one was around, I stepped closer for a better look.

Brands were bunched together, organised by 'flow'. What kind of flow was post-birth? Why didn't she tell me? I didn't want to call her in case she was sleeping. I could ask someone, but I didn't want to admit that I didn't know what the mother of my baby needed; I'd look like an arsehole for not knowing.

Why so much bloody choice?

I picked up one box with 'wings'. Christ did women want them to fucking fly or something? Next to the wings was night-time ultra; I picked it up. And there were also extra long ones. Did it matter what size underwear you had? She was quite petite so she would want smaller ones, right? But did the flow matter?

Oh, this is just fucking ridiculous!

How much choice did you need for that type of thing? Jesus! "Jasper?"

No! I spun around, holding a box of wings and night-time ultra. My mouth dropped. I hadn't expected to run into Abby, especially not down the Feminine Hygiene aisle.

She was gripping onto a small trolley with her baby. The little boy was tucked up in his car seat. The baby that I thought, for a little while, was mine. He was cute. I thought it would hurt when I saw him, but it didn't. Seeing Abby and her son did nothing to me but make me wish I was back at Holly's parents' with her and Sophia.

I was over Abby. Looking at her now, I felt nothing. It didn't hurt and although the memory of how our marriage ended hurt, it didn't bother me the way it used to.

I smiled. "Abby, how are you?"

She looked at the items in my hands and then laughed quietly. "I'm doing really good, thanks. You?"

"I'm great. How's…"

I trailed off, realising I didn't even know her baby's name. Not that I particularly should. We hadn't spoken in months, and the only communication was through our lawyers, which was soon to end as our divorce was in the final stages.

"Jacob. He's doing well. He's ten days old now. What about you?"

"Everything's good. Sophia is perfect."

She smiled. "That's great. I knew Holly was due soon, but I wasn't sure when."

I didn't like the way she said Holly as if she hated her. I knew she wasn't a fan before, but Holly had done nothing wrong. If it wasn't for Abby cheating, I would have never been with Holly in the first place.

I was suddenly very grateful to Abby.

"Soph was due on the 9th of April, but she was early, born three days ago," I said proudly. "Anyway, I really need to get back to my girls so I'll see you around. Take care of yourself, Abby."

I threw the two boxes in the trolley and Abby walked off. I still wasn't sure if I was getting the right type, so I picked up a few others, chucking them in. I had ones with wings, short ones, long ones, ultra absorbent ones, night-time ones.... One of them had to be right, surely?

Holly burst out laughing at the full shopping bags I clung to. "Did you buy the whole shop?"

"Hey, they give you too much choice! There can't possibly be a need for so many variations!" I ranted.

"I'm sorry. Thank you for getting them for me." She took the bags off me and tipped them out on the sofa. The boxes covered two seats. Stifling a laugh, she searched through them.

"So which ones do you have?" I asked when she didn't pick anything up.

"All of these are fine. It was very sweet of you," she replied, dodging my question.

There was literally no other type left on the shelf that I didn't pick up so what was wrong?

"What? It's none of them, isn't it? Jesus, I picked one of everything, how could I still get it wrong."

"Hey, no, you did nothing wrong."

"You're just saying that to make me feel better. Tell me, Holly."

"Well, I've been using the maternity ones. They're down the baby aisle, but these are fine, they all work the same."

What the fuck! Why would they put them somewhere else? How the hell were you supposed to know they did maternity ones if they weren't with the others?

"I can go back."

"No, don't be silly. These are honestly okay. All these night-time ones will be fine now and the others in a couple of days."

"I told you I'd get whatever you need."

"And you have."

"I haven't. I'm such an idiot. When you said maternity pads I didn't think they did something separate to all the others. I didn't want to call in case you'd fallen asleep."

"Jasper, stop. You're not an idiot. You're incredibly sweet. How many other men would get every variety and every brand just because they didn't want to risk waking someone up?"

"They're really okay?"

"Yes, I promise. Thank you."

I smiled and sat down, wrapping my arm around her. Ever since I'd seen Abby in the shop I'd wanted to hold Holly.

"Are you tired?" I whispered. She nodded, pulling the blanket up and snuggling into my side. "Sleep then."

If Holly was right, we had about another hour and a half before Sophia would wake up.

"I like having you around," she whispered and yawned.

"I like being around. I'll be here as much as you let me."

"I'd never tell you not to come. You know you can see Sophia whenever you want."

Of course I knew that. Holly would never try to keep me from our daughter; she loved Sophia too much to be selfish with her.

"I saw Abby today," I said.

I wasn't sure if it was deliberate or not, but she pressed her body against mine a little harder.

"Yeah? How is she?"

"Fine. She has a son called Jacob. He's about a month older than Sophia. They both looked well."

"That's good. How do you feel after seeing her again?"

"I feel fine. Thought it'd make me miss her but I don't. I care about her in the way I care about any other human, but I don't have any feelings for her, good or bad."

Holly looked up at me, her blue eyes brighter than ever. "That's great."

"Yeah, it is. Seeing her made everything clear. What I want. Who I want."

"Who you want?"

I narrowed my eyes. "You're being very coy considering you already know it's you."

She didn't move.

"I thought I was ruined for relationships. I was so sure I'd never want anything real again. When Abby cheated I thought that was it for me, that I'd never be able to trust anyone again and that I wouldn't be brave enough to take a chance. But I trust you, Holly. It's not taking a chance because we're already there, aren't we? We've been in a relationship since your aunt's wedding but without the label."

She gripped my jacket, tearing up.

"Good," I said. "I knew you felt it, too. I'm not scared to let you in, or acknowledge that I already have. I'm not worried about you crushing me because you won't and you don't ever have to worry because I will never hurt you; either of you."

"Jasper," she whispered.

"I know." I pressed my forehead against hers. "God, you really have no idea how beautiful you are, do you?"

Her cheeks turned pink, proving my point. "You are, and so is Sophia. I'm a very lucky man to have you both."

"I think I'm the lucky one," she said.

I tucked her hair behind her ear, wanting to see more of that face I'd grown to love so much. She really was stunning. Her striking blue eyes sparkled. How could I not have seen how I felt about her before? Was it masked by the sudden pregnancy and my divorce? I'd been so consumed by everything else that I'd almost let her slip through my fingers.

"I'm never letting you go," I whispered and kissed her.

CHAPTER
Thirty-Seven

Jasper

I got out of the shower that I'd had to have after my little angel puked her milk all over me. For something so tiny, she could really let it all go. It was like a fountain. Thank God, I had spare clothes at Holly's place. I changed in the bathroom and went into Holly's room to pack my old stuff in a bag.

My makeshift bed – a blow-up one – on the floor beside Sophia's Moses basket laid unused. For the last couple of nights I'd slept beside Holly, cuddled up to her. I folded the fleece blanket up and pulled the plug out of the bed.

Everyone knew we were together now – we got a chorus of 'about time' or 'weren't you already together?' thrown at us – so there was no point having the second bed down there.

I put the pillow back on Holly's bed and saw an envelope. My name in Holly's handwriting was scribbled on the front. A few things ran through my head, the scariest one: she's breaking up with me and doesn't know how to do it face-to-face. I picked it up, heart in my mouth as I opened it. I pulled the piece of paper out and started to read.

Jasper, I don't know how to say this to you, so I thought writing it would be easier. I hope. Sometimes I feel that your protectiveness, although completely understandable, is an insult to me. I love Sophia as much as you do and I would NEVER allow anyone to hurt her, nor would I leave her alone with anyone I don't trust.

You've been through something so terrible that, you're right, I don't get but that doesn't mean that I'm not capable of making the right choices for Sophia and that I can't adequately protect her.

I love that you want to be around, WE love having you around, but I want to be able to take my daughter out for a walk and not worry about checking in with you. And I want you to be comfortable with us going out. We both have to give and take here, or we're going to suffocate each other. I think it's pretty obvious that I want to be with you by now, and you've said you want the same, so maybe once you've read this and understand a little more how I feel, we can talk. I want this to work. I want our little family together.

Holly X

I gripped her letter in my hand and closed my eyes, taking a deep breath through my nose. I was gutted that I'd made her feel like I thought she was a bad or an incapable mum. That was the last thing I felt. And I hated Max impossibly more because of it.

Folding the letter and shoving it in my pocket, I walked downstairs to find her. I wasn't going to let my past and my insecurities mess this up for us. We'd only been together for two bloody days, and Max was coming between us already!

He wasn't going to win.

"Holly?" I called at the bottom of the stairs.

"In the kitchen," she replied. She sounded nervous, knowing I'd read the letter.

Holly and her mum sat around the kitchen table. Sylvie was giving Sophia Holly's expressed milk from a bottle – something she'd finally agreed to do so I could help with the night feeds.

"How's my girl?" I asked, brushing the back of my fingers over her baby-soft hair.

"Hungry. But we're fixing that now, aren't we, sweet girl," she said to Sophia.

Holly gnawed at her lip, tapping the table. She was nervous, and I didn't want to make her suffer any longer.

"Sylvie, do you think you could look after Soph while Holly and I go for a drive?"

She nodded and her smile gave her away, she knew about the letter and Holly's feelings.

"Yes, of course."

I let Holly walk out first after she'd kissed Soph, and she kept her eyes on the floor, avoiding me. I took one last look at Sophia necking her bottle and followed. I would do anything for them both, including facing my biggest fear.

Holly slung her coat on and left the house, not bothering to wait. She was nervous. I knew she found it hard to express herself or say what she wanted, so I didn't mind that I was being ignored and would have to start the conversation.

"Where to?" I asked as I got in and switched the ignition on.

She shrugged, clicking her seatbelt in.

"Okay, maybe just McDonalds drive-thru for a coffee? I'd quite like to stay in the car for privacy." And we both needed caffeine for this talk.

"Sounds good," she replied, finally looking over at me.

I pulled out of her parents' drive.

"Your letter gutted me," I said.

She visibly shrank in the seat.

"Sorry," she whispered.

"No, don't be sorry, I want you to be honest. I'm sorry for making you feel that way."

We quickly fell silent. I wanted to give her time to think everything through, even though I wanted to have it out now. Holly was the type to close up if she was pushed. Pulling up at the drive-thru, I placed our order and wiped my hands on my jeans. The silence was killing me. I wanted it sorted out now so we could move on, but she bottled things away, fearing confrontation.

I paid for the coffees and handed them to Holly while I parked the car.

"You're too quiet," I said as I turned the engine off and turned to her.

"Sorry," she replied.

I sipped my coffee as the silence stretched out again.

"Holly, you're an incredible mum. Sophia is lucky to have you. I've never thought that you can't cope, or you can't protect her. I trust you one hundred per cent to do what's best for her."

"Then why are you so hostile to my family and friends?"

"Because I don't know them."

"I do."

"Yeah, but you can never know someone completely."

"You don't know me completely, but you trust me with her,

right?" She raised her eyebrows, challenging me to say no.

"Of course I do. Look, I can't help who I trust and who I don't. It's not easy for me to trust anyone, and I'm sorry, but if I'm not comfortable with someone around my daughter I'm not leaving them with her."

"Jasper, we were in the same room, and you still looked like you wanted to kill them all."

"They were holding her." That was enough. When someone had her that I didn't know, all I could see in my head was her silently crying.

"In front of us!"

Sighing, I ran my hand through my hair. I couldn't make her understand, not properly, but I was sure I knew someone that could help.

"We're going to see Carol," I said. "We need to sort this properly, or we're gonna screw this up before it's properly begun."

Her eyes softened. "Okay. I want this to work."

"Good. Me too."

"I should be more understanding."

I shrugged.

"I think we both should but it's hard to understand where each other is coming from sometimes, especially with something as big as this. It's about our daughter's safety."

"Tell me it'll be okay," she whispered. "I've wanted this for months and I'm afraid of losing it."

Leaning over, I kissed her soft lips.

"It's going to be okay. I told you I'm not letting you go, and I meant it. I'd just like to avoid you hating me if we carry on like this. Don't give up on us."

She shook her head. "I won't."

Carol was good; she got me talking and realising shit that I never thought was there. I believed that she could help us both understand each other more. Neither I nor Holly were willing to give up, so we'd make it work, whatever it took.

CHAPTER
Thirty-Eight

Jasper

Holly looked like me when it was my first time in here. She sat stiffly on the sofa, visibly wanting to be anywhere else. It wasn't exactly my favourite place to be either, but I'd had to admit I was wrong, and therapy worked.

"I appreciate you coming today, Holly, and congratulations to you both," Carol said.

"Thank you," Holly and I replied at the same time.

"How is parenthood treating you both?"

"Good," Holly said. "Sophia is such a good baby."

For now.

Carol nodded. "Is she with family?"

"Yes, with Jasper's mum."

"It's always good when you have plenty of willing volunteers to watch them for you."

I flinched. No, it wasn't.

"Jasper?" Carol said. "Why don't you start?"

"Fine. Me and Holly have been talking about my fears about Sophia. And Max."

"You were toying with the idea of visiting him. Have you made a decision yet?"

"Yeah, I'm going to do it. I just don't know if it'll help and if it doesn't…"

She smiled. "Then you don't know if the worry will ever ease?"

"Pretty much."

"What do you think, Holly?"

Holly hated being put on the spot.

"Um, I don't know really. I want things to be easier for Jasper, but I'm worried that visiting his dad will make it worse."

Carol nodded. "How does Jasper's anxiety affect you?"

I looked at Holly. That I didn't know. She played with the ends of her sleeves.

"It makes me uncomfortable when he's hovering around my family. Don't get me wrong, I understand, but they're my family, and I don't want them to feel like we don't trust them with our daughter."

"I think that's the issue here, Holly, Jasper doesn't. It's nothing personal, and he's not questioning your judgement, but trust for Jasper is hard to gain and easy to lose."

That about summed it up. Carol was worth every penny I paid her. I could count on one hand the amount of people I trusted completely with Sophia.

"I don't know what I can do to convince him they can be trusted, and I sometimes do feel like he doesn't trust me to keep her safe."

"Don't think that, Holly." Shit I hated that she felt like that.

"You're an amazing mum and I know you'd never let anyone near her you weren't sure about, but we were once sure about Max."

"See and that's what makes me feel like you don't trust me," she said. "You're basically saying I don't know my family."

"No, I'm saying we don't really know anyone."

She shook her head; lips pursed, looking pissed at me.

"I know my family."

"Okay," Carol said, putting an end to our discussion before it turned into an argument.

I got where Holly was coming from, but she hadn't been on the other end of it when you found out someone you thought was your hero was really a monster.

"Until Jasper has worked through his anxiety we need to find a way of getting you both to understand where the other one is coming from. Jasper, do you trust Holly?"

"Yes," I replied.

"Then do you think you could go out while she has someone over to see Sophia?"

I gulped. Holly was petite and had not long given birth. Would she be able to protect Sophia? And herself?

"Jasper," Holly whispered. The tone in her voice froze me on the spot. Tears welled in her eyes.

"I trust you," I said, taking her hand in mine. "I worry about you, too."

"I'm a big girl and if anyone tried to hurt my daughter I'd kill them. I may not be particularly strong, but you find the strength for that. No one is going to hurt her. Not ever."

I heard the words, and I knew she'd protect her, but I couldn't help thinking I should be there to be certain nothing happened to either of them.

"I know. I get it, Holly, I really do, but I can't help how I feel.

We're just going round in circles."

"What do you think will help you achieve closure?" Carol asked.

"Oakley thinks going to see him will." It kept coming back to Max.

She nodded. "Do you think that?"

"I'm leaning more towards yes. I'll give just about anything a go to not feel so scared and helpless or have Holly think I don't trust her. I just don't know how I'm going to deal with seeing him."

"And that's why you're here?"

"That and I want me and Holly to be able to talk about it without arguing. I hate arguing with her."

"I hate arguing with you, too," she replied, squeezing my hand.

"What are you most scared of happening if you visited him? Your anger getting the better of you?"

I gulped. "No, I'm most scared of remembering who he was before."

Carol left the words to hang in the air. Holly froze.

"That would be perfectly normal if you did," Carol said. "You could remember plenty of good things right now if you allowed yourself to."

"Well, I won't."

She nodded. "I know. That's fine too; some people are capable of forgetting and not having it interfere with their lives. When it eats away at you and affects your life though, that's the time to face it."

"You may as well have just said 'Jasper, face it'," I replied.

"Do you believe it affects your life?"

I diverted my eyes, looking at the back of the sofa beside her shoulder.

"Yes," I admitted. "But I don't want it to."

"And you don't want anyone to know it does," Holly said and covered my hand with her own.

"I don't want other people having to deal with my problems."

Carol nodded again.

"We're talking about your mum and Oakley. Jasper, I can tell you that Oakley is doing very well and from what she tells me your mother is too. Now it's time to focus on you. They *want* to offer you the same support. You're not putting anything on them, but taking it off."

I frowned. That was a crock of shit. How could telling them help them?

"You don't believe me," she said. "Do you know Oakley's main concern now? The thing that we go over the most?"

When I didn't reply she said, "You, Jasper. She worries about you."

"I don't want them to worry about me, and I don't want to be a mess every time I'm away from Sophia. Tell me what I have to do."

"We'll start by talking," she said. "About everything you're comfortable with."

"I'll wait outside," Holly said, squeezing my hand before she let go.

"You don't have to." The thought of losing Holly before I even properly had her was terrifying. If hearing my deepest, darkest fears would make her understand me and not give up, then I'd go with it.

She seemed to realise my fear and kissed my cheek.

"It's okay. I'll be right outside. I'm not going anywhere, Jasper."

I watched her leave, a little overwhelmed that she could make me love her more and more when I hadn't wanted to love anyone ever again.

"You're happy with Holly," Carol said, gaining my attention.

"Yeah. I didn't think that'd happen again, especially not so soon."

"Ah, it usually happens when you least expect it. So, where do you want to start?"

"The day Max was arrested," I replied, and she nodded. "At first I was certain they'd got it wrong. I would have put any money on it being a mistake. I kept going over it; *there must be another Max Farrell*. The second Oakley said 'It is true' my whole world collapsed. Ever since then, I see Oakley as a little girl, in distress, everywhere. I dream about it all the time."

Carol looks at me intently. "Oh? You've not mentioned this before."

"No one knows."

"You say you see her?"

"Not like an imaginary friend, I'm not four, but I picture her aged five, in a long pink nightdress, clutching her teddy and crying. Tears are rolling down her face, but she never makes a sound. Then I saw Everleigh like that too. And now…"

"You see Sophia."

I swallowed a lump in my throat. "Yeah."

"What about the dreams?"

"Always the same," I said. "Always Oakley as a kid again, silently screaming my name. I've wondered too many times if she did that when Frank…"

Carol nodded, letting me know she got it because, Christ, I could not finish that sentence.

"I need it to stop," I said, inwardly wincing at the desperation in my voice.

"We'll work on that."

"How?"

"The same way Oakley ended her nightmares."

I gave a quick nod. "Facing it. Right." *Man up and fucking do it.*

"I don't hate the man I thought he was."

It was out in the open, and I hated myself more than I ever had before.

Carol smiled reassuringly. "Of course not. He was your dad, and you loved him. I understand that your feelings for him now have changed– "

"That's putting it fucking lightly."

"–but you should never feel bad about remembering affection for someone who was once everything to you."

Her words were like the light bulb effect.

"Remembered affection," I said. "Shit, that's it. This whole time I've been hating him more because I thought a part of me still cared or something fucked up like that. I hate the bastard; I really do, but I remember loving him. Still, it doesn't help me understand."

"Do you ever think you'll understand?"

"No. I've wanted to ask him so many times why he did it to her, but I was scared that if I saw him I'd just go crazy."

"And you'd be asking the wrong question. You need to know why he did it to you."

Like Oakley said. I blinked, clenching my jaw so I wouldn't bloody cry. He was supposed to be my dad, a good man, but that didn't stop him from doing what he did. He didn't love any of us enough. My mind was made up. I needed to know why he didn't love his wife and children enough. I was going to see him.

CHAPTER
Thirty-Nine

Jasper

"I don't know if I can go in," I said.

"You don't have to, but I really think you need this," Oakley replied down the phone.

"I hate him."

"I know you do. But you didn't used to. You deserve answers, or at the very least to face him and realise it's not worth letting his mistakes ruin your life."

"Mistakes? Christ, that's a small word for what he did."

"Whatever. It doesn't matter what you call it, the fact is, it's screwing with you and you need to do something about it. Now get out of the car and do this for yourself."

"Whoa, yes, mum!" I got out. The next hurdle was forcing myself to walk into that building.

"I don't know how I'm going to keep my cool, especially if he mentions you. Or Everleigh."

"So what if he does, he's stuck in there."

She was bothered by the idea that he might mention them and Mum; I knew she was.

"We don't even know if he knows about Everleigh."

"Come on," I said. Now she was just clutching at straws. His mum, who we rarely speak to now, visited him. I knew he was her son, but I couldn't get past the fact that she still wanted to see him after what he did to her granddaughter.

"Okay, fine. He probably does, but he'll never get anywhere near her, so it's a non-issue. I've got to go; Bentley's kicking my bladder. Call me when you get out."

"Alright. Bye."

I slipped my phone in my pocket and walked to the visitor's entrance, but I couldn't go through the door. My muscles had frozen in fear. Seeing him again felt wrong, I didn't want to have anything to do with him. I didn't want seeing him to be the thing that helped me move on. And what if Holly was right, what if it didn't help? I could walk away today feeling worse, hating him more and having my fears for Sophia's safety double.

This was either going to be really good for me or really bad. Either way, I had to try. Me and Holly wouldn't work if I didn't get myself sorted out. It was worth trying; anything was worth trying. I'd face the devil for her, and my father came pretty damn close.

For Holly and Soph.

I walked through the door, swallowing my fear.

Inside was dim with pale green walls and an old dark wooden reception desk. A few people were hovering around, waiting to go through.

I cleared my throat. "I'm Jasper Scofield, here to see Max Farrell."

The woman behind the desk barely looked up. She tapped a few things on her keyboard.

"Okay. Take a seat and you'll be called through in a minute," she said, even though the six seats were clearly taken.

"Thanks."

I stood by the window and concentrated on keeping my breathing even. This was the last place on earth I wanted to be, and I had to force myself to stay still and not flee out the door.

I sat on the metal chair and waited as the inmates walked through the barred door into the visiting room. A few people stood up to greet their loved ones briefly before being told to break it off. I kept still on the chair, tapping my foot anxiously.

Then I saw him, and my world clouded.

He was dressed in dark blue sweats and a black jumper. I'd never seen him like that before. He usually wore suits, smart jeans, and shirts. It was like watching another person. I bet he hated it, but I doubt there was a huge range of choice in prison. Good.

His hair had greyed more at the sides, and he'd put on some weight. His clean shaven face was the same as always, but with the addition of a few wrinkles around his evil eyes.

He knew I was coming, but he still looked shocked to see me. Maybe he didn't think I'd really come.

"Son," he said as he sat down.

I wasn't sure if he'd said it to get to me, or if he still thought of me as his son; either way I wasn't going to let him get to me.

"Let's be clear about this, I don't want a relationship with you. After today, you'll never see me again so don't get any ideas. And don't call me son. I want answers; that's it. I think you owe me that much."

His expression was impassive, and I had no idea what was going through his head. I used to think I knew what he was thinking, what punishment I'd get for swearing or how he'd react to a bad grade. Turns out, I never knew him at all.

"I understand," he finally said. "I am sorry for what I did, Jasper. I've been receiving treatment in here."

"Don't," I growled. "There is nothing you can say that'll ever make up for what you did, so don't go there. If you even mention her name, I'll be out of here and you can rot."

He nodded once.

"I want to know why."

"I was sick, Jasper."

I closed my eyes and took a deep breath.

"Most parents would die for their children. They'd give them their heart if they needed it. Why were we not enough?"

His mouth pressed into a thin line.

"I regret my actions, and I'm trying to get better. I'm truly sorry that I hurt you, all of you, but I can't change the past."

"You broke our family up, betrayed us all in the worst way, and all you can say is sorry. Mum cried every night. You have any idea of the guilt Mum and I feel over this? We did nothing, yet we're the ones that feel we let her down. You sit there saying you're all better, well, fucking great for you, but what about us? Do you have any idea what you've done?"

"I understand the repercussions of my actions, Jasper, of course. It was never my intention to hurt any of you."

Was he for real?

"You're not answering me. Why did you do it?"

"I honestly do not know. I've gone over that in treatment, but I still don't know. The answer you're looking for, I don't have. I was ill, Jasper."

"Ill. Like the way you tried to make the court believe Oakley was? Were you ill when you researched a personality disorder that could have explained her being mute for eleven fucking years? Was it the illness that drove you to do that?"

"You're angry. I am, too."

I stood up. This was going nowhere. He wasn't going to accept responsibility for anything. In his head, he was still the respectable father and businessman. He'd made things acceptable in his head. He could say sorry a million times, but it was all for show. It was always all for show.

"You know what, you're a sad, lonely, old man. Think what you like but we all know what your sickness is. You're hiding behind something that makes you the victim. I don't know why I even wasted time being angry with you. You're a coward. Goodbye, Max."

I stormed past him towards the exit. A guard opened the door as he saw me approach. My clenched hands shook, but I felt about a stone lighter. Like storm clouds had passed and I could finally see the possibility of clear skies.

I'd got no answers, but that was okay because I didn't really need them. What I'd needed all along was to say the things to him I just had: I had to look him in the eye and dismiss him from my life. I hadn't had closure before, but that was what it felt like I'd just found. I'd closed that chapter of my life, and I could move on without hating him with a vengeance every single day. I didn't have to feel anything for him at all.

He was no one.

Epilogue

Jasper

I parked outside our old house and stared at it. It held so many good memories and one massive bad one. It wasn't just a house. It was my childhood, and the place my family turned to shit. Sure, we'd still been Mum, Oakley and Jasper, but it wasn't the same. We'd been fucked up, all of us. We'd carried around insecurities, fear, and anger and to some degree still did.

Oakley had been back here and turned a tormenting house into a pile of bricks in her head. I wanted it just to be a house again. Since Oakley's visit there had been new owners. The day I saw a picture of it staring back at me from the estate agent's window still haunted me. I hadn't expected it. I thought it was nothing. I thought it was all nothing but I couldn't push it to the back of my head any more, it had fucked me up.

Now it was time to take control and face it all.

I didn't need to go inside; just looking at the exterior was enough. Gripping the steering wheel, I let the memories flood my mind. Some were good – most were good.

Water fights with Dad in the summer and snowball fights in the winter. Him teaching me to ride a bike. Birthday parties we'd had in the house and back garden. Him giving me 'the talk' when I was sixteen – though it was awkward and two years too late. Playing football on the lawn against Cole and his dad, David.

Oakley was right; he was the perfect dad to me until I was a teenager. I thought I couldn't have good memories of him because, why should I, when hers ended at the age of five? But I did, and nothing could change that – not even me.

And it was okay. It was okay because I hadn't known about any of it. It was okay because my idolised vision of my dad disappeared the second I found out what he really was. It was okay because I could have good memories that would never change how he was nothing to me.

Closing my eyes, I reached for the key and turned the ignition on. I'd be okay. As much as I hated relying on something, I was going to keep seeing Carol. She helped, and, like Oakley, I wasn't stupid enough to think that you do one thing, and all your problems magically disappear. This was more like another step towards letting it all go.

Making another appointment could wait until tomorrow. Right now I just wanted to be with my girlfriend and my daughter.

Holly smiled as I walked into her parents' living room.

"Hey, I thought you'd be back earlier."

"Sorry, I had something to take care of. Where's Sophia?"

"Mum's taken her out for a walk so I could have a bath in peace." She twirled her damp hair around her finger. "Though I think she just wanted to show her off to my aunts."

I sat beside her. *Sophia's okay; Sylvie would never let anyone hurt her.*

"Alright, maybe it's a good thing. I don't want Sophia around when I talk about this."

A frown filled with worry marred her flawless face. She pushed her long hair behind her ears. "What? Is everything okay?"

"Yeah, actually. I went to see my father today."

Holly looked anxiously at me. "How did it go?"

"About as well as I expected. He gave me nothing but a lot of shit about getting better. Point is, he's history."

She pursed her lips, not even trying to hide her doubt.

"Alright, I know I should still talk about the past, but he's not going to screw up the present. I doubt I'll ever stop worrying about Sophia or Everleigh and nothing will change that."

I exhaled sharply. I wasn't doing a very good job of this.

"What I'm trying to say is that I've put something to rest, and I want to move on. Finally. A massive part of that moving on is telling you…" I took her hand. "Telling you that I love you, Holly. I love you so fucking much. And I love Sophia. Move in with me."

I wasn't sure whether her stunned silence was a good thing or not.

"Holly?"

"Are you sure?" She whispered.

"What? Yeah, of course I'm sure."

"You love me? Not just because I'm Sophia's mum?"

"I fell in love with you as we spent more time together and I watched our baby grow inside you."

She raised her eyebrow. "You fell in love with me when I was getting fat?"

"Well, you were never fat, but yeah. You're smart, funny, caring, beautiful, and you're the best mum in the world. What's not to love?"

Her eyes glazed as if she was about to cry. "I love you, too, Jasper. I tried to stop because you said so many times that you didn't want another relationship, but I couldn't help it. There's no way I would ever hurt you."

I reached over and wiped a tear before it fell.

"I know you wouldn't. I trust you, Holly. Now, about moving in?"

A smile lit up her face, and she launched herself at me. I caught her and immediately worried she'd hurt herself, sometimes when she moved too quickly she winced. It had only been a few weeks since she'd given birth.

"Are you okay?"

"Hell, yes, and of course we'll move in with you!" She pulled back. "Is this why you didn't buy another cot?"

I shrugged. "We don't need two. How long until your mum brings Soph back?"

"She was taking her around the block and then to my aunt Sheila's for her bottle." She looked at the clock, calculating Sophia's feeding times. "Probably about another ten or fifteen minutes."

I laid her down on the sofa, and she frowned.

"You know I can't do that."

"You've got a one-track mind, Holly. I kind of love you even more for that. But that's not where I was going with this. And for the record, we'd need longer than fifteen minutes!" I pressed my lips to hers and curled my arms around her.

Books by Natasha Preston

Silence
Broken Silence
Players, Bumps and Cocktail Sausages
Covert
The Cellar
Second Chance
Save Me

Connect with Natasha Preston

Website
Facebook
Twitter

9 781496 153463